FATAL DOSE

A Caitlyn Jamison Mystery

M. E. Maki

Visit the author at www.CaitlynJamisonMysteries.blogspot.com

Published in the United States by Mary E. Maki

ISBN-13: 9781974305650
ISBN-10: 1974305651

Cover photo: Joseph Scaglione III - Joe Scaglione Photography
Cover Design: Suzette Young
Author photo: Raymond Maki

Printed in the United States of America

This book is dedicated to the Caitlyn Jamison mystery fans. Thank you for your support and encouragement.

~ EDDA ~

August 1968
Riverview, New York

Edda van der Molen pushed away from the stained kitchen sink and sighed. She tucked several stray strands of hair behind her ear and surveyed the dismal state of her kitchen—a room that reflected her life.

She'd escaped a dysfunctional family only to find herself trapped in a loveless and sometimes abusive marriage.

She slowly rubbed the top of her bulging stomach, her way of communicating with the life within. A life she didn't want to bring into *her* world. But here she was, six months pregnant.

Then she thought about Jonathan. And today was Thursday.

~

On Thursdays she'd wait for the little rust-covered pickup to stop in front of the house. The driver would get out and explain what seasonal vegetables were available that week. As tempting as the fresh vegetables were, it wasn't the vegetables Edda longed to see. It was the roguish driver, just about her age, and from the first day they met he provided her with the company she craved.

He told stories about how the residents of the commune, where he lived, were free from the rules of "the establishment." They grew vegetables without the use of pesticides and their drinking water was uncontaminated.

With each visit their conversations delved deeper into the aspects of communal living. At first Edda was curious and intrigued and then she was envious.

By mid-July the commune sold wildflower bouquets. Edda longed to brighten her dreary existence with one, but she knew their meager income should not be spent on frivolities.

One day the driver presented her with an arrangement featuring black-eyed Susans and Queen Anne's lace.

"I can't afford those."

"They aren't for sale. They're a gift. And call me Jon."

"Would that be short for Jonathan?" she'd asked, tilting her head and with a shy smile, flirting with him.

"You're correct," he answered with a laugh and a wink.

A relationship had begun. First with small talk, then flowers, and one day he presented her with a packet. She remembered the exact moment he held the small bag out to her and said, "Take it. It'll help you feel better."

What did she really know about him? She didn't want to believe an attentive and caring man like Jon would harm her. He was different from any man she had ever known. He made her feel beautiful, even in her condition.

~

Edda's feelings for Jon were unsettling.

Was it love, infatuation or hormones?

She didn't care. His visits were the highlight of her week. And those visits prompted her to question the state of her marriage. Her husband, Palle, worked long hours at the mill, came home, ate dinner and fell asleep. That was on the good nights. On the bad, well, she feared his temper.

Their marriage wasn't built on love. Rather, it resulted from pushback against their parents' plans. She and Palle had been impulsive, married by a JP, with no money and no place to live. Only because Palle's family had this empty farmhouse did they have a roof over their heads. She should have listened to her mother about getting married so young. She should have stayed in school and not abandoned her plans of becoming a fashion designer.

Edda made her way into the sparsely furnished living room carefully cradling a cup of tea made from the special dried leaves Jon had given her that morning. She plopped down on the sagging old couch and watched as a gentle breeze played with the lone tattered window curtain. Pixie, their tortoiseshell cat, curled up next to her and purred loudly. The cat didn't seem to mind that the couch was as worn as the rest of the house.

A rustling sound; Palle was at the door. She finished her tea, scooped the spent leaves into a napkin, placed it into her pocket, and then sat back to enjoy the euphoric feeling the tea provided.

Palle entered the room carrying a small bag, but his downcast expression set off Edda's internal alarms. Something was wrong. Would he take out his frustration on her?

"Did you get some grain?" She asked tentatively, eyeing the bag and hoping to set a positive tone. They depended on the stolen grain to supplement their income.

Palle snarled, "The boss was standing near the wheat bin. He's on to what we're doing. I snuck back into the mill and grabbed a bag of rye."

This statement startled her. Memories she'd worked hard to suppress flooded her mind. She knew the family stories; she was sure she carried the genes and consequently had fought the temptation all her life. But the voice in her head was back, stronger than ever.

Her problem could be solved . . .

Palle, oblivious to Edda's turmoil, said, "The bag'll be in the kitchen. When's dinner?"

Edda, paralyzed by the family stories that had invaded her psyche, didn't respond.

~ ONE ~

August 2017

Steven Sullivan resisted his compulsion to push down on the accelerator. He was in no hurry to reach his destination. The reason being—for the first time in his life, he felt fear. He popped another antacid into his mouth with the hope it would do the trick.

This undercover assignment would test his limits. He knew he wasn't as quick and agile as he was a few years ago, an unpleasant reminder of his age.

He was told that federal agents, younger then he, had been assigned to Upstate New York over the past couple of months with no appreciable results. So, he wondered, how did they expect him, at age fifty-seven, to accomplish what those agents had failed to do?

He had asked that question, brought up his age, and the fact he had family in the upstate area. Nothing seemed to matter, another reason he'd lost faith in the agency. It was apparent that the government didn't care about him or his family; the end result took priority over any casualties along the way. As a psychologist and a trained police officer he understood the reasoning, but this was personal. For him, it boiled down to the fact that he didn't want to play the game any longer.

Why do I even bother? For each one caught, two more take their place.

He was also uncomfortable with the cover story the agency provided—a college lecturer. Forensic psychology he knew, for it was his profession, but teaching a bunch of college kids? Not good.

To further his frustration with this assignment, today's grueling six-hour drive from Boston to Upstate New York was only adding to his discomfort. The heat wave that had paralyzed the East Coast for the last two weeks was unrelenting, and he had a car with a malfunctioning air conditioner.

He wiped his brow and turned the fan to its highest setting in an attempt to move the hot humid air. His right hand explored the passenger seat for *anything* to wipe away the sweat that poured down his face. His fingers touched the only option available, the saturated handkerchief he'd been using.

Damn!

His cell phone emitted a familiar ring and he glanced down at the number.

Why don't they leave me alone?

With a sigh of resignation he touched the accept icon and put the phone on speaker. Pleasantries were not expected.

"Almost to the exit; ETA within the hour." Steven abruptly ended the call, demonstrating his annoyance. He didn't want any discussion that would nurture more doubts about the job.

Leaving the thruway, he headed south along one of the Finger Lakes. To his left, the rippling blue water provided the first cool breeze of the day. He slowed, opened his windows, and took several deep breaths.

As he traveled south, the landscape transformed into rolling hills and vineyards began to appear. Did one of these vineyards belong to his niece? He debated whether to contact her. He didn't want to put her in danger.

Thirty miles south of the thruway he slowed and looked for the route that would take him into the town of Riverview, a small town, he learned, experiencing growing pains due to the opening of the university's new satellite campus. This campus would be his base. Although he didn't like his cover, he had to admit it gave him the networking opportunities he'd need.

He had identified key businessmen in the area as well as the police officers in Renwick and Riverview. The key was to identify those he could trust.

Steven understood that although crime was usually associated with big cities, it didn't discriminate. That was the reason he was assigned to this bucolic area.

Work fast. In and out—that was his life—for now.

~ TWO ~

Late September 2017

Caitlyn Jamison drove north as fast as her conscience and the law allowed. She *had* to arrive at Winding Creek Winery in Upstate New York by early afternoon because the weatherman had *promised* a perfect day.

The winery was in a geographic area known for its cloudy days and fickle weather. That meant finding consecutive days of clear blue skies was a challenge. The forecast for the end of the week was hopeful and was the reason she'd left her Arlington, Virginia apartment early this morning. She'd arrive at the winery in time to capture mid-day photos, assuming Mother Nature didn't pull any tricks. Time was running out. The winery's brochure couldn't wait; the fall wine trail season was upon them.

If the pressure of finding a good weather window wasn't bad enough, her friend, Abbie Hetherington, had sent multiple emails over the last few weeks, each one more anxious than the last. The winery's busiest season had arrived and they *had to have* updated brochures. They were starting a wine club this year and the membership application was included in the brochure. They were losing business. If Caitlyn didn't get the job done, her friend would hire someone else.

~

The sun was on the horizon when Caitlyn stopped for gas and a cup of coffee. She'd been so caught up in her clients' projects she'd not taken adequate time to prepare for the trip, and by the Pennsylvania border, she noted how low her fuel was.

Caitlyn looked forward to her time in Riverview, even though technically, she'd be working, taking photos for the winery's brochure. At least she wouldn't be sitting alone in front of a computer screen, in her efficiency apartment that served as her graphic design office. Instead, she'd be out in the fresh air among the grape vines, and at the end of the day she'd enjoy the fruit of her friend's labor—a chilled glass of Winding Creek Riesling.

With the gas tank filled, and sustained by a cup of java, she climbed back behind the wheel and placed her cup in the holder. She glanced over at the passenger seat where Summit, her white Shih Tzu, was snoring away. He was not going to let a short stop interrupt his morning nap.

I'd like to do that. Hmm, when would self-driving cars be available? Better question, could I ever afford one?

She hoped the seven-hour drive to New York would be without interruption so she'd have time to plan the photo shoot, and time to sort out her future. A big part of that "future" was her relationship with Riverview's sheriff, Ethan Ewing.

Last spring when she flew to New York after hearing about her cousin's murder, her only thought was to catch the culprit. Her brash approach to assisting Riverview's sheriff with the investigation had not put Ethan off; instead he had welcomed her help. There was nothing legal or appropriate about her role in the investigation, but she learned Ethan was a renegade and did whatever was needed to get the job done. It wasn't long before her role was more than note taking. She became his confidant.

It also didn't hurt he was good looking. She liked the way his wavy brown hair flopped over his forehead, and she still wondered about the scar across his right forehead, just at the hairline. She'd refrained from asking about it, as it seemed too personal a question, so she fantasized that the scar was the result of defending an innocent victim on the streets of New York.

She liked the way his brown eyes twinkled when he discovered some new information, and she knew he worked hard to keep extra weight off his six-foot frame. Close in age, mid-thirties, they had connected socially and culturally. They realized they formed a perfect partnership in solving the crime.

Their time together was brief and consumed by the murder investigation. As soon as the culprit was caught, Caitlyn returned to the Washington metropolitan area. They'd kept in touch over the summer, though neither wanted to broach the subject of their relationship, each uncertain what the other's answer might be.

Riverview's population influx, due to the new satellite campus, had wreaked havoc on the sheriff's office workload, and on one particularly difficult day Ethan called Caitlyn and said, "There's been another murder and I was wondering ..."

She didn't realize he was teasing, so her immediate response was, "You've got to be kidding! No way!" When he explained he *was* kidding, he told her *if* there had been a murder, he'd probably be the main suspect. The added workload was stressful on him and his staff. Increased traffic, residents' complaints, and petty crimes were issues with which they now dealt, with no extra help in the foreseeable future.

~

Caitlyn exited Route 15 onto I-81 north just west of Harrisburg, Pennsylvania. She kept an eye out for the Statue of Liberty replica mounted on an old railroad pier in the middle of the Susquehanna River. The original replica was made of venetian blinds, but in 1992 Harrisburg residents made a stronger version to reign over the Susquehanna's Dauphin Narrows. As she drove past the small towns along the Susquehanna, her thoughts returned to life in Riverview.

Her time in Riverview had been brief, but she'd fallen in love with the area—swimming in the lake and picnicking in Riverview Park. She loved to walk the gorge trails as she watched the river deliver its bounty into the lake. While in high school, she'd volunteered at the local historical society and could still recite the history of the area, especially the Indian legend of the Great Spirit's role in the formation of the Finger Lakes. It was the lakes, rolling hills, and fertile farmland that Caitlyn loved best about the area.

One thing she was sure of—Riverview was drawing her back.

~ THREE ~

A cold blast of air hit Sheriff Ethan Ewing as he stepped out onto the front porch, forcing him back into the house to grab something warmer. Fall in Upstate New York had arrived.

Back outside, he settled into his Adirondack chair and ignored the fact the old wooden chair needed a coat of stain. That project would have to wait; he had no time for chores.

Chores aside, his thoughts wandered as he watched the steam curl up from his coffee mug.

He took a tentative sip of the hot liquid and gazed out at the horizon. He'd been too busy lately to notice that the trees had shed enough of their leaves to provide him the first-of-the-season glimpse of the lake beyond. When he moved to Riverview last October, most of the leaves had dropped and he had taken this view for granted until mid-May when the foliage returned. By then, he was too busy to appreciate much of anything in his yard.

His thoughts segued to the circumstances that had brought him to this location in Upstate New York. There really wasn't an *exact* moment when he decided to leave the city, because unrest with his job and his life had brewed for a while. Though he remembered the defining moment in that decision was his captain's pay-to-play talk. It was clear if Ethan expected promotion, he'd have to pay his dues. Sometimes those "dues" included unethical, even illegal behavior, as in turning a blind eye when certain crimes were committed. That wasn't Ethan's style.

Leaving the captain's office that day, he noticed an ad for a sheriff's position in a small rural community upstate. It would be a one-eighty from walking his beat in the Bronx, but maybe it was the job he needed right now. He'd be more in control of his life, in charge, no longer a small cog in a large wheel, and most of all, not wondering whom to trust among his colleagues. He tore the ad off the bulletin board and stuffed it in his pocket.

Ethan applied on a whim, and to his surprise he was offered the sheriff's position in the town of Riverview, New York. He thought his application was such a long shot he didn't even know where the place was. A map of New York indicated Riverview was situated just west of one of the Finger Lakes in Central New York. When the offer arrived, he immediately accepted the position. He didn't want time to change his mind, but then he had second thoughts. What if the quiet life didn't suit him? Crime and politics didn't discriminate, but he didn't believe they would be as rampant as in the city. Would he be happy giving out speeding tickets? What else could possibly happen in a rural community?

He justified accepting the position by deciding to take it on a one-year trial basis. If he couldn't adjust to the slower pace of rural life, he'd go back. Big cities were always looking for experienced police officers.

~

Ethan learned it would take time to be accepted by Riverview's ingrained "born here" culture. He was a newcomer, and not from an upstate family. He had to work to win the confidence and friendship of the residents, and after a year, he thought he'd been accepted by most.

He smiled at the thought and took another sip of his cooling coffee. Life in Riverview was never boring; some of the residents were like characters out of a Norman Rockwell painting. He loved walking the main street, peeking into the quaint shops, and meeting the proprietors. At first he was concerned whether the small shops, struggling financially, would make it. That worry dissipated when the university's satellite campus, located a few miles south of town, opened this summer.

The downside of having a campus in this rural community was the conflict created by the arrival of students and faculty. Riverview residents didn't like the added traffic, noise, and college kids taking

11

over the town, but shop owners loved the new business. The overall economy of Riverview was better by the day, and Ethan figured in time tensions between the factions would iron themselves out. In the meantime, his office would keep busy ironing out the differences.

Increased growth meant escalating crime. Ethan didn't know how much longer he and his deputy Tom Snow could keep up with the calls. Ethan's quiet mornings were starting earlier and getting shorter, while the workdays were getting longer.

~

Six months after his arrival this sleepy community was shocked by two murders. The first involved a teenage boy, the son of a prominent member of the community; the other, a descendant of one of the founding families of Riverview. The situation couldn't have been worse; pressure to solve the crimes intense.

Those events had brought Caitlyn Jamison into his life. He'd bent every rule and allowed her, a relative of the murdered teenager, access to the investigation. But she was the asset he needed, and as they worked to solve the crime, a personal relationship developed. *That* was not in the plan.

He hadn't heard from her in a while, so he wasn't sure when she'd be returning to photograph her friend's winery; it had to be soon. The fall colors wouldn't last much longer.

Would he get to see her?

Ethan sighed. He missed her mischievous smile, and her beautiful blue eyes, set off by reddish-brown hair that sometimes curled around her face. Just thinking about her put a smile on his face. Ethan realized that if he was going to have a chance at any kind of relationship, *he* had to make some decisions about his life.

But this morning, he couldn't think about his failed marriage, and so he shook off those thoughts with no resolution. He shifted forward, elbows resting on his knees as he thought about what he was going to do, personally and professionally. So much weighed on him at this early hour.

Instead, he decided to focus on the pros and cons of continuing as sheriff. He enjoyed working with his deputy, Tom, and dispatcher, Maddie. They made a great team. He liked being sheriff of Riverview, liked the residents, the tourists, and he was even getting used to the college kids. He enjoyed his bungalow with the wide front porch that overlooked the expanse of lawn to the tree line beyond. With his self-imposed deadline almost up, at this moment, as he gazed through the trees to the lake beyond, Ethan decided to exercise the option on his rent-to-own agreement. He wanted to continue as sheriff of Riverview, and he could do that as long as he didn't cross the line with the captain too many more times. He'd have to watch his step.

Exhaling, he relaxed back into his chair, hands warmed by the coffee mug, and enjoyed the peaceful setting until his phone emitted a familiar ding and a calendar reminder appeared.

Meeting w/ Capt Robertson in 30 minutes.

Damn!

He'd forgotten he had a meeting with the captain first thing this morning, and for good reason. The reporting hierarchy had recently changed, temporarily, he hoped. The increase in crime had created a budget crisis. To mange this crisis, rural law enforcement officers were asked to meet with Captain Robertson once a month to discuss budgets and any other issues that might affect funding.

He sighed, pushed himself out of the comfortable chair, and took one last look at the lake.

Another day had begun.

~ FOUR ~

Steven Sullivan's fingers drummed Tracy's antique oak desk as he debated what to do. The phone call he'd received a half hour ago had surprised him; he didn't think his informant would be ready this soon.

He should've been better prepared. In any case, he'd be at the agreed upon place and hope for the best. There was no time to call for backup.

Should I alert Tracy?

By agreeing to bunk at her place, he'd put her in a compromising position. They had been colleagues, once, but when she left Boston they had had no further contact and he had no idea she lived in this area until that hot August day when he showed up at her real estate agency. However, Steven suspected his boss knew, and had set them up. What did his boss think would happen? Was it a plan to get Tracy back into the fold?

Tracy suspected the reason he was in Riverview and they both understood the possible repercussions of his job. They just hadn't discussed it.

Steven checked his watch. Tracy was taking her time this morning. He didn't want her to sense his impatience, but it was almost time for him to leave.

~

In her upstairs bedroom, Tracy Connor hummed as she checked her hair and makeup one last time. Mirrors don't lie. Her bathroom mirror reflected a woman with a flawless complexion that belied her fifty-six years. She leaned in to check every detail, and then made a slight touch-up to the eyeliner that defined her deep blue eyes. She ran her fingers through her hair and noted she'd need highlights soon. That worry was for another day. For now, she fluffed the thick tumble that flowed gently to her shoulders.

She paused and looked deep into her soul. She'd accomplished a lot in her life. She'd overcome childhood health issues, issues that forced her into special classes, because of her learning difficulties.

When she reached the age of four, her parents explained she was adopted, but she was their chosen child and was loved unconditionally. Consequently, Tracy blamed her learning disabilities on her birth parents, whoever they were. She wondered why she was given up. She didn't want to think it was because she wasn't wanted.

Tracy worked hard to overcome her disabilities, and by junior high she was mainstreamed back into a regular classroom. After high school she attended college, then went through police academy and gained the highest marks, and then midlife crisis hit her hard. She was tired of the violence she encountered while doing her job. She was afraid of being killed, just because she was a police officer. She needed to make changes in her life, and she did.

And then Steven's arrival in Riverview had changed her life once again. When she couldn't find him a suitable rental, she reluctantly offered him a room in her house.

Tracy had learned that life consisted of roles to be played, and she now loved her role as manager of a successful real estate office. No one, not even Steven, was going to change that.

~

The new campus in Riverview was a boon for the real estate market. Professors and staff were moving to Riverview to be closer to their jobs. Students were grabbing up all the rental properties she managed.

Tracy allowed one more glance in the full-length mirror.

"Steven?" Tracy yelled as she headed down the stairs. "I'm on my way to work."

She stopped on the bottom step, paused and entertained a moment of guilt about not allowing him to talk about his assignment. She refused to relive those days.

15

She never understood why Steven, with his doctorate in forensic psychology, didn't go into private practice, make piles of money, and have weekends and holidays off. But, she learned, that wasn't who he was. He went into the police academy for training, and served as a consultant to the Boston PD to provide psychological profiles for the worst criminals. He undertook specialized training, which brought him to the dangerous work he was engaged in today.

She knew that some assignments took years. Relationships had to be built before the opportunity arose to go in for the kill. The little he had shared about this assignment was that he thought he could wrap it up quickly. She hoped so, too. She'd created a new life. Her business was booming and it needed her full attention. She refused to be distracted by him and his assignment.

She checked her watch. Was he scheduled to be on campus today? She'd been so wrapped up in her own business issues she hadn't been paying attention to his schedule. They had agreed to let each other know when they'd be back at the end of the day.

Had he violated that agreement already? Why isn't he responding?

"Steven?" She called again, this time louder.

Where could he be?

"I'm here," Steven said, stepping out of the small den at the end of the hall.

"The door was closed; didn't hear you at first. Off to work?" He said, disguising his relief. He'd decided not to tell her about the meeting with his informant.

Looking at her watch, she realized she was late and didn't have time to talk.

"Yes, off to a busy day. Have executives arriving in about an hour. Don't think they'll stay long. I won't make them feel welcome," she responded with a laugh.

"I don't know what my day will bring, but you have a good one."

Tracy turned and faced Steven. "Be careful, okay?"

"Always," he replied with a grin.

~

Steven turned back into the office and shut the door; images of their previous relationship flashed through his mind. They had met in Boston and served on a few cases together. They made a good team, and when the case was over they started meeting for drinks. A brief affair followed before they went their separate ways. Married to their jobs, neither had time for a relationship.

And now he was assigned to a case in an area where she lived and worked. When he showed up at her office looking for a rental, there were a few awkward moments.

They'd reviewed the rental listing, and when nothing came up as acceptable, resigned, Tracy took Steven to her house, a small Cape Cod on a quiet cul-de-sac in Riverview. It fit his needs perfectly. It featured two spacious bedrooms, two full baths, and a den for him to use during his stay.

She'd explained that she had to escape Boston and what it represented—the big city and the inherent crime and violence. It seemed only natural for her to return to her hometown.

Steven hoped that Tracy would be a good sounding board, someone he could trust, but it didn't take long for him to understand she was no longer interested in law enforcement. She'd lost her desire to make the world right, and she continued to have nightmares.

She'd made it clear that although they'd share living quarters, each would go their own way. She wasn't interested in his case. He cared little about the real estate market, unless it applied to a person of interest. He trusted Tracy's instincts would let him know if that happened.

She might be an asset after all.

~

After arriving in Riverview on that hot August day, he'd unpacked his duffle, and then driven into town. He noted some of the historic houses in the downtown area had been turned into government offices. The buildings had been saved from being demolished. Apparently, the town fathers had foreseen the future

17

enough to create an historic district to protect these "painted ladies." Mature maple trees along the main street provided much needed shade.

He walked down Main Street to where it ended at River Road Park, a place that featured benches, picnic tables, and a playground for residents and visitors. He noticed construction was starting on some sort of monument.

On the way back to the car he stopped at a small coffee shop and treated himself to a latte and a bagel smothered with cream cheese. As he continued his walk he noticed a store called Notions and Things. He walked in and met the owner, Anna Jones. He learned that her family members were long time residents of Riverview, and she regaled him with tales of local history, and explained the plans for the veteran's memorial being constructed in the park. The dedication was planned for the end of September. Steven silently hoped his job was finished by then, but his conversation with Anna had provided him background information he needed about the major players in town.

Walking down Main Street, Steven decided Riverview was one of the more peaceful locales in which he'd been assigned. He hated to think evil lurked beneath the surface of such a beautiful place, but the reality was, evil was everywhere, and his job was to find it and flush it out.

When this job is finished, could I retire here? What would Tracy think about that?

He continued to struggle with whether or not he should introduce himself to the local sheriff. The usual modus operandi was to remain anonymous, get the job done and don't involve the locals. Sometimes working with the local police agencies was helpful, but he'd have to wait and see.

~

Steven enjoyed working for the Boston Police Department, interviewing and writing up psychological assessments of those involved in the criminal system. His reputation grew over the years, and his services were requested throughout the state.

Then one day his life changed. His boss called him into the office and told him how the Boston PD was developing a specially trained law enforcement unit. This unit would also be available to federal agencies, for a fee.

Steven always looked for the next challenge, so he didn't give the offer a second thought. He embarked on months of training, and was then available to any government agency that needed assistance or undercover work.

His position as floating agent was unique. The downside was his exciting and dangerous lifestyle left no time for personal relationships, much less marriage and children. He loved living on the edge and without personal complications. Now, he realized, he was paying a price for those decisions.

He was still sore from his last assignment. A fight with a hired thug was a turning point for him. He had ended up in the hospital, and before he could voice his concerns about his job, his boss was at his bedside giving him the details of his next assignment. Following a week's rest he was instructed to drive to Central New York, pose as a college lecturer, and get the job done.

During his week of "rest" he gathered intelligence on Upstate New York. Steven was chosen for this assignment because he was good at making the right connections. That was how he managed to get the meeting this morning.

He checked his watch. He had decided to walk what he estimated to be a mile to the designated location. He didn't want his presence given away by the car's engine. If he saw anyone other than his contact, he'd abort.

Steven knew his informant would be nervous, so it was up to him to remain calm, reassuring, and in control. He would get the information he was sent to discover. He'd make sure his informant was protected, and then be on his way.

He decided to travel light. Trust was everything and with this informant, he needed to be cautious. He had to get it right. The information was critical; nothing could go wrong.

Steven yanked on the desk drawer. It stuck and needed to be jiggled just the right way for it to open. He had no right to complain; this was Tracy's house, Tracy's furniture. He had to make do. He pulled out the crumbled papers and placed his firearm, cell phone and wallet in the back. He replaced the papers, giving the appearance of a normal messy desk drawer. He locked the desk and hid the key.

"I'm ready."

He stood and thought through possible scenarios. If his contact decided to search him, Steven didn't want to be carrying a gun. He hated to leave it behind, but in this particular instance, with this particular informant, it was the right decision. Instead, he retrieved his knife and slid it into a sheath that was hooked to his belt and hidden from view by his jacket.

Steven closed the back door, listened for the latch, turned and walked away.

~ FIVE ~

Verna Adams's day started normally enough. Each morning since she moved back to her hometown of Riverview, she and her miniature collie Oliver took their constitutional on Old Mill Road. Verna preferred this route because the dirt road was full of nasty ruts that didn't encourage traffic. She liked the way the trees created an umbrella effect as they arched over the road, and she was drawn to this location because of the presence of her long-abandoned family homestead. To her dismay the house was in disrepair and overgrown with weeds. How many more years before it fell into complete ruin?

Verna stopped to gaze at the house and to remember. Or was it to torture herself? Her parents and grandparents raised their families here; they'd farmed the land. Childhood memories flooded into her mind and tears filled her eyes. Why did she do this to herself? What could be gained by reliving these memories when she should be concentrating on finding answers?

Since her return to Riverview, the question that haunted her most was what had happened to her brother Palle. The last contact with him was in June 1968 after he and Edda married and moved into this house after their parents had moved out. *Everyone* knew the rumors about Edda Villetta's ancestors and how they poisoned their spouses. Even though they were just rumors, Verna's family believed them and therefore much angst was felt about the marriage. But Verna's brother was strong willed, so it was no surprise that Palle, at age nineteen and with no money, married Edda anyway. How he thought he could support them, Verna hadn't a clue. Their parents gave in and allowed the newlyweds to move into the old homestead. Verna was furious. She'd set her sights on occupying the family homestead one day.

It was the line in the sand as far as Verna was concerned. She applied for a teaching position in Florida, the furthest she could get away from her family. The day she left, she'd made one last stop at the house to say a final goodbye to her brother, only to realize he'd left for work already, and Verna had nothing to say to her sister-in-law.

It was now time to bring closure. She regretted her stubbornness in shutting her family out all these years, and now Palle haunted her dreams.

Verna brought her thoughts back to the present. She resolved to begin the search to learn what happened to her brother. When she returned home she'd pull the boxes of family papers from the attic and start going through them.

With that decision made, she straightened her spine and continued her walk, tucking her hands up into her oversized sweater for warmth. She chided herself for forgetting her walking stick; she'd have to watch her step.

She loved the rustling sound as she shuffled through newly fallen leaves on this late September day. She tipped her face to the sun, as it filtered through the trees, and soaked in its warmth. She took a deep breath of the crisp fall air. Mornings like this reminded her that life might be worth living after all.

This road provided the peace and quiet Verna craved. In her opinion, Riverview was getting too crowded and too noisy, and she blamed it on the newly arrived college students. She'd been appalled when the university announced they were renovating the old mill for a satellite campus. Palle had worked in that mill and if she had a say, the old brick building would be reused as age-restricted apartments or boutique shops.

Riverview just wasn't the same town as in her childhood. She'd come back, but now she couldn't wait to leave. This morning as she and Oliver walked the familiar route, she planned her annual trip south. She and Oliver usually went south just after the New Year, but if they went *before* the holidays, like mid-November, she'd avoid the obligatory family gatherings she abhorred.

She had no immediate family of her own, so her late husband's nieces and nephews had always included her in their holiday gatherings. She didn't mind when they described her as their "old maid schoolteacher aunt"—the younger generation didn't know the difference between being a widow and an unmarried woman. What she did mind, however, was the constant arguing over politics and sports teams. Who cares, really?

But they were her only family, so she drove back to New Jersey, and put up with the arguing and the wayward children. It wasn't her idea of a pleasant holiday. Why had she put up with it this long? The old saying you can pick your friends but not your relatives held more than a kernel of truth.

She smiled, and her head nodded in affirmation as her early departure plan came together. She was pleased she'd figured out how to avoid any more family dinners. But before she went south, she had to know what happened to her brother. Her plan was in place; she would now get it done.

As all these thoughts collided in her head, Oliver jerked his leash. He made an abrupt turn off the road that pulled her into the weeds as he searched for the right spot to attend to business.

Verna, her mind still in mental disarray, was taken off guard. Her thoughts were on Palle and not on her dog's needs. Because the dog pulled so abruptly, she lost her balance, but remained somewhat upright thanks to a strategically placed sapling. Oliver continued his quest, pulling a stumbling Verna along. She took a few staggering steps in an attempt to regain her balance before she tripped over a log cleverly disguised by overgrowth. Down she went, grabbing another sapling to cushion her fall. In the process she lost control of the leash and Oliver was off, enjoying his newfound freedom.

Verna struggled to get back on her feet using the sapling to steady herself. She bent over, hands on her knees, gasping for breath. Whenever something like this happened, she was painfully reminded of her age.

She brushed herself off, observing the bleeding scratches on her hands and arms. *Damn! That hurt.*

She surveyed the area for Oliver, and it was then she saw *him*. There, in the weeds, was a man lying face down, but with his head slightly turned so that she could see his eyes were closed. Was that blood on his head? Was the ground damp below?

Verna didn't know what to do. She turned her head; she didn't want to look at *him*. If he was dead she didn't want to touch him, but what if he was still alive? She had watched enough TV to know she should put two fingers to his throat to check for a pulse. If he was alive and she didn't help, would she be able to live with herself?

Was this road jinxed? A distant memory flashed through her mind.

~

Putting her anger aside, she wanted to see her brother, Palle, to make sure he was all right before she headed to Florida. But Palle had left for work and she was forced to acknowledge Edda. All she could remember from that day was Edda's statement, "It's not my fault." What did Edda mean by that and did it have anything to do with Palle's disappearance?

~

Verna jerked back to the present. She had a crisis to deal with.

She came up with a compromise. Keeping her eyes averted, she pulled the cell phone from her vest pocket and willing her hands to stop shaking, she opened the flap and hit 911. There was nothing she could do for this young man, dead or alive, but paramedics could. After reporting what she saw, she returned the phone to her pocket. With her back to the body, she debated what to do. She checked for any sign the assailant might still be in the vicinity, and shaking with fright, she strode quickly back to the road to wait for the police and paramedics to arrive, calling to Oliver as she went.

~ SIX ~

Deputy Tom Snow raced through town with lights flashing. Dispatcher Maddie Smith had sent him to Old Mill Road because some woman, "Thinks she found a body and she doesn't know whether he's dead or alive."

How could she "think" it was a body? It was or it wasn't. And if it was, didn't she have the wherewithal to check for a pulse?

Tom was starting his second year with the Riverview Police Department, and he was frustrated. He was still a deputy in a rural community with no chance for promotion. His girlfriend Sarah had ended their relationship when she'd had enough of broken dates due to his constant work demands. To put a final note to their relationship, she had moved out of state.

Tom had transferred to Riverview from the Buffalo Police Department two years before. When the previous sheriff of Riverview announced his retirement, Tom figured with his experience in a large city, he'd be a shoo-in. That proved not to be the case, as the town council instead chose a beat cop from New York City. It was a crushing disappointment and Tom had hoped the new sheriff, Ethan Ewing, wouldn't fit into the Upstate New York culture. Unfortunately, Ethan did, and despite Tom's initial disappointment, he liked working with Ethan.

Tom had watched Ethan settle into the job and thrive in the rural environment. With Maddie managing the office and the dispatch console, Tom had to admit they made a good team. It just wasn't what he'd planned. He was still determined, though, to continue to pursue his career goals.

The quiet rural community was no more. The new satellite campus brought inherent crime and social issues to this sleepy village. Because of the increased population, Tom was sure another deputy would be hired and that would provide Tom the opportunity to move up the ladder. Maybe they'd add a detective position; he was ready for the challenge. One thing for sure was that he and Ethan couldn't cover all the bases; they needed help.

Tom knew Ethan had been diligent in following up on their repeated requests for additional officers. A good case was made, but the wheels of the state budget office turned slowly and their requests seemed to fall on deaf ears.

Another reason Tom was frustrated was the fact he was assigned to digitize a stack of cold cases. It was a tedious job, and this morning he planned to get through a number of them. Just get it done was his mantra until Maddie got the call about a body being found.

His thoughts were interrupted as he turned onto a dirt road. He stopped, checked his GPS. Yes, this was Old Mill Road, one of the few roads he'd never been on. He would've remembered this rutted pathway, because it wasn't much more than that, narrowed by trees and overhanging branches. His patrol car would acquire a few new scratches.

He pulled up to the spot where the "alleged" body was reported and saw an older woman standing by the side of the road. She was slight of frame, her grey hair pulled back in a bun. The bulky red sweater she wore appeared at least two sizes too big.

What's a woman her age doing out here so early?

It was then he saw the retractable leash hanging from her right hand.

Ah, a dog walker. But where's the dog?

He glanced at the information Maddie handed him as he left the office. Verna Adams made the report. Tom climbed out of his cruiser, straightened his uniform, shifted his holster into position, and walked towards the woman he assumed to be Verna Adams.

~

Verna turned at the sound of a car approaching. She waved at the car, like the driver wouldn't notice her standing alone in the road. She was dismayed when she realized the person responding to her call wasn't the nice sheriff.

"What've we got here, ma'am?" Tom asked, trying his best to be polite, though unable to keep a bit of sarcasm out of his tone. He was still upset his morning routine had been interrupted.

Verna's hand and voice shook as she pointed in the direction of the abandoned house.

"There's a body over there, in the brush. Not quite to the house. Don't know if he's still alive. Didn't want to disturb anything. Will the paramedics get here soon?" Verna said in a rush. The fact she didn't have the courage to check for a pulse or do anything to help the victim made her feel inadequate.

"Are you sure there's a body? Maybe just an old log or something," Tom suggested. He didn't want to go through the brush if he didn't have to.

At her age Verna was used to sarcasm, so she gave him one of her schoolmarm looks.

How I hate this younger generation. They think because we're old, we're daft!

Verna jutted her hip to the right, with her hand on her hip, and replied just as sarcastically, "Young fella, it could be a log, but I've never seen a log that bled."

Tom was saved from responding to Verna's irreverent remark by the arrival of the paramedics. He realized the report was real. He turned away from Verna and took control of the situation, assuming his own authoritative stance and instructed the paramedics, "Through there she says. Follow the path into the brush. Hurry!"

Tom took a look around. What was this place, anyway? The trees that arched over the road gave a tunnel-like appearance. It might feel comforting to some, but to him, it was creepy. It was like the trees planned to trap you in their deadly embrace.

He then noticed the crumbling old farmhouse beyond where the paramedics were headed. It, too, was being swallowed up by nature.

I wonder what story this place has to tell? It'd make the perfect spot for all sorts of illegal liaisons.

He didn't have time to think about that now as he followed the paramedics. He pushed his way through the saplings and tall weeds, trying not to get his pants dirty.

~

Verna watched as the men trampled through the bushes in search of the body she reported. Just after their arrival, Oliver came bounding back out of the brush, apparently more curious about what was happening on the road than anything he was tracking.

"Finally you return from your adventure," Verna said to her dog as she securely fastened his leash. "Well, I've had an adventure of my own."

With Oliver corralled and safely fastened, Verna stayed put. She was sure there would be more questions once the body was discovered. She looked for somewhere to sit, but there was only the ground. If she chose that option she'd have difficulty getting up. Maybe she'd lean on the bumper of Deputy Snow's patrol car. After all, she was a taxpayer.

A few minutes later another car approached, this time a vehicle marked with a decal indicating the Office of the Medical Examiner. Verna watched as Doc Morse got out of the driver's side, but who was the young woman with him? The two scrambled to get their equipment out of the back of the van, and then each donned protective clothing. She watched doc and the young woman traipse into the weeds, following the path made by the paramedics. She tried to catch their attention, but they were far too intent on their purpose to even notice her.

Never mind. She had her ways.

~ SEVEN ~

Doc Morse nodded to the paramedics when he arrived. He didn't invite conversation before he'd had a chance to observe the scene and examine the body. It was his clean slate approach. He donned a mask and gloves. He checked for signs of life, going through the proper procedures. Flies had begun to land on the body, which gave him the answer, but he wanted to see for himself.

The paramedics were thorough in their job, but it was his job to make sure there was no doubt. He remembered the time when … but back to this gentleman. He checked the man's pockets and found a credit card. It could or could not have relevance. He handed the card to his assistant for bagging. He then turned the body over.

The head wound showed blood, but it didn't take Doc long by looking at the young man's face and arms to realize this was a drug overdose.

A cursory exam was done with his assistant, also wearing the requisite mask and gloves, close at hand, taking notes, bagging evidence. He stood up and nodded to his assistant. She measured air temperature, and prepared evidence bags. She photographed the scene and asked Tom and the paramedics to step back.

"Take the swabs, now, Carrie, if you would be so kind," Doc instructed.

When Doc stood up and took a step back so the woman could do her work, Tom approached.

"What do'ya think, Doc?" Tom asked after Doc broke the silence. "I noticed a look of surprise on your face when you saw the card. Do you know the victim?"

"How intuitive. I recognized the name on the card, and if the card belongs to the victim, then it's Steven Sullivan. I attended one of the university's town-gown receptions and noticed the name on the program. I'm not sure if he was there or not, because I didn't have a chance to meet him. I was at the reception because I wanted to meet the professors in the science department."

Doc scratched his head, his usual thinking pose.

"If I remember correctly, one of the secretaries mentioned Mr. Sullivan was renting a room, maybe about a mile from here," Doc responded. "I haven't the foggiest notion what anybody would be doing out in this remote area, at this time of the morning. From what I see on a cursory examination, and the marks on his arms, this is not the first time he's shot up. Not something I want to associate with a university professor. But heaven knows these days. It seems anything goes."

Tom shook his head while jotting down notes on the victim's appearance, clean cut, dark blue shirt with collar, tan slacks, loafers.

"And your assistant?" Tom whispered, nodding at the woman taking samples. He was going to like working with her.

"Actually, Tom, she's the new medical examiner, Carrie Young. We're working together for a few months while she gets to know the area. Then I'll step down."

Carrie must have heard the conversation as she turned and gave Tom a knowing smile.

"Oh . . . I didn't know," Tom responded, kicking himself for bringing up what appeared to be a touchy subject.

"Not many know about it yet. We're trying to make the transition without much pomp and circumstance. I've been meaning to tell Ethan. Just couldn't bring myself . . ." Doc's voice trailed off.

It was evident Doc was conflicted about the upcoming changes in his status and wasn't entirely comfortable with the conversation, so Tom stopped the chitchat.

"I'll finish securing the scene. Is there anything more you can tell me about cause of death?"

"Not at this time. The bruise on his head was likely from that rock, but it certainly wasn't enough to kill him. I suspect it was whatever drug or drugs he was taking. We'll have to do an autopsy to determine the exact cause."

~

It was nearly fifteen minutes later when Verna saw the paramedics coming towards her in a slow trot. As they passed, she noticed the victim's head was covered.

Doc Morse and the woman followed the paramedics. They all acted business-like. Verna didn't dare approach them.

Darn! She wanted to be the fountain of information when she went to the senior center later today. Well, she could certainly tell them she'd found a body, and she could make up the details.

Tom came and stood beside her. His attitude changed once he realized there was a body.

"How long was he . . . ?" Verna stuttered, having trouble finishing her sentence. She needed to be reassured that the man hadn't died moments before their arrival due to her lack of courage. She needed to know he was dead a long time and that there was *nothing* she could have done to change the outcome.

Tom didn't answer her question. Instead he pulled out his notepad.

"I need to know," Verna demanded, pulling on Tom's arm. She refused to be treated like a child.

Tom hesitated. He didn't like this pushy old woman.

"He's been dead a few hours, ma'am. There was nothing you could have done. Did you recognize him?"

Verna thought a minute.

"I'm not sure. It was such a surprise, him lying there like that. My dog dragged me through the weeds. I lost my balance. It was so upsetting. I was a little dizzy by it all. But, no. I don't think he was familiar, but it was such a shock. All I could think about was calling for help, getting back to the road, and finding Oliver. Sorry I'm not being helpful."

"That's fine, ma'am. You've had quite a morning. Just tell me again how you came to find the victim, and then if you will provide me with your contact information, you can go on home and we'll be in touch if we have more questions."

"What happened?" Verna asked.

"We don't know yet," was all Tom was willing to share with her, his patience running out. "Now, please, ma'am, answer my questions, and then you are free to go."

Verna grudgingly accepted the fact that Tom was not going to give her any more information, though she felt she was owed more. After all, she was the one who found the man. If she hadn't come by when she did, he'd still be in the weeds rotting away.

"Well," she began. "He appeared to be a young man wearing a dark shirt, light colored pants. He was clean cut, you know. Do you think he could be a university student? Oh, I'm sorry. I wish I could remember more, but it was all such a blur."

"That's fine," Tom said, putting his notebook in his pocket. "Would you like a ride back to your house?"

"No, no. Oliver and I will walk back to my car. Thanks for the offer," Verna said as she turned and walked Oliver down the middle of Old Mill Road, checking behind her as she went. What if the culprit was still out there?

~ EIGHT ~

Ethan arrived at the Renwick police station with not a minute to spare. He'd scrambled to get dressed and out the door, his relaxed early morning ritual forgotten. The early morning meeting turned out to be a discussion regarding the mayor's new drug task force. Ethan figured the reason he was chosen was because of his NYPD background. Or maybe it was because the captain wanted to keep a tighter rein on Ethan's schedule.

Ethan hurried into the meeting and pulled a pad and pencil from his briefcase to take notes. There were two others seated at the table. One was a city cop, and the other an older gentleman, obviously a businessman. Since Ethan was late and introductions had already been made, he wasn't acknowledged. Another game Captain Robertson played.

Without preamble, the captain stated the latest statistics on heroin use in Upstate New York. "We've a double-edged sword, I'm afraid," Captain Robertson began.

"From the information I have been supplied by the Centers for Disease Control and the U.S. Drug Enforcement Agency, between the years 2007 and 2015 the total grams of oxycodone increased by triple-digit percentages in the Albany Region, Southern Tier and Lower Hudson Valley."

"What do you mean by a double-edged sword?" Ethan asked.

"We are up against the drug cartels trucking in illegal drugs, mostly heroin from Mexico, as well as pharmaceutical drug wholesalers the supply the pain medication that certain doctors are overprescribing," Captain Robertson responded. "The Centers for Disease Control have identified the three pharmaceutical wholesalers who control 85% of the distribution market. Here is the list. We are working with our state senators to develop legislation to deal with these issues."

"The reality is that we would be going up against the large pharmaceutical companies supplying the warehouses and their 'donations' to the reelection campaigns of those very legislators," Ethan added. "How do you plan to take on the big pharmaceutical companies and the Mexican cartels?"

"We have to try," the man to Ethan's right replied. "It isn't easy. If I don't get pain medications for my customers, they'll go to the chain pharmacy across town. When I see an inordinate amount of pain pills prescribed, I call the doctor. One day a man came in with a prescription for 180 hydrocordone pills and said he told the doctor he only wanted Tylenol. It's that type of prescription abuse we're fighting. Once the person is addicted, the cartels can take over. The pharmaceutical companies continue to supply the addictive drugs as well as the rescue drugs. Do you know that in 2015 over 50,000 Americans were killed by drug overdoses?"

"And you are?" Ethan asked. He hadn't been introduced, so he had no idea who was at the table.

"Sorry, I should have introduced myself. I'm Harold Johansson, a local pharmacist."

"Harold Johansson is one of our celebrated long-time residents of Renwick," Captain Robertson added in a tone to put Ethan in his place.

But Ethan wasn't listening. The numbers just quoted were staggering, and almost too much to grasp. Crime in the tri-state area was escalating so rapidly statisticians couldn't keep up with the current figures. Law enforcement agencies were ramping up to deal with more thefts and murders; hospitals were struggling with how to deal with the number of overdose emergencies.

Drug use was nothing new. The difference was the drug of choice, and the rapid escalation of addiction. Law enforcement couldn't keep up, nor was the usual way of dealing with this issue any longer relevant.

The captain put forth a possible solution.

"The mayor wants to treat overdose cases in specialized care centers instead of hospital emergency rooms. Abusers would be treated at these care centers instead of sending them to the emergency room or jail. We may even go so far as to provide safe places for addicts to shoot up."

Ethan was surprised that Renwick's mayor had come up with this out-of-the-box plan. At first glance it appeared to be an outrageous idea, but as he thought it through, it was pure genius. His skeptical side told him when something seemed too good to be true . . . follow the money. Was there money to be made by the mayor or someone else in setting up these centers? He drew a dollar sign on his pad followed by a question mark.

The captain continued unaware of Ethan's thoughts.

"As usual, the proposed solution comes down to funding. Emergency care centers are expensive. New York residents are already being crushed under the state's tax burden."

The captain then talked about the area's college campuses, their campus security procedures, and how campus health centers, under this new plan, would have to deal with the influx of student addicts. The cost would be the university's burden.

"Now that a campus is located in Riverview, the village will be a ripe target for increased crime. Will we have more deputies assigned to our location?" Ethan asked.

"Probably not," the captain replied. "Budgets are tight. Towns throughout the state have requested more staff, and those requests are being filled on a first-come first-served basis. Riverview has to wait its turn."

Not surprised by this response, Ethan continued to take copious notes about everything discussed in order to share the information with Tom and Maddie. Their work was cut out for them, and it was important that they remain a strong team. Ethan didn't want to lose his staff from the heavy workload. No matter how much a person liked or was loyal to their job, there was a limit. They *needed* more help.

When the meeting was adjourned, Ethan joined Captain Robertson in his office for their monthly appointment. The captain was a crusty old guy who'd climbed the police ranks until he hit the top—a perfect example of the Peter Principle. It wasn't that the captain was a bad police officer. From what Ethan was told, the captain had been an outstanding officer, but then he was promoted to his level of incompetence, which was management. Since he had to start reporting to Robertson on funding, they had gone head-to-head on several issues. Additional staff for the Riverview office would be one more argument that Ethan would most likely lose.

Ethan settled into the uncomfortable wooden chair and waited for the captain to get himself situated in his padded office chair. Before the captain took control of the conversation, which was his wont, Ethan spoke up.

"Sorry I was late this morning, and sorry to miss the introductions. Can you tell me who else was at the table?"

"As I said, Harold Johansson's the home-town druggist. There's more than one drug store in Renwick, but we think of Harold's pharmacy as the best, the preferred, if you will. His family was one of the founding families of Renwick, and we take care of our own," Captain Robertson replied with a wink. "The police officer is my son-in-law, James Bradley. Very proud of him."

Ethan couldn't believe how that deck was stacked. So much for a well-rounded committee. It will be interesting to see who shows up for the first task force meeting. He sat back and prepared himself for the minutia the captain usually covered at these meetings. Ethan would be given a bunch of irrelevant instructions, which he'd completely ignore.

~

Leaving his meeting with Captain Robertson, Ethan checked his watch and thought an early lunch at Riverview's new restaurant would hit the spot. He turned his phone on, and he listened to a voicemail from Maddie alerting him to the situation on Old Mill Road.

36

"Body found on Old Mill Road about an hour ago. Tom there, paramedics have arrived; Doc Morse on his way. Call in as soon as you get this message."

Ethan called Maddie immediately to get the latest information on the body. Maddie briefed him on what Tom reported.

"The body's at the morgue and nothing can be learned until Doc Morse has a chance to run some tests. And, you've got several phone messages here that need your immediate attention," Maddie said. "Do you want them now?"

"No. I'm almost to the office. I'll deal with them then."

~

What Ethan didn't plan on was seeing the Mayor of Renwick in the Riverview Sheriff's office.

"Mayor, to what do we owe this visit?" Ethan asked, breathless from his race up the front steps. In the year Ethan was sheriff, the mayor of the neighboring town had never visited Riverview. Their paths never crossed, and this fact made Ethan immediately suspicious.

Before the mayor could answer, Maddie stepped back out of the mayor's line of vision, rolled her eyes indicating her annoyance, and returned to the dispatch console.

"I'm visiting the area towns, the town supervisors, councilmen, and sheriff's offices. As you know, I'm concerned about the escalating drug traffic, and I want to let each municipality know that I'm working on a plan to deal with this," Mayor Goodrich stated. "We're going to have to work together to address this horrendous issue, and that's the reason for my new task force. I suggested you be appointed to serve, because with your background, you'll bring much to the table. I also wanted to introduce myself to your staff." He turned and gave Maddie a nod.

Ethan was tuned into the mayor's obvious ploy. He had learned of the mayor's plan at the morning's meeting. It was a good idea, though it would cost communities a lot of money, and should go through a vetting process first. Ethan took a deep breath, smiled and replied to the mayor's comment.

"Of course I'm honored to be chosen for your task force, but there's one problem. As you see, Mayor, we're a small office. The staff consists of my deputy, Tom Snow, Maddie, our dispatcher, and me. I've requested additional support, but was told to wait in line. I can't afford time away," Ethan said with a sad smile. He loved it when he could use his diplomatic and acting skills.

"Never you mind. We'll find you help," Mayor Goodrich blustered. "In the meantime, I expect to see you at the meeting. Captain Robertson will let you know when that will be. I've more towns to visit today," the mayor stated as he shook Ethan's hand, nodded to Maddie, donned his hat and left the building.

"What the hell was that about?" Maddie asked in anger. Before she could continue Ethan cut in, his own anger apparent.

"You know what that was all about. Politics. He, with every other politico in New York, wants to climb the ladder. He has a scheme to deal with the drug problem and if he can make something of that, he'll make a name for himself. It all comes down to politics, and that leads to money and power. I've seen it too many times. I guess I should be honored that he thinks I could help make his plan work—even if it creates havoc with the localities."

He failed to notice Maddie's agitation, and that she had something more on her mind. She started to say something, but he cut her off.

"Do you have any words of wisdom?"

Maddie, short for Madeleine, with her curly red hair and freckles to match, usually had an answer for every situation, but in this regard, she stood firm with arms crossed as if she were ready for battle.

"I'll answer your question, if you will then hear me out," Maddie responded.

"I think you are stuck with this assignment, but in the process you'll learn about the powerbase in Renwick. That networking will work to our advantage in the future."

"What do you mean?" Ethan asked.

"Budgets and stuff like that. It's not what you know, but who you know."

Ethan nodded in acknowledgement. "You're right, of course. Besides, it appears I don't have a say, so I'd better buck up and deal with it."

Ethan's appreciation of Maddie rose even higher at her common sense insights. She handled calls with efficiency, having the knack for knowing when there was an emergency and when there was not. It was a valuable skill so their manpower wasn't wasted on false alarms. Her best attribute, however, was her encyclopedic knowledge when it came to the residents of Riverview. She'd lived in the town long enough to be considered an "old timer," and Ethan was thankful for the fount of Maddie's knowledge of the townspeople, the politics and the culture of the area.

In the end, Ethan admitted Maddie was right. There was nothing he could do. There was too much power behind the request and if he stood his ground, the department and maybe even the residents of Riverview would suffer.

Resigned, he looked at her and he finally realized her anxious expression didn't have anything to do with his being appointed to the mayor's task force.

"You've got something on your mind, don't you," he said, immediately regretting he had ignored her obvious distress.

~ NINE ~

"You bet I do! Don't you check your text messages?" Her voice raised in exasperation. "I sent a text asking you to call back."

Ethan pulled the phone from his pocket. Embarrassed, he responded, "I guess I didn't hear the text come in. Sorry. What's up?"

"I wanted to fill you in on the situation this morning and suggest you go to the morgue."

"Fill me in," Ethan said, looking adequately chastised.

"The report was called in by Verna Adams. She's a retired schoolteacher. During her morning walk she came across a man's body near the old van der Molen place on Old Mill Road. She was so shocked she didn't know if he were dead or alive, so instead of checking, she called 911."

"Okay, what else?" Ethan asked. He didn't know why Maddie was wound up. He sensed there was a lot more to the story.

"I sent Tom to check the situation and he reported that it was a body, apparently the victim of a drug overdose. The only ID near or on the body was a credit card. Tom called in to say they thought the victim might be Steven Sullivan, a new professor at the campus here in town. He was dead when they arrived. The body was taken to the medical examiner's office for an autopsy," Maddie explained. "It's just too awful. Tracy's going to be devastated."

"Who's Tracy?" Ethan asked making a downward motion with his hands to encourage Maddie to slow down. She retained so many details, she tended to mind dump names and places, and sometimes it was more than Ethan could comprehend. He wasn't familiar with everyone in town, so it took time for him to make the connections.

"Tracy Connor's a local real estate agent, and Steven is staying with her until he finds a place. I think they may have worked together in Boston, or something, and now he's a part-time lecturer assigned to the satellite campus," Maddie replied. "I met him when out walking. They seem like nice folks."

"You said, 'they think' it is this Sullivan guy?" Ethan said.

"Yeah, that's the funny thing. Like I said, the only ID near the victim was a credit card. Doc said he heard of a lecturer at the new campus named Steven Sullivan, but Doc isn't sure. He can't say anything definite until a positive identification is made. It's a strange situation, so I thought you'd better look into it."

"Where's Tom now?" Ethan asked, looking over at Tom's empty desk. "He must have left in a hurry. A bag of carrot sticks is sitting on his desk."

"He was about to have his morning snack when the call came in. Right now he's at the morgue getting more details. He got a statement from Verna and sent her home. You should go talk with Verna and Doc Morse. They might have more information," Maddie instructed, shooing him out the door.

"Don't you trust Tom to do the job?" Ethan asked, standing his ground, not wanting Maddie to control his schedule.

"It's not that I don't trust him, I just want to make sure everything possible is done to find out what happened to this guy. Two heads are better than one," Maddie explained.

Ethan didn't want to argue with Maddie, because he respected her professional instincts. There was something else going on.

"You're right, Maddie," Ethan said as he turned towards the door, "but I still think Tom will do a thorough job."

"And I *still think* you should check in with the doc," Maddie said with defiance, twisting her hands.

"Okay," Ethan agreed, because there must be more to Maddie's request than what she was sharing. He suspected in time it would come out. Maddie wasn't going to back down and she did have a point.

"I'll see what Doc has to say."

41

Ethan walked by Tom's desk and thumbed through the pile of manila folders.

"How do you think the cold case project is coming?" Ethan asked.

Maddie hesitated before answering.

"Okay, I guess. Tom's been down lately. I don't know what's bothering him. Well, actually I do. I wasn't going to say anything, because it isn't my news to share. But his mood is starting to affect the office. I know he was disappointed he didn't get your position last year, but he seemed to accept that fact. He applied for a position in the Adirondacks and didn't get that either. He's bummed, and I don't blame him. To top things off, I think he and his girlfriend have split. He works too many hours, which resulted in too many broken dates. I know he's frustrated, but he can't bring that baggage into the office. You should have a talk with him," Maddie stated.

Ethan nodded in understanding. "I suspected he was getting itchy and hasn't been his happy self. I guess we've all been so busy we haven't taken time for each other. I'll talk with him and let him know I'll stand behind him if he wants to try for other positions. He's a good deputy, and once he gets a few more years experience behind him, he will make a hell of a good police officer."

"He's in here by eight, sometimes earlier, and I think he takes pride in having everything under control by the time you arrive. One thing I've noticed is Tom is pretty rigid in his schedule. In fact he was working on those damn files when the 911 call came in. He's not happy about the cold case file assignment, but he's determined to do a good job and get it done. I admire him for that," Maddie continued.

Ethan wasn't happy about the assignment either, but it would be a huge benefit in bringing criminals to justice. Several months earlier the state legislature, in its infinite wisdom, decided cold cases should be digitized so that police departments across the state had access. The policy made sense, but what didn't make sense was the mandate carried no funding. The state police were the repository of cold case files and didn't want to carry the burden. Each sheriff's office within their jurisdiction received numerous boxes filled with manila folders. The local police departments were to pick up the workload as well as the tab. When the boxes arrived and Ethan realized how much work it was going to mean for his office, he requested funds to hire a temporary worker—a request that was immediately denied by the state budget office. No surprise there.

Ethan turned from Tom's desk. With the heavier workload and longer hours, Ethan had neglected to keep a finger on the pulse of his staff. He'd find time to talk with Tom.

He turned back to the business at hand. "Going to the morgue," Ethan said with a sigh as he grabbed his cap off the rack, and headed out the door.

~ TEN ~

At Maddie's insistence, Ethan drove back to the medical examiner's office, located a few miles outside Renwick. His plan to catch an early lunch at the Garden of Eatin' was forgotten.

Until recently the medical examiner's office was located in a wing of the building Doc Morse used for his Riverview office. Over the summer the state legislature decided to consolidate each county's medical examiner offices into one central location. Riverview's office was the first to be moved to the lower level of the Renwick Hospital. The remaining towns had until January 1 to comply. The rural municipalities put up resistance, as they didn't want to give up home rule. The consolidation was supposed to save money, but in reality the inconvenience with time and travel for the medical examiners and police officers would offset any saving. Ethan didn't like this arrangement and Doc Morse disliked it even more.

When Ethan pulled up to the building, he noticed Tom sitting in his car with cell phone to his ear. Ethan hoped he was giving Maddie more details to add to the case file.

As Ethan approached, Tom quickly ended his call and got out of his patrol car.

"I'm surprised to see you here, sheriff. Is there a problem?"

"No problem, Tom. Just thought I'd see what Doc has to say about the victim, and Maddie thinks she might know the guy."

"She didn't let on when I called it in," Tom responded with annoyance, slipping the phone back into its case.

Ethan ignored Tom's abrupt response and instead focused on the reason they were there.

"Do we know anything more about the deceased?" Ethan asked.

"Only the guy's name. He didn't have anything in his pockets except a credit card. Strange. Usually people have something more on them, even if it's only a cell phone. Doc Morse thinks the guy might have a connection with the university."

~

Ethan felt a chill as they entered the morgue. Was it his imagination or was this wing of the building kept cooler in deference to the dead?

He nodded to the receptionist, showed his ID and indicated Tom should follow him down the long hallway. When they reached the last door on the left, the autopsy suite, Ethan paused. He wasn't sure how comfortable Tom was with bodies and autopsies. Ethan dreaded this part of his job. The bodies, the equipment, and the smells at times were more than he could handle. He hated the way the room's odors permeated his clothing, his hair and his skin. It was the reason he kept a change of clothes at the office, and why his dry cleaning bills were so high.

A young woman greeted them. She appeared to be in her late twenties, five four, shoulder length brown hair, blue eyes, and an engaging smile. Not the usual description Ethan would attribute to a woman working in this environment. She extended her hand and introduced herself.

"Carrie Young, and you must be Sheriff Ewing."

She winked at Tom and said with a smile, "I met Deputy Snow at the crime scene. We weren't formally introduced, but I asked Doc Morse on the way back and he told me who you were. By the way, I'm the new medical examiner."

Ethan took a step back, a look of surprise on his face. He recovered, shook her hand, and then looked around for Doc Morse.

"Where's Doc?" Ethan asked, upset by the news.

Why hadn't Doc mentioned this?

"Oh, he went to get supplies. You'd think he'd keep this room stocked," replied Carrie, looking around at the cabinets that lined the back wall. "That won't happen when I take over."

Ethan was put off by Carrie's cavalier attitude, but held his tongue. He'd find out what was going on, peeved that Doc hadn't mentioned the impending change.

Ethan swallowed, and said, "And when will that be?"

Before Carrie could respond Doc Morse entered the room.

"Ethan, and Tom. Good to see you both. Though I'm not sure why you're here."

Ethan detected Doc's somber mood.

Ethan replied to Doc's question, ignoring Carrie and getting down to business.

"Good to see you, too. What can you tell me about the body found this morning?"

Doc Morse stepped closer to the autopsy table. He detected Ethan's impatience and wondered what that was about.

"It's too soon to have much information, but I can tell you it's possible the gentleman is Steven Sullivan. I say 'possible' because the only identification found on the body was a worn credit card. I'll need conclusive verification.

If it is Mr. Sullivan, then I believe he works for the university as a part-time lecturer. I noticed his name on a university program listing of new professors and lecturers. Having said that, I'll get a positive ID before I state his identity."

"Interesting. What about cause of death?" Ethan asked.

"I can't provide that information for sure until an autopsy has been performed and blood tests have been run. A preliminary guess would be a massive drug overdose with complicating bleed out from hitting his head on a rock. But this whole thing doesn't add up," Doc replied, his voice starting to shake.

Ethan had noted Doc was tense, definitely not himself. Was he upset about being replaced as medical examiner? Or was he upset about the workload, or the time it now took to get to the new state-mandated autopsy suite . . . or something else? Ethan had to find

46

out, but right now they had to put those things aside and focus on the victim.

"When will you have results, Doc?" Ethan said, his patience getting thin.

"In due time," Doc responded back with impatience of his own.

"Sorry," Ethan responded. "I've had a tough morning."

"And so has this gentleman," Doc retorted, pointing to the victim.

"It's my determination, after superficial examination …" Carrie jumped in.

The men turned to her out of politeness, but she got the message, backed away, and deferred to Doc Morse. Her frustration at being ignored was evident in her stance.

Doc was agitated, and Ethan needed to keep the situation under control if they were going to get the information needed and get on with the investigation.

"Doc, can we talk?" Ethan asked in a whisper. He nodded to the other side of the room.

"Carrie, you fill Deputy Snow in on the rest. I'll be right back," Doc instructed.

~ ELEVEN ~

Ethan followed Doc to the end of the autopsy suite, a long narrow room with refrigerated units lining one side.

While he waited for them both to calm down, Ethan noticed how much Doc had aged. Over the past year Ethan had depended on this man. Doc was a person of intelligence and stability, and someone who helped make sense out of chaotic situations. But now Doc's gait was slower, his hair whiter and thinner, and the twinkle in Doc's green-gray eyes was missing. Was it the move or the increased workload aging him? Emotions were high today and Ethan had to get to the bottom of what was going on. They couldn't afford to lose this man.

"I apologize for my impatience," Ethan began. "I know the move to this new facility must be hard on you."

"It is, Ethan. My Riverview office had everything at hand. Now I'm not sure where anything is. I'm off my game. And the commute back and forth . . . well, that isn't the only problem."

"If that isn't the problem, what is? Is it that young lady at the other end of the room?"

Doc hesitated, sighed, and said, "Partly. It's difficult to realize you are past your prime; that you have to let the next generation take over. But mostly, Ethan . . .," Doc looked down the line of autopsy tables.

"Do you know why we were given this section of the hospital?"

"Because of the consolidation mandated by the state?" Ethan replied.

"Partly, but mostly because it's a large space with room for expansion. And this morning, well, a death in Riverview . . ." Doc took a deep breath, "means this insidious addiction has reached into

48

my home territory. It's going to affect my friends and neighbors. It's taking hold everywhere."

Ethan nodded, understanding that Doc experienced a lot of bad situations during his professional life, and if this situation was upsetting him so . . . what did it foretell?

"Did you read about the situation in West Virginia? There were so many overdose deaths within a short period of time it overwhelmed the medical examiner, and paramedics started to quit. They were seeing the same overdose victims they had revived before. The stress was too much even for the specially trained. Will this happen here? Will we see our communities destroyed? How can it be stopped? We've never had a situation quite like this," Doc stated, allowing his thoughts to tumble out.

"I understand," Ethan said softly, placing his hand on Doc's shoulder. "But I think it goes deeper. You're a professional. You've seen a lot of situations. What's at the root of this for you, Doc?"

Doc Morse looked up and surveyed the room. He knew how many bodies were in the coolers and how many more were to come.

"I'm guilty," Doc whispered.

"What do you mean?" Ethan stated, lowering his voice. "You can't help what's going on out there."

"But I could have. Don't you see? All my years as a practicing physician I tried to help my patients live a better life. When the new painkillers became available and the reps were giving out generous samples, and pushing them as miracle drugs, I believed them and prescribed the drugs just like everyone else. I liked the money and the perks offered by the pharmaceutical companies. Now I'm paying the price. I had no idea the drugs were so addictive and that my patients wouldn't be able to get off of them, ever. I didn't know their lives, and the lives of those around them, would be ruined. I don't know how I'm going to live with this guilt. I'm relieved Carrie is here to take my place. I can't do this anymore."

Doc's revelation stunned Ethan and his heart went out to his colleague.

49

"Doc, you can't hold yourself responsible. You did what you thought was best at the time. You thought you were providing much needed pain relief. It's not too late. You can educate your fellow physicians on the dangers of these painkillers."

"Don't you see, Ethan? The gentleman, on the table over there, is a perfect example. His clothes tell us he's upper middle class. Maybe he was doing something important; something that would improve the lives of many. But because of his addiction to this noxious drug, and the ease with which he could get it, that potential is gone."

Doc continued his thought. "So many of my colleagues, if you can call them that, continue to prescribe these painkillers even when they're not necessary. The money coming in is too good to pass up. It's criminal, and those physicians should be brought up on charges."

Ethan agreed, but today, right now, was not the time. They needed to get back on task and deal with the victim and his untimely death.

"Doc, I've been assigned to a task force to address how local communities can deal with the situation. I'll make sure discussions are streamlined so our victims get the help they need and first responders are protected."

Ethan waited for Doc's response.

"I'm not supposed to say anything, but I think you should know," Doc whispered.

"Know what?"

"This death in Riverview. It's the county's hundredth overdose victim this month. That number triggers emergency response units to be set up. The state health department has us under strict instructions to not release these numbers, but I wanted you to know. The legislators in Albany are scrambling to find a solution, but I, for one, don't hold any hope. The drug cartels and the pharmaceutical companies are too powerful. They have the money and power to buy off anyone they wish," Doc continued. "I fear it's hopeless. And, Ethan, I have never been so frightened of the outcome."

Ethan agreed, and as much as he wanted Doc to feel better, he couldn't argue the point.

~

The two men walked soberly back to Tom and Carrie. They looked at Ethan and Doc with questioning expressions, expressions that received no explanation.

"Tom, make sure they send the samples to Bode Labs," Ethan instructed.

~

Doc's confession had put him in a combative mood. Baring his soul to Ethan made him even more depressed and angry about the situation.

"Wait a minute, Ethan. This is still my lab and I'll send the samples where I want them to go. We use the state lab. You've got to stop ruining our budget. We can't afford private labs."

Ethan took a breath. The battle wasn't over and the conversation was getting out of hand again. He had to bring it back to a civilized level.

"I understand that," Ethan said quietly, straining to keep his temper, his attempt to lower Doc's stress level, "But it's *my* job to learn the cause of death as soon as possible. If a crime has been committed, I need to act on that information. We know test results from the state lab can take months. We don't have that much time. You *suspect* this guy died of a drug overdose. We need verification of that fact, and we need it fast."

"I know test results from the state can take an inordinate amount of time, but damn it, I don't have a choice," Doc responded, his body tensing for another verbal fight.

Ethan continued, "We need to find out who this guy is and what he was doing in that out of the way place. That's why we need to use a private lab—to get quick results."

"There's another problem," Doc said. "I don't know when we'll have time to perform an autopsy. There are several cases ahead of

51

this. Now that all county deaths come through this facility, there are a lot more bodies coming, especially with the drug overdoses. The other MEs aren't here that much, so most of the work is up to the two of us. In a word, we're overwhelmed." Doc took a breath, squared his shoulders and reestablished his professional demeanor. "But we'll be as efficient as possible, right Carrie?"

Ethan turned to the young woman, feeling a bit ashamed that he had dismissed her earlier.

"That's right, doctor," Carrie responded, still miffed at the fact these men didn't respect her status.

Doc turned from the body and looked from Carrie to Ethan.

"Please excuse my manners. Let me introduce the new medical examiner, Carrie Young. She'll be taking over in a few weeks. I'll remain on to assist until the end of the year. I'm not completely retiring, just giving up as medical examiner. A decision was made that someone younger and more adept at new technology should have the position. I'll continue to see my patients, and then phase into retirement over the next year."

The elephant in the room remained after Doc's explanation of why he was being replaced. It was now essential that the medical examiner's office be in the 21st century. Unfortunately, it meant pushing aside people who had given so much to the community. Doc's comments showed he was ambivalent about the situation, but in any case, Ethan was glad Doc would still be around, though he wondered how effective Doc would be with his patients' pain management.

"Welcome to Riverview," Ethan said to Carrie and put out his hand in greeting.

After pleasantries were exchanged, Ethan turned back to the body. He wasn't happy to learn that his case was being put in the queue. It was apparent the medical examiner's office needed additional staff. Maybe Doc shouldn't retire just yet. There was more than enough work for several medical examiner positions. Once again the budget monster raised its ugly head.

"Doc, there are too many unknowns with this case. Is there any way you can speed things up?"

"Afraid not. I know you want to solve this case, but we have to follow protocol," Doc responded.

Before Ethan could argue the point further the phone rang. Doc answered, then turned to the group and said, "Tracy Connor is at the front desk and she's frantic to see the body."

~ TWELVE ~

"Why was she called?" Ethan asked, his voice rising with each word. "We don't know for sure who the victim is."

Ethan was exasperated. The situation was out of hand.

"I understand your frustration, Ethan, but when a body comes here with identification, the next of kin is notified. This body was identified as Steven Sullivan, so the call was made. I didn't mean for it to happen this way, because in this case we're not sure about the victim's identity. It's a communication error that we can blame on the new set-up here. But since she was called, let's be honest about the fact that she's the only one who can tell us whether or not this is Mr. Sullivan."

Ethan wanted to argue more, but knew it was too late. He stood back while Doc called the receptionist.

"You can walk Ms. Connor down now," Doc instructed.

The group waited, wondering what the next few minutes would bring.

~

Doc Morse met Tracy Connor at the door and walked her into the autopsy suite, talking softly, preparing her for what she would see. She appeared in control, a real cool customer.

"Would you like to sit a minute?" He asked.

"No, let's get it over with," Tracy replied. She put on a stalwart expression, but Ethan detected a twitch in her cheek that indicated stress. Her complexion was pale, and even her expertly applied makeup couldn't disguise that. He noticed how she quickly surveyed the room and those in the room. She was a trained

54

professional, and his instincts immediately told him there was more to Tracy Connor than a small town real estate agent.

Doc was coaching Tracy, preparing her for the viewing. Ethan wished he would just get it over with. There was work to be done.

Tracy stood at the autopsy table where the victim was covered by a crisp white sheet.

She took a deep breath.

"Are you okay?" Doc asked, as they reached the table. "I have to warn you that we aren't sure this is Steven. You are the one who will know."

Doc and Tracy stood next to the body as Doc painstakingly pulled the sheet down enough to reveal the head. Tracy took a long look. She gasped, stepped back, and turned to Ethan and Tom.

She shook her head and said, "That's not Steven."

~

Given Doc's earlier suspicions, they weren't surprised by Tracy's response. But if it wasn't Steven Sullivan, who was it and how did the credit card get into the victim's pocket?

When Tracy had recovered enough to talk, Ethan stepped forward, introduced himself and Tom, and asked, "Ms. Connor, you rent a room to Steven Sullivan?"

"Yes. He's a lecturer at the satellite campus. He came to my real estate office looking for a rental. We couldn't find anything appropriate. Time was running out, so I offered him a spare room until he could get familiar with the area."

The way she looked down, and then up at him with a toss of her hair, was a signal she wasn't telling the truth, or at least not all of it. He didn't want to confront her here in the morgue.

"Do you normally rent rooms in your home to men you just met?" Ethan asked.

Tracy glared at him. Doc took a step forward in dismay.

"We had met before, long ago, so he wasn't a complete stranger," Tracy responded in a huff.

That's more like it, Ethan thought.

"One more thing, Ms. Connor. Do you know where Mr. Sullivan is now? I believe his campus office was contacted and he didn't show up for a meeting this morning."

"I don't know where he is. I have a real estate office to run in Renwick, so I am not always privy to his schedule."

"And something else, do you know the deceased? Do you have any idea why he would have a credit card with Mr. Sullivan's name on it?"

Tracy fidgeted, which meant Ethan's questions were unwelcome.

"I've never seen the deceased before and I don't know how he would have gotten Steven's credit card. Except, maybe if he," Tracy replied, nodding toward the autopsy table, "was on campus, he stole the card."

"Thanks, again, Ms. Connor. You can go now," Ethan said, dismissing her.

As Carrie covered the body, Doc put his arm around Tracy and walked her from the room, retaining his country doctor manners.

Ethan turned to Carrie and instructed, "Run whatever tests you need to identify the body. When we get those results, they might help us learn why the credit card was on the body, and in the meantime my office will work on locating Sullivan."

Carrie nodded, acknowledging the instructions as she wheeled the body back to the cooler.

Walking down the corridor toward the reception area, Ethan turned to Tom, "Did you thoroughly search the crime scene and secure it?"

"Yes I did, and I planned to return. I wanted to accompany the body to the morgue to see if the doc could tell me anything more."

"Okay. We need to get back there and look around."

"What're you thinking, boss?"

"This crime isn't what we think, not the victim we thought. Why was that young man there this morning?" Ethan sighed. He suspected what was going on, a drug deal gone wrong, but he needed proof.

"There has to be more evidence, because every time someone enters a space, they leave something behind," Ethan said.

"The Locard Exchange Principle, I know, I know," Tom replied, not wanting to be lectured on Investigation 101. "I learned that the first week in the academy."

"Just seeing if you remember your lessons," Ethan replied with a smile, his way of lessening the stress they felt with a murder and a possible missing person on their hands.

"It's our job to find that something, and it's going to be a challenge because the crime scene is outside and in a remote area. At least we aren't faced with an impending storm," Ethan said, remembering the last murder crime scene he faced. "I'm up for the challenge, are you?"

Tom shuffled the dirt at his feet, thinking. "You're right. There was something about the scene that didn't sit right with me, and yes, I'm up for the challenge. Let's go."

Ethan watched Tom jump into his patrol car and pull away.

A death in Riverview.

Doc's statement resonated in Ethan's mind. He never thought this one death would tip the area's social, medical, and political balance into an extraordinary and dangerous situation.

~ THIRTEEN ~

While Ethan waited for Tom to point out the spot where the body was found this morning, he stood alongside the road looking through the tall brush toward a structure known by the locals as the van der Molen place. Maddie had told him at some point that a house on this road was abandoned, though she didn't expand on the history. All she said was something happened there, and just as she was about to expound on the story, someone entered the office to ask directions, and the moment was lost. He had made a mental note to get the rest of the story.

The house sat a distance from the road, was boarded up and covered with invasive plants. It appeared to not have been occupied in a long time, but he suspected that over the years partying teenagers had congregated in this out-of-the-way place. His curiosity was aroused and he made a mental note to ask the town historian what he knew about the van der Molens.

Tom parked behind Ethan's car, got out and pointed to a spot a few yards away where Ethan noticed weeds were worn down by foot traffic.

"Over here is where we went in and found the body," Tom said as he pointed towards where the weeds were trampled.

Ethan handed Tom a mask, gloves and booties. Ethan didn't know how much they'd come up with because the crime scene had been contaminated by the paramedics, medical examiners, Tom, and the woman who found the body.

"I'll go first, you come right behind stepping where I step, understood?" Ethan instructed. He wanted to avoid any more contamination of the scene.

The two men trod through the tall weeds with Tom carrying the crime scene kit that contained the supplies they might need. Ethan stopped at the point where the weeds were trampled and a jutting rock displayed blood.

"Take more samples from where the victim's head hit the rock and work out through the surrounding area," Ethan instructed as he swatted flies from around his face.

Tom followed the instructions while Ethan surveyed the area. There wasn't much to see with the naked eye, and trying to find a piece of evidence in the heavy tangle of weeds was going to be like finding a needle in a haystack.

Using a thin metal rod with a small hook at the end that he brought for this occasion, Ethan methodically searched the perimeter from the point where the body was located to several yards away. Finding nothing, he stood silently, observed, and listened.

"Tom, does this look like someone went through here, or has it been worn down by an animal?" Ethan asked, pointing in a westerly direction.

Tom walked over and looked at what Ethan had pointed out. Tom hesitated as he studied the path.

"It could be where someone or something walked, but if so, it did a damn good job of not disturbing much," Tom replied. "A deer maybe?"

"I think it's more than animal tracks. Look at the way it winds through there," Ethan said as he pointed back towards the house. "I think there was at least one other person here. They were careful about leaving tracks, but if you look closely, you'll notice broken stems."

Tom walked the route Ethan pointed out.

"Found something!" Tom called out.

Ethan followed Tom's trail and saw what he'd found—a partial shoe print. So not a deer.

Ethan snapped photos of the print and the trail that led towards the house, and then the two set off to follow the path.

When Ethan stopped abruptly, Tom almost collided into him. Ethan pointed to something shiny in the tall grass. Tom nodded, and stepped into the weeds, praying there was no poison ivy. With gloved hands, he picked up a knife.

Tom bagged the knife and the two men continued towards the house.

The trail ended at the house's overgrown driveway.

"A vehicle was here recently," Ethan said as he knelt down and touched the oil drips, bringing his finger close to his nose for a confirming smell. He stood up and surveyed the house's sagging roof and missing windows. "Let's check it out."

Tom followed as Ethan made his way to the back door. The front entrance did not allow entry as it was blocked by a thick mass of forsythia bushes. It was apparent no one had entered through the front door in a very long time. The back door, on the other hand, wasn't completely blocked, so Ethan used his pocketknife to cut through the few stems that stood in their way.

The door opened easily, as the wood around the hinges had rotted away. Before stepping over the threshold into the circa 1950s kitchen, they checked to make sure the ceiling wasn't going to fall down around them, and that the floor was solid. The rusted rectangular kitchen sink was of the old farm variety now in vogue. The Formica countertops were curled and stained. The metal table in the middle of the room was rusted to the point of disintegrating.

They walked down the short hallway and entered a small parlor. Two windows flanked the walls with one lone curtain gently swaying in and out on the breath of the breeze. They climbed the stairs, testing each one to make sure it would carry their weight, holding onto the handrail just in case. The single bedroom on the second floor contained a three quarter bed and one dresser.

Whoever lived here didn't have much, Ethan thought as he surveyed the small room. The men went back down the stairs, and returned to the kitchen. Ethan turned to Tom and said, "Interesting place, but I don't see any sign of recent activity."

"Neither do I," replied Tom, covering a sneeze and anxious to leave the dust-covered surroundings.

Ethan hesitated at the door and turned to face Tom.

"Tom, I've made a decision. If Doc's finding on cause of death is confirmed, and I think it will be, that the victim died of a massive drug overdose, I'm going to rule this young man's death a homicide."

Tom was stunned. No one, to his knowledge in this state, had ruled a drug overdose as murder. Ethan tended to be a renegade when it came to certain things, and so far his hunches played out. But this was a different story. They were going to set the trend, buck the system, whatever you wanted to call it, and they could end up the laughingstock of New York law enforcement. Or worse. He and Ethan could find themselves on a cartel hit list. He shuddered at the thought.

"Are you sure you want to do that?" Tom asked tentatively. "You'd be up against the system, and maybe even undermining the mayor's task force."

Ethan tilted his head up giving his neck a good stretch. He closed his eyes as his neck and shoulder muscles eased with the gentle movement as he considered Tom's sage advice.

"You're quite right, of course, but I am so damned tired of the status quo. These victims have suffered; their families have suffered. The community suffers as we spin our wheels. If we rule this case a homicide, that gives us the opportunity to go after the suppliers and charge them with murder instead of dealing."

"We could be in trouble for going this route," Tom said.

"Yeah, I know, and if you're not comfortable with it, I understand. You can handle other cases that come through."

Tom shifted his weight from one side to the other, weighing his options. Finally he replied, "Of course I'll back you up, boss. We're a team."

Ethan patted Tom on the back, nodding assent.

"I don't think there's much else we can do here. Let's get back to the office," Ethan said with a sigh.

Tom nodded as he took another look at the disintegrating house. *Definitely a creepy place.*

~ FOURTEEN ~

The day was as promised when Caitlyn Jamison arrived at Winding Creek Winery. She was eager to start the photo shoot before the weather changed. She remembered the saying—if you don't like the weather in upstate, just wait a minute—it will change.

She parked far off the road to allow Summit some off-leash time. Over the summer she'd worked on obedience training with him, and was confident he'd return to her side as soon as she gave the signal.

The hillside was covered with grapevines dressed in various shades of yellow and green. She turned to admire the deep blue lake below. Deciduous trees across the lake had begun to wear their fall colors and that would provide a vibrant background. She rubbed her hands in anticipation—this photo shoot was going to be better than she expected.

Caitlyn got right to work, taking photos from every angle, and finally satisfied with her efforts, she called Summit to her side and placed him onto the passenger seat. Her equipment was stored on the back seat, and now she was ready to drive up to the winery's tasting room.

~

Abbie Hetherington rushed out the door to greet her friend.

"Caitlyn, I'm so glad you're here," Abbie cried as she embraced her.

"Actually, I've been 'here' for over an hour," Caitlyn said with a laugh. "I took advantage of the day, the light, everything, while I could. Sorry I forgot to let you know."

"No problem. I've been busy overseeing the harvest. Come in, sit down, how was your drive?"

"Dry roads and little traffic, so the drive was fine. And, of course, Summit is great company," Caitlyn said with a laugh.

~

Just then Abbie's husband Tim raced through the door.

"Abbie," he said, breathless, just as he noticed Caitlyn standing next to his wife.

"Oh, Caitlyn. I forgot you were arriving today."

"Tim, what's the rush? How could you forget Caitlyn was coming to take photos for the brochure?" Abbie asked, annoyed that he rudely interrupted their conversation and that the winery's new brochure wasn't foremost on his mind.

Ignoring his wife's comment, Tim asked, "Have you heard from your uncle today?"

"No, of course not. You know Uncle Steven. He's not the stay-in-touch-with-family type. In fact, I'm surprised he even let us know he's in the area," Abbie responded with sarcasm, her arms folded across her chest in defiance. "Why?"

"Well, he didn't show up for an important department meeting this morning. He didn't answer his phone when Janie, our secretary, called him, and then a rumor started around campus about a death on Old Mill Road," Tim said, still breathless.

"Oh my god, that's awful. Does anyone know who it is?" Abbie exclaimed, not yet making the connection between the two statements.

Caitlyn looked from one to the other, confused, and shocked that there was a suspicious death in Riverview.

"Who's Steven?" She stammered.

"Steven's my uncle," Abbie explained, turning to face Caitlyn.

"I didn't know you had a uncle. Well, actually I guess I didn't live here long enough to get to know any of my friends' extended families."

"You wouldn't have gotten to know my uncle even if you were here," Abbie explained, sighing. "He never had much to do with the family. He lives in Boston, and when he did show up he'd be vague about what he did for a living. He talked about teaching, working for the Boston PD, but we could never pin him down as to *exactly* what he did. As youngsters we'd speculate he might be doing something more exotic, but we were just kids using our imaginations."

"So, what's he doing here, now?" Caitlyn asked.

"We got a brief phone call when he arrived a couple of months ago, and he mentioned something about teaching a college course. He's a forensic psychologist, and he's been in Boston for as long as I can remember. When he called he said he'd be busy getting ready for his courses, so he wouldn't be able to see us very soon, but promised when he got settled . . . yeah, right."

"We think there's more to Uncle Steven than what he lets on," Tim added.

Tim's cell phone rang and he excused himself.

"Tim likes to think Steven's a spy," Abbie replied with a laugh. "We like to imagine that someone in our family is doing something different and exciting."

"You and Tim are doing something exciting, starting a winery," Caitlyn replied.

Tim came back into the room. "That was Janie, the department secretary. She said when she couldn't get hold of Steven she called Tracy at work."

Tim looked at Caitlyn to explain.

"Tracy Connor offered Uncle Steven a room in her house until he got settled. Just before noon she was notified a body was found and the authorities thought it might be Steven. I don't know why. When she went to the morgue to identify it, it wasn't him."

Abbie's expression went from horror to relief as Tim related the information.

"How bizarre," Caitlyn remarked. Now she had an excuse to connect with Ethan, and soon, to get the rest of this story.

"Could he be visiting a colleague or doing research? And I'm also curious as to why you were on campus, Tim."

"Oh, yeah, we owe you that. A little background, because things happened so quickly I don't believe Abbie told you . . ."

"Told me what?" Caitlyn said, concerned again.

"Just before classes started at the new satellite campus, actually just three weeks ago, the science department chair asked me to teach an enology course. The course was labeled wines and vines. Since we've been successful growing unique grape vines in various soil types, the university wanted me to share our experience and expertise. Abbie's feeling better and can handle more responsibility at the winery, so we thought it would be okay if I taught a course. The extra money during the winter months will come in handy."

"Lots of changes here," Caitlyn said, looking from Tim to Abbie. "So why do you think something happened to her uncle?"

Tim answered before Abbie could respond.

"Abbie and I disagree about her uncle. I think he's here for some other reason," Tim stated.

"Interesting, and what might that be?" Caitlyn asked. She'd been in Riverview a couple of hours and this trip was already intriguing.

"Oh, I don't know," Tim said, backing down from his earlier comment.

Caitlyn had had enough of the speculation. "If I get a chance to talk to the sheriff, I'll ask if there are any secret agents operating in the area," she said with a laugh.

Tim looked annoyed at her response, and seemed to have more on his mind as he paced back and forth.

"One day after work a few of us went for a drink . . .," Tim began.

"You never told me that," Abbie interrupted with hands on her hips.

"There wasn't anything to tell. I drank one beer and left. But I saw your uncle over in a corner talking to someone who appeared to be a student. I tried to catch his eye, and have him join us, but he was too deep in conversation," Tim explained. "I gathered from the body language that the talk was serious, so I didn't interrupt."

Abbie and Caitlyn were silent. There was nothing to say to discount what Tim suggested, nor did they want to get into an argument.

Caitlyn was first to break the silence.

"Tim, you don't have any solid evidence to substantiate what you are implying."

"You're right. So can you ask Ethan if he knows anything about where Abbie's uncle might be?" Tim asked, not willing to let go.

Resigned, Caitlyn responded, "Okay, I'll talk to Ethan."

Abbie added, "Thank you. We're not close, though Uncle Steven *is* family, and we'd feel awful if we didn't check on him."

~

"Excuse me, Mrs. Hetherington?"

Caitlyn turned to see a young woman in her early twenties, standing in the doorway. She was anorexic-thin, her complexion pale, and her hair scraggly. Caitlyn didn't have any idea what someone in her condition was doing at the winery.

Abbie got up to confer with the young woman, and once the issue was dealt with, she returned to the table.

"That's one of our part timers, Lizzie Bradley. She's a gem and a quick learner. She's doing what we call the grunt work now, but we have plans for her to learn more about the business. Tim has taken her under his wing and is teaching her the chemistry involved in wine production," Abbie explained.

Caitlyn wasn't sure how to broach the subject of the girl's appearance, but her curiosity got the better of her. She spoke out with the hope she wasn't overstepping. "She looks kind of frail for this kind of work."

Abbie and Tim looked at each other before Abbie responded.

"Lizzie is in a drug abuse recovery program. Area businesses were encouraged to help addicts recover by giving them work opportunities, so they can dig themselves out of the abyss. We were reluctant, because of the wine production, but she seems to be working out okay. We keep a close eye on her, and are hoping for the best."

Caitlyn nodded, though she had reservations about how the girl would work out. There was a lot going on in this small community, and they each had much to think about. With a glass of wine in hand, they sat and looked out over the vineyards to the lake beyond.

~ FIFTEEN ~

Doug Mitchell, Town Historian. It had a nice ring to it.

This morning, Doug watched the office supply delivery guy position the fourth and last Steelcase file cabinet neatly against the wall in his home office. He was pleased with how the room was finally coming together.

Early retirement was great so far, and he was excited to throw himself into the position as Riverview's next town historian. He'd been appointed at the first of the year, but he couldn't do much until he officially retired from his job on September 1.

His wife Penny stood at the door, coffee cup in hand. "Looks like the cabinets finally arrived."

"Yes, and I'm about to open the boxes of Pendaflex folders and set them into their file drawer cradles."

"Don't open them all. You won't need them yet, and they'll be easier to store on your newly installed closet shelves."

"I'm glad you showed up to supervise my new office," Doug replied with a smile, happy that his wife showed interest in his new pursuit.

"That's all the supervision you get for today. I'm off to work. A town clerk's job is never done," she said as she raised her cup in salute.

Doug had decided his first goal would be to develop a list of the town's oldest families and start work on their genealogies, incorporating as much of each person's social history as he could find. Unfortunately, that project had to be put aside when he realized how much organizing there was to be done before he could begin what he considered the fun part of his job.

He walked over to the corner of the room where boxes holding the town's history were stacked and wondered how he was going to get through it all. The amount of time it would take to make sense of the documents contained in the twenty-something boxes was overwhelming. The previous historian had given up the position when she arrived at the ripe old age of ninety and no longer had the energy to maintain the files. She should have given up the position twenty years before. When her helpers came to pack up the town's history that was scattered throughout her house, they dumped the files and loose papers into the boxes in no particular order.

He hadn't done his due diligence when he volunteered for the position. He didn't realize what he was getting into or in what condition the town's history would be in when he took possession. In reality, even if he'd been aware, it wouldn't have made a difference. He wanted the job.

Doug was downsized when his company decided to cleanse its payroll of the higher-paid staff. He quickly learned about the gray ceiling, so he decided to take the "early retirement" option.

He and Penny had talked about leaving the area for a place where he might secure employment. In the end they decided to limp along financially, on her salary, until they were eligible for social security and his pension money.

Doug loved history and was now at the age when genealogy became a driving interest. He enjoyed living in Riverview, and he felt it would be a great service to the town if he researched the founding families. Maybe they could plan an event around his research to bring the townspeople together and be a tourist draw. His long-term plan was to charge for his genealogy research services, but he'd have to conquer a steep learning curve first.

One benefit of the surrounding chaos was he and Penny could work together to bring order. It'd give them something to talk about, like how to best organize the files. She had a knack for that.

With those happy thoughts, Doug pulled out his pocketknife and opened the first box of folders.

~ SIXTEEN ~

Back at the office, Ethan instructed Tom to send the items collected from the crime scene to the private lab in Virginia, which prompted him to remember the trouble he had gotten into last spring when using this lab.

Ethan felt that a quick turnaround from the evidence they'd collected was the only thing that mattered, even if the captain, who now had a close eye on the budget, raised hell over the cost. Because he received fast results last spring, they'd been able to identify the murderer quicker. Since he'd classified this morning's death a homicide, he hoped the evidence would be assigned a higher priority. Ethan didn't have the patience to wait months to solve a case.

While Tom prepared the evidence for shipment, Ethan said, "I should talk with Tracy Connor again to see if she will tell me more about Steven Sullivan. Is he missing or just off on a tangent? There could be any number of reasons the guy is out of touch, and it isn't any of our business."

He then noted Maddie's disappointed look, which told him she wanted action taken on the disappearance of her neighbor.

"Okay, Maddie, I'll talk with Ms. Connor."

Ethan jotted down the address as Maddie recited it to him.

Maddie explained, "I talked with her a while ago. She's at the house now before going back to work. Not a surprise she needed some time after getting a call to come to the morgue."

Maddie handed Ethan his cap, her subtle way of telling him to move along.

~

When Ethan arrived at the address Maddie provided, he noticed a late model silver metallic Toyota Camry in the drive.

Tracy answered the door after several moments, and Ethan introduced himself again.

She reluctantly allowed him in and he followed her into a cozy living room. It had that lived-in feel, and not the formal staged arrangement he associated with real estate agents. That assumption wasn't fair; he shouldn't profile her.

The room contained a comfortable couch, upholstered side chairs, and an old wooden coffee table cluttered with books and magazines. It was a room in which he'd have no trouble relaxing and putting his feet up, with beer in hand.

When Tracy settled into one of the side chairs, Ethan took the other, holding his cap and fingering the brim. "I know this has been a difficult morning for you, Ms. Connor, thinking Steven might be dead when in fact he's not. Do you think he's missing?"

"Well . . ." Tracy stopped. She debated how much she should tell the sheriff about the real reason Steven was in Riverview. It was not her business to say, and Steven hadn't mentioned anything about working with local law enforcement.

Ethan sat, waiting for her to decide what, if anything, she wanted to tell him; her silence spoke volumes. As far as he was concerned, there was nothing for him to follow-up on at this point. No missing persons report could be filed for twenty-four hours. He did, however, need to identify the body in the morgue, find the drug supplier that caused the young man's death, and know why Sullivan's credit card was on the victim's body.

Tracy shifted in her seat, knowing Ethan suspected she knew more than she was telling.

"I can't tell you anything that will help. We met each other in Boston a long time ago," Tracy began.

Ethan nodded, encouraging her to continue.

"He came here to take a position at the university and to look around the area. I offered him a room until he could find something suitable. I handle rentals, but the students have scooped up all that are available."

She took a breath, deciding what information she could share.

"As for our relationship, Steven usually mentions when he's going out, but this morning he didn't. Actually, he said something like he didn't have plans, or something. I was distracted and in too much of a hurry to pay attention. I realize now that he had a meeting on campus, but he didn't mention that. Or, if he did, I didn't pay attention. We've gotten into a dinner routine and it's a little disconcerting that he didn't leave a note saying when he would return. I'm sorry to bother you with these domestic trivialities. You have more important things on your plate."

Ethan suspected there was more to their relationship than Tracy was sharing. He knew his life would get more complicated if Steven Sullivan didn't turn up.

"You understand I can't do anything officially, but is there anything I can do for you? Put out feelers?" Ethan asked.

"No. There's nothing to be done. I'm sure he'll show up. Now, if you don't mind, I have to get back to work," Tracy stated as she stood, signaling the end to their conversation.

Ethan didn't budge.

"Does Steven have a room he uses for an office?"

Tracy hesitated.

"Yes, down the hall," Tracy said as she waved her hand in the direction of a hallway running off the foyer. "I've been too busy to figure out a use for that room, so I let him use it while he's here. Why?"

"May I take a look? I won't pry into anything that looks too personal, but I may notice a simple reason why he left without telling you. It's helpful to have a second pair of eyes."

Tracy considered the request. She didn't want the sheriff poking around in Steven's office, but if she put up too much of a fuss, the sheriff might suspect something amiss. Better to play along. She was sure Steven would have been careful about leaving anything out.

"This way," she said as she walked down the hall. "He didn't bring much with him, and what he did bring he keeps at his campus office."

Ethan went to Steven's desk and noticed it held a few papers, but nothing jumped out at him. They were mostly scientific articles. The laptop was there, but he suspected it was password protected. If Steven didn't return, they'd get a court order if necessary to take that, as well as any other electronics.

Ethan sat down at the desk, his hand reaching for the side drawer.

"Please don't touch that," Tracy said. "I've told you all I know, and you have no right to go through that desk without a warrant."

Tracy's abrupt change in attitude startled Ethan, and he stopped as his fingers rested on the desk drawer's handle. He had to do what she asked. This was not an official visit; he had no official standing here.

"I understand. I didn't mean to go beyond the bounds."

With hands behind his back, Ethan walked around the room as he made his way to the door. The room contained three metal file cabinets, a bookcase with a few books, and two comfortable reading chairs. The windows looked out onto the backyard and into the woods beyond. It was a pleasant room where a person could spend quiet time. Except for the slightly cluttered desk, the rest of the room was neat. Ethan walked over to the bookshelf and drew his finger across the teak wood shelves.

With nothing more to be done, he turned to Tracy, and gave her his card with his personal cell phone number on the back. "Call me tonight, either way," he instructed.

"I will."

Ethan positioned his cap on his head, thanked her and left.

~ SEVENTEEN ~

Caitlyn eased her light green Prius into the driveway of the sprawling white clapboard farmhouse—the home of her uncle and aunt, Jerry and Myra Tilton.

She climbed out of the car and grabbed the bags from the back seat, her mind still spinning from what Abbie and Tim shared. A possible missing uncle, a recovering addict employee, a death in Riverview.

What have I come into? This sleepy town's becoming more big city-like. Maybe this visit won't be as happy as I hoped.

Caitlyn pushed those thoughts aside and looked forward to spending time with her Aunt Myra. She hoped Uncle Jerry was still in Albany.

~

Her uncle was a conundrum. His long-term goal was realized last spring when he was appointed to fill out the term of the late Senator Smith. Her uncle was ambitious, and his position as the local bank president was only a step on his career ladder.

It was a tumultuous time in Albany, and as soon as he took his senate seat he was faced with a vote on whether hydraulic fracturing should continue to be allowed in New York State, thereby ending home rule. Jerry, who sat on an oil company's board, appeared to be a shoo-in by the senior senators who were in favor of hydraulic fracturing. But when Jerry learned about the secret plan for the Catskill region that had nothing to do with energy, his conscience wouldn't allow him to follow the dictates of the oil company or the senior senators.

Caitlyn was proud of her uncle for overcoming his desire for power and monetary gain. His stance almost caused his professional demise, and she suspected he'd been working hard to regain the approval of his colleagues. She wondered what the elected officials—she refused to call them 'leaders'—and the Wall Street bankers were up to now. Had they learned their lesson? Probably not.

~

"Myra, I'm here," Caitlyn called as she walked in the front door with Summit at her feet. She stopped to watch the dog's reaction. Would he remember the house? Remember his young master? Summit stepped over the threshold and sniffed around the doorframe. A worried look passed briefly over this face. He remembered. Was he happy to be back in the big house?

As for her, there was a different atmosphere from the last time, and she suspected Summit sensed that as well, as he hesitated a moment before charging into the house.

Myra Tilton came running from the kitchen, arms spread.

"Oh, Caitlyn, it's good to see you. Take off your coat, and come with me. I want you to meet someone," Myra said, her tone suddenly turning somber.

Caitlyn followed Myra into the kitchen wondering why her aunt's expression had turned serious. Not more bad news, she prayed. Entering the kitchen, Caitlyn saw a woman sitting at the kitchen table. The table was covered with colored pencils and coloring books.

Not waiting for an introduction, Caitlyn asked, "What are you two doing?"

"Why, Caitlyn, it's the newest rage," Myra replied. "Adult coloring books. Verna and I get together once a week to color. It helps relieve stress. We needed an additional session today. Verna found a body this morning while walking her dog. Oh, and Caitlyn, this is my friend, Verna Adams, and Verna, this is my niece Caitlyn that I've told you so much about," Myra said in a rush.

"It's nice to meet you, Verna," Caitlyn replied with a smile. "I'm sorry to hear about your experience this morning. It must have been upsetting."

"It was, but you know, the most upsetting part was I didn't know what to do," Verna replied. "You'd think after all my years teaching elementary school that I'd be prepared for any emergency. This morning I froze. I'm so ashamed. I keep telling myself that even if I had felt for a pulse or tried to resuscitate him, it wouldn't have done any good. I'm so glad I can talk to Myra. She's made me feel better about myself."

Caitlyn nodded. She knew how important it was to have a friend and confidant, but she wanted to get off the subject of the body.

"Hmm, adult coloring books. I read an article about that craze. Interesting. I'm glad you've found something to do together that helps you relax."

"It's much more than relaxing," Myra said as she gave Verna a big smile. "It's art therapy."

Caitlyn couldn't help but laugh at her aunt's new hobby.

"Verna was just telling me about her experience this morning," Myra said, wanting to continue talking about the topic of the day.

Caitlyn paused, and then said, "Could that be the body they found on Old Mill Road?"

Myra gasped, hand to her chest. "It wasn't murder was it?"

Myra's son, Todd, was murdered not six months ago and the pain remained. They said time would heal the sadness in her heart, but so far, for her, that hadn't been the case.

"I don't know the particulars yet, but I'm sure the news will be out soon," Caitlyn responded.

"How did you know?" Myra was finally able to say.

"I was taking photos at the winery all afternoon. After that I went up to see Abbie and Tim. Tim came in with the news. They were nervous that the body might be Abbie's uncle, Steven Sullivan," Caitlyn explained. "Mr. Sullivan missed a meeting this morning on campus and you know how the academic gossip mill operates. The news is coming in bits and pieces, so I don't think Tim knows the whole story."

Myra closed her eyes and took a deep breath. "You never cease to amaze me," she said, giving Caitlyn a hug.

"Do you know anything more?" Verna finally asked.

"No, and I won't know until I have a chance to talk with Sheriff Ewing. Tim thinks Abbie's uncle might be in danger," Caitlyn explained. "I don't see the big deal. It's only been a few hours, but I promised to ask, so I will. I'll try to find out as much information as I can. Do you mind if I leave Summit with you?"

"Of course, dear, but don't get involved in anything," her aunt warned, shaking her finger.

"Don't worry. I learned my lesson," Caitlyn responded with a smile.

She waved good-by to the two women, who had turned their attention back to their coloring projects.

~ EIGHTEEN ~

Caitlyn didn't know what to expect when she drove down Riverview's main street. At first glance it looked the same, except the maple trees, now dressed in shades of red and orange, and had begun to drop leaves to the sidewalk below. There were more people, mostly students, walking around, frequenting the restaurants and bars, but otherwise the street looked the same.

Her nerves tingled as she approached the sheriff's office. She remembered her last act before leaving Riverview in the spring. Ethan tried to contact her several times soon after, but she refused to answer his call. She didn't want to talk about it. She'd closed that chapter. When she finally talked with him, he told her the coach had been arrested. She didn't want to hear the rest. She had faith the law would bring justice to him, and peace to his victims.

She pushed these unpleasant memories aside as she climbed the steps onto the veranda of the renovated Victorian house that now served as the sheriff's office. Her hand hovered over the doorknob as she took a deep breath. It was going to be okay. She'd share the information Tim provided and be on her way.

~

Deputy Tom Snow was the first to see her. He jumped up and rushed over to give her a hug. "Caitlyn, what brings you back to Riverview?"

Caitlyn felt her tension ease at the welcome.

"Working on a new brochure for Winding Creek Winery," was her reply.

Maddie flipped off her headset and raced over to give Caitlyn a welcome hug.

"We're so glad to see you again, and I know the sheriff will be delighted. Does he know you're here?" Maddie asked, unable to hide her curiosity. She tried to stay informed on every subject, especially the sheriff's love life. She was miffed that the sheriff might have known of Caitlyn's arrival and did not tell her.

"I told him I was working on the winery's brochure, and needed to take photos. My life has been in turmoil lately with client crises, so I'm not sure I told him when I was coming. My trip was completely dependent on the weather, and consequently the dates changed a couple of times," Caitlyn replied, catching her breath.

"I'm sure he'll be glad to see you, though unfortunately, he'll be busy. A body was found this morning," Maddie said.

"I heard. That's why I need to see him," Caitlyn said, stealing a glance towards the sheriff's small office.

"What do you mean?" Tom asked. "Do you know something about this incident? Didn't you just arrive in town?"

"Yes, I did, but I went straight to the winery and took photos for over an hour. After that I talked with Tim and Abbie. Tim told us about the events of this morning, and they think Abbie's uncle, Steven Sullivan, might be missing."

Before Tom could respond the door opened and Ethan rushed in yelling instructions.

"Maddie, what do you know about Steven Sullivan and . . ."

Ethan stopped mid sentence, his jaw dropped.

"Caitlyn, what are you doing here?"

"I'm here to take photos for Winding Creek. I mentioned that to you," she replied. "But then the dates changed. Several client projects came up unexpectedly . . . and I forgot to keep you in the loop."

"That's okay. I'm just glad to see you," Ethan responded breathlessly. "We've been a little busy here, too. This morning a woman walking her dog found a body off Old Mill Road."

"I know!" Caitlyn jumped in before Ethan could finish. "I heard about it from Abbie and Tim, and then from Aunt Myra's friend, Verna Adams. She found the body." Not wanting to waste any more time, she continued, motioning towards his office, "Ethan, can we talk?"

"Sure, yeah, come in," Ethan responded, shaking his head at the amount of information Caitlyn had gathered in the few hours she'd been in town.

They entered his office where she noticed changes since the last time she was there.

The space originally served as an oversized pantry in the old Victorian house, but Ethan didn't mind using it as his office. He didn't plan to spend time there anyway. He preferred to be out and about, meeting people and being a presence in town. He believed crime could be deterred with police presence, a result of his experience with the New York City Police Department.

"I like the new wall color," Caitlyn said.

"It was overdue. I did it one weekend. Didn't take long in this small space," Ethan responded looking around, pleased with his handiwork.

"I also like the fact you have your diplomas on the wall, and a local painting," Caitlyn further remarked.

"There was controversy over that," Ethan said. "I wanted to brighten the place. There were those on the town council, the ones who didn't want to hire me in the first place, who stated a sheriff's office should have only professional certificates on the wall. I disagreed, and that's why I painted the room myself and chose a pale yellow. The room doesn't have windows, so the soft color fights the somberness. I purchased the painting at a local art show. I'm glad you approve."

"Politics and power struggles are everywhere, aren't they? Even over the silliest things," Caitlyn said as she sat down and admired the room's new look. "You'd think the town council would have better use of their time and efforts than determining whether you can have a landscape painting on your wall. When will people concentrate on what's important?"

Ethan didn't need to comment. She was right.

Caitlyn brought herself back to the reason why she was there and moved to the edge of her seat, resting her arms on his desk in order to make her point.

"I heard you mention Steven Sullivan when you came in."

"Yes, I did. How do you know him?"

"I don't. But Abbie and Tim do. Tim thinks something has happened to Steven because he didn't show up for his class today, and missed a department meeting. They're concerned because this guy is Abbie's uncle. Kind of a long-lost type. Tim and Abbie are worried and asked me to talk to you about it."

The situation wasn't funny, but Ethan chuckled.

"You've been in town a couple of hours and you're already involved in police business," Ethan said with a smile.

"Just trying to help a friend," Caitlyn replied as she slid back into her chair. She, too, laughed at the irony.

The door opened and Maddie poked her head in. "Sheriff, that new girl in the medical examiner's office just called. Carrie?"

"Carrie Young," Ethan said.

"She said the victim's fingerprints belong to," Maddie checked her note, "Richard Kent. I guess it was fortunate he had been fingerprinted in order to volunteer at a school sometime in the past. Tom's running a background check now."

"Thanks Maddie. Let me know as soon as Tom gets the information. Maybe we can figure out what the hell he was doing out there this morning and what got him killed."

"Don't forget to return those phone calls. They seemed urgent," Maddie reminded him.

"I will," Ethan responded without enthusiasm.

He turned back to Caitlyn. "We've got a couple of situations going right now. The guy in the morgue, as you heard, has been identified as Richard Kent. He's young, clean cut, possibly a college student, and, unfortunately, into drugs. Now that he's been identified, and when Tom gets more information, we'll notify next of kin. Not my favorite thing to do. As far as Steven Sullivan is concerned, he might be missing or might not. I just talked with the woman he's renting from, and she said he usually told her when he was going out. This morning he didn't. Just said he didn't know what his day would bring. She felt it violated their protocol. I've asked her to call me this evening if he doesn't appear. Until then, there's nothing we can do about him."

Caitlyn nodded, understanding the laws regarding missing persons.

"Your use of the term 'violated protocol' makes me think there's more to this case than you're letting on," Caitlyn said.

Ethan didn't respond to her insightful comment. He was letting this situation get the better of him, and he had to stick with realities.

"Sorry, used the wrong term. I'm used to police procedure," Ethan said with a smile. "Let me rephrase, he violated their 'agreement.' Is that better?"

Caitlyn smiled at his attempt to please her.

"But seriously, did Tim tell you anything more about what's happening on campus? That might be important if this guy doesn't show up."

Caitlyn took a deep breath before responding. It was important to relay exactly what Tim told her and not add her prejudices or embellishments.

"According to Tim, several things are brewing. Students are starting to protest, because, according to Tim, that's what students do. He says certain faculty members are fueling the flame regarding rumors of a huge tuition hike next year. In addition, it was leaked that the reason for the satellite campus was not to better serve residential or commuter students, but to offer massive open online courses, otherwise known as MOOCs. Again, another rumor that MOOCs would increase the university's bottom line while overloading professors and not providing onsite students with the individual attention they believe they're entitled to. No one knows what impact the change will have on the residential student population, but it adds fuel to the fire of student protests."

"I doubt any of those issues are relevant to Steven Sullivan," Ethan interjected. He had no patience for campus politics.

"Probably not. The campus issues are background noise. From talking with Steven's colleagues, Tim suspects Steven's involved with more than teaching."

"What did he mean by that?" Ethan asked.

"I don't know and Tim didn't elaborate. Maybe he meant a union organizer? To be honest," Caitlyn said, and paused.

"Yes?"

"Tim thinks Abbie's uncle is a spy."

Ethan laughed out loud.

"This day is getting stranger by the minute."

Ethan caught his breath and turned serious.

"I've got to get back to the morgue to talk with the new medical examiner. She might have more information on our victim that could help us figure out what he was doing on Old Mill Road this morning. Besides, I was rude to Carrie and I need to apologize," Ethan explained.

"Carrie? Who's Carrie and where's Doc Morse?" Caitlyn asked.

"Doc's still there, but he's stepping back in his responsibilities. They've hired a woman, Carrie Young, to take over the medical examiner position. Doc will stay in Riverview and tend to his live patients," Ethan explained. "Why don't you come with me and we can catch up on news other than crime scenes."

Caitlyn looked at her watch. She didn't want to be late getting back to the house, but she couldn't pass up time with Ethan, even if it was in a police car and he was working a case.

"Love to," she replied.

~ NINETEEN ~

The Medical Examiner's office, now inconveniently located in the basement of the Renwick hospital, was quiet when Ethan and Caitlyn walked in. The receptionist was filing her nails and concentrating on a crossword puzzle. Ethan was tempted to make a joke about a five-letter word for not enough to do, but thought better of it. The reality was this office was incredibly busy, and the poor woman deserved some free time.

"Sorry to interrupt," Ethan said as he looked down at the crossword puzzle she was working.

"Not a problem. We're so busy these days I don't dare take lunch, so I eat at my desk and take five-minute breaks through the day. Not the best situation, but until we get more funding . . ."

"I understand completely," Ethan said as he showed the woman his badge and introduced Caitlyn. Once the receptionist was satisfied with the credentials, she nodded permission for them to enter the hallway leading to the autopsy suite.

They entered the medical examiner's office and found Carrie Young working at a desk situated against the back wall. She turned at the sound of the door opening.

"Carrie, uh, Dr. Young, sorry to bother you," Ethan said as he stopped just inside the door. He didn't want to cross a professional boundary and create another embarrassing situation.

"No bother, please come in, Sheriff."

Still concerned about professional courtesy, Ethan asked, "Do you prefer Carrie or Dr. Young?"

"You can call me Carrie. I want to set an informal tone with my colleagues. I think it makes for a closer working relationship. And may I call you Ethan or do you prefer Sheriff Ewing?"

"Ethan's fine," he responded with a smile.

"So, what can I do for you?" Carrie asked as she glanced over at Caitlyn.

"I apologize for my rudeness this morning. I shouldn't have been so quick to judge. I was distracted by the circumstances surrounding this morning's victim, but that was no excuse."

"No need to apologize. I know it's unsettling when a new person shows up to replace someone everyone respects. Doc Morse's shoes will be hard to fill, and that's why I insisted that I shadow him for a few months. I want a smooth transition," Carrie explained, and then went on, "even though it's created havoc with the state's budget office. But that's not something you need to be bothered with."

"I'm fighting the same budget battle. We're all expected to do more with less," Ethan replied as he turned to Caitlyn. "Before we get to the reason for our visit, let me introduce you to Caitlyn Jamison."

Caitlyn and Carrie shook hands, sizing up each other.

Ethan noticed Carrie's curious expression so he explained.

"Last spring, Caitlyn helped solve the murder of her cousin, Todd Tilton. You may have heard about that. The situation was very upsetting for the town, and Caitlyn worked with me, taking notes from interviews, being a good listener. I bounced ideas off her and, to tell the truth, it was Caitlyn who caught the murderer."

"Whoa, I'm impressed. I heard about the tragic death of the teenager. Please accept my belated condolences, Caitlyn."

Caitlyn smiled and nodded. She was beginning to like Carrie, even if she was replacing their beloved Doc Morse.

"Just to be clear, on this trip I'm here to do a photo shoot and that's all," Caitlyn said with a smile.

Carrie nodded, though she didn't believe a word. She had a feeling Caitlyn was going to end up doing more than taking photos; she knew the type. To be polite, she responded without emotion, "Sounds like the right decision."

Carrie decided to make her position clear.

"Just so we all understand, I'll explain a couple of things before we get into the specifics surrounding Mr. Kent's death."

"Okay," Ethan said, not understanding why Carrie's mood had changed and that she felt the need for an explanation.

Carrie took a breath and looked Caitlyn in the eye.

"The job of the medical examiner is to determine the cause and manner of death. The cause of death is determined from the etiologically specific disease or injury. That starts the sequence of events that leads to death. It answers the 'what' question. The 'what' is the event that starts the chain of events, and then we have to answer the 'how' question. Again, as a medical examiner it's *my job* to determine the cause and manner of death."

Carrie hesitated to see if Ethan was going to argue the point. He didn't.

"Deaths are grouped into six categories: homicide, suicide, accident, natural disease, therapeutic complication, and undetermined. Our main goal is to *not* have any of our autopsies come out with 'undetermined' as the cause of death. To me that indicates failure. I either missed something in the autopsy, in the x-rays, in the accident scene report, or the information wasn't provided and I have to go back to the investigation team and get what's needed. That's not a popular option. Time is wasted. Science should provide the answer with the assistance of the many tools available to us now."

Caitlyn felt she was being targeted with this diatribe. Although interesting, she was not a fool and she was going to let Carrie understand that fact.

"This is all very interesting, but I'm not as naïve as you might think. I understand the process."

Carrie ignored Caitlyn's remark, and continued. She wanted no misunderstanding about her role in the process.

"The manner of death affects a whole range of institutions like insurance companies, district attorneys, police, and of course, families. As a medical examiner I have to be concise and accurate; I have to count fingers and toes, go over every inch and document,

document, document. Every scrape, bruise, and cut tells a story. I can't miss a detail or my findings will be in question. And when that happens, my credibility is gone, maybe forever."

Carrie's explanation and the passion with which she detailed the specifics of what her job entailed, in addition to the skills she needed in performing an autopsy, were sobering.

"Nicely explained," Ethan said with a smile. "Your job is a combination of medical skills, careful paperwork management, and being able to accurately present details without prejudice in a court of law."

Caitlyn noticed he shifted his position in order to give Carrie a pat on the back, but at the last minute held back his desire to touch her.

"That's correct," Carrie said, her emotion spent. "And that's the reason I've been sent to Renwick. And the reason it is up to this office to make the determination. In addition, the county's recent growth prompted the medical community to review services here. That review showed a lack of resources. For years Riverview residents, as well as the other rural towns, have depended on Renwick to supplement their forensic services. With the added satellite campus drawing more students, faculty and staff to the area, the medical facilities were deemed lacking. In January, a medicolegal investigator will be in charge of this office. That person will be specially trained and certified in forensic investigations. Several surrounding counties already employ a medicolegal investigator, as well as a coroner or medical examiner."

"And Mr. Kent?" Ethan didn't care how the medical examiner's office was organized. He had a murder to solve.

"He, and others like him are another reason I've been sent here," Carrie stated.

"What do you mean by that?"

Her answer didn't make sense unless there was another side to this death.

"Mr. Kent is an overdose victim. And not just any overdose. Either he took or someone gave him a hit of a combo drug that killed him," Carrie explained. "The state's been fighting the illegal drug trade for years, but overdose deaths are happening so frequently we can't keep up. Central New York is considered a hot spot for drugs, and that's why I was sent to work at this lab. When the other towns have finished their consolidation, then we'll have a team of medical examiners on site. But for now, it's just Doc Morse, me, and a couple of part-timers. The medical examiners have been charged with coming up with solutions to stem the tide of overdose deaths, and that's going to be a challenge."

Carrie took a deep breath before continuing. This story was getting old. She'd told it so many times, and there didn't seem to be an end.

"Back to Mr. Kent. I've sent samples off to the state lab, with little hope of getting anything back for a number of weeks. But when we do, those findings should help us learn more about him, and I can provide you an official manner of death."

"Thanks for giving us background," Ethan said. "I'm having the items we collected at the scene sent to a private lab in Virginia. If they are as backed up as the state labs, I might lose my job. But it's worth the chance if I can find the reason for this young man's death. Too many people are dying or destroying their lives. So unnecessary," Ethan said, shaking his head.

"I'll run tests that I can do here, and hope those results give us some answers. Again, these tests take time, so we have to be patient. Labs don't turn results around as fast as they do on CSI or NCIS."

"I understand, and in the meantime, we'll notify his next of kin," Ethan said.

"Great. Let me know what you find. Any information as to his previous activities could be the clue we need."

Ethan turned to go, then stopped.

"Carrie, one more thing you should know."

"Yes?"

"I've ruled this young man's death a homicide."

"What? How can you do that without our final report? It's an apparent drug overdose, but critical test results aren't in, and this office has not confirmed the manner of death."

"You're correct. But the victim was given enough drugs for a deadly dose, and to me, that's murder. It's time we go after the dealers," Ethan responded.

Carrie was dumbfounded.

Ethan saw she was speechless, and so he continued as if his decision wasn't out of the ordinary.

"Thanks for the information, Carrie. It'll be nice working with you and I'm pleased you're easing Doc out of his medical examiner role with dignity."

Caitlyn, too, was shocked at Ethan's revelation. What is he getting himself into? She watched the exchange between the two with interest because, from what she observed, even with their differences, Ethan and Carrie were connecting on more than a professional basis. She chided herself for feeling jealous, especially under the circumstances.

They said their good-byes, and as Ethan and Caitlyn took their leave, Carrie gave Ethan one more glance, shaking her head in dismay.

As they walked down the hall toward the reception area, Caitlyn thought about Ethan's decision, and what repercussions that decision would have on Ethan's job. She also wondered about the budding relationship with the new medical examiner.

~ TWENTY ~

Outside the morgue Ethan turned to Caitlyn. "I know you need to get back to your aunt's, but do you have time for a quick stop at the campus? Until Tom can provide us with information on our victim, it might be productive to talk with Steven Sullivan's colleagues before they leave for the day just in case he is missing. Maybe we can learn how Richard Kent came into possession of Sullivan's credit card. It'll also give you an opportunity to see our newest Riverview feature—the satellite campus."

Caitlyn balked, her emotions conflicted. She should get back to the house. She appreciated the fact Ethan was interested in the whereabouts of Abbie's uncle, although she didn't like the term "our" with victim. She was *not* getting involved in another murder investigation. On the other hand, she was curious about Steven Sullivan's whereabouts.

Maybe Ethan's suggestion was an excuse to spend time with her, though more likely he, too, was curious about Steven and didn't want to take the time to drop her off at the station.

She glanced at her watch, not wanting to seem too eager, and responded, "Sure. I've got time. I appreciate the fact you're taking an interest in Abbie's uncle, but what about *your murder* victim?"

"That tone tells me you're skeptical about ruling Mr. Kent's death a homicide."

"I don't want you to get into more trouble, that's all."

"Don't worry. I've got Tom working on the guy's background. As soon as I get back to the office, I'll decide the best way to investigate his death. In the meantime, I have a gut feeling about Steven Sullivan," Ethan replied.

"What gut feeling?" Caitlyn asked as she stopped walking.

"I don't believe in coincidences. It's a 'coincidence' that Richard Kent was murdered the same morning that Steven Sullivan went missing. And a 'coincidence' that Sullivan's credit card was found on the body. To me that's not coincidence, but evidence."

His explanation made sense, but Caitlyn didn't want to consider the fact that Abbie's uncle might be connected with a possible homicide.

On the drive to the campus Ethan filled her in on all things happening in Riverview.

"The new campus has already made an impact on the community. Business owners are delighted, but residents not so much. Maddie fields a lot of complaint calls about students taking over the town, filling up the restaurants, causing traffic issues and increasing crime."

"Doesn't a healthy economy benefit everyone?"

"Yes, but residents don't want to admit it. The change is happening too quickly for some."

Caitlyn realized Riverview was a community experiencing change. The NIMBY principle—not in my backyard—was alive and well.

"In addition, residents are installing alarm systems in their homes, something they'd never had to do before. I've attended meetings hosted by various town organizations that wanted an explanation as to how we're going to handle the population influx."

"I didn't think about that part," Caitlyn said. "Do you think there'll be a lot of new houses built?"

"No doubt. It'll put pressure on the farmers to sell their land for development."

"Which means less local produce," Caitlyn finished his thought.

"Here we are," Ethan said as he pulled into the campus parking lot. "What do you think of our new university campus?"

Caitlyn couldn't believe what she saw. She was awed by how the brick building had been transformed. The university and its contractors did a splendid job in turning the defunct structure into usable space while preserving the integrity of the old mill.

Ethan urged her along, "It's getting late. Let's see who we can catch before they head out."

~

The building was a maze of hallways, so it took a while to find the science department wing. Ethan wondered how students found their way to class on time. They finally noticed signage pointing them in the right direction and came upon a door marked Science Department.

The receptionist immediately acknowledged Ethan and Caitlyn. The stacks of papers and folders on the desk made it apparent that this woman was more than a receptionist. She pulled off her headphones and gave them a smile that featured a mouth full of perfect white teeth. Ethan looked at Caitlyn. They were both thinking the same thing.

I wonder what whitening agent she uses?

"Welcome, I'm Janie," she said.

Ethan showed his badge, and in a lowered voice introduced Caitlyn as his assistant.

"I'm here to talk with colleagues of Steven Sullivan. We were notified he didn't show up today as scheduled." Ethan said.

"That's correct. He didn't show up for a department meeting this morning, and then right after he missed an appointment with the dean. In fact, it was Steven who made the appointment. He seemed quite intense, so I juggled meetings around in order to accommodate his request," Janie explained, her annoyance evident. "Things are a bit upside down, getting used to new offices, settling in, helping the new professors and lecturers, to say nothing of welcoming the students."

"I understand. Can you give me a list of Steven's colleagues in the science department, and anyone else he might have come in contact with?" Ethan asked.

"Sorry, but it is university policy that we not give out that information," Janie responded. "But, if you want to walk down the hallway, knock on a few doors, I can't stop you from doing that."

"Can you tell me if many professors are on campus now?"

Janie glanced at the clock.

"I doubt it. Most of their courses are held in the morning, but you're free to check."

~

They walked down the long corridor that housed offices and classrooms for the sciences. Ethan took one side of the hall and Caitlyn the other, knocking on each door. Nothing. It appeared faculty had gone for the day. They were about to give up when a voice behind them said, "Can I help you?"

They turned to see a middle-aged gentleman emerge from the men's bathroom.

Ethan introduced himself, showing his badge. He then introduced Caitlyn as his assistant who'd be taking notes.

"It seems Dr. Steven Sullivan didn't show up for his commitments today, and a friend is worried about him, so we're making informal inquiries," Ethan explained.

"Well, you're in luck. I'm Dr. Brant Jordan, and I share an office with Steven. Come on in and we can talk," Dr. Jordan said as he pointed Ethan and Caitlyn to an office door marked 320.

~ TWENTY-ONE ~

The office shared by Drs. Brant Jordan and Steven Sullivan was the epitome of how Caitlyn pictured a college professor's office would look. Two desks facing opposite walls with two chairs each. A large bookcase that sat along the outside wall was filled with books, papers, and paraphernalia. The bookshelves resembled a dumping ground for whatever the professors wanted to unload. Caitlyn's sense of neatness made her cringe at the sight. Before she could take in any more of the clutter, Dr. Jordan cleared spaces for them to sit.

"Sorry about the mess," Brant said as he pulled a stack of papers from two chairs. "I get involved in projects and coursework and don't notice things are piling up."

That's an understatement, Caitlyn thought.

After introductions were made, Ethan said, "Can you tell me if Dr. Sullivan was working on anything in particular, besides his coursework?"

"First let me ask, you said this was purely informal," Dr. Jordan said.

"Yes. You may have heard that a body was found this morning, about the time Dr. Sullivan left his house. I'm trying to figure out if the two are related. If they are, the faster I can get up to speed on what Dr. Sullivan was working on, who he was meeting with, the better. So, with that, can you tell me if he was working on anything special, who he talked to, his closest colleagues?"

"We've been busy getting our coursework together. Steven is new to the area, so he was getting oriented to the town, and developing his lesson plans."

Ethan nodded, encouraging him to continue.

Dr. Jordan paused, deciding how much he should say. Ethan caught this expression and wondered what was going through Dr. Jordan's head. Ethan let the man process and then pounced.

"What should you tell me that you aren't sure you should say?"

Dr. Jordan looked up, surprised.

"I believe in professional courtesy, you know," Dr. Jordan responded testily.

"I understand, but if Dr. Sullivan is in fact missing, then professional courtesy isn't going to help him, is it?" Ethan responded curtly. "Now, what's bothering you?"

Dr. Jordan stared past their heads, searching for the appropriate words. He, too, was good at psychology, baiting his audience and keeping them waiting.

Ethan was losing patience. Just before he was about to explode, Dr. Jordan spoke.

"I've been a bit uncomfortable with Steven. He comes here as a part-time lecturer, and at his age, you know it's not a long-term career choice. He asks me questions about the area, and then he seems to focus on Renwick. I've lived in the area a long time, but my wife and I live outside the city limits, and we aren't involved with the organizations in town. Consequently, I can't answer Steven's questions. I tell him the best restaurants, where to get his clothes dry-cleaned, stuff like that, but that doesn't seem to be what he's after. So I wonder. Why *is* he here?"

He sighed, took a breath and continued.

"One day after he left, I looked at the reference books and articles on his desk. That was not very professional, but I was curious. We felt comfortable leaving stuff on our desk, because we're both careful about locking up when we leave. The articles were about genetically modified organisms, and then painkillers and their side effects; articles that I didn't think were related to what I thought he was here to teach. He had maps of the state, roads, waterways, and that kind of thing. So these articles had me stumped. We are academics, so it's possible he's working on an article of some kind. As you can see, we have piles of books and

96

papers everywhere, projects we're working on, but there was something about these particular articles that gave me pause. A funny thing for a psychologist to admit."

"Does anyone else know about these articles?" Caitlyn asked.

Dr. Jordan thought a minute. "I'm not sure, actually. But when he dropped one the other day and I leaned over to pick it up, he grabbed it, and then apologized. He said it was a private project and could I not mention these articles to anyone. I haven't."

"It sounds like he was sensitive of others finding out what he was doing," Caitlyn wondered out loud. "Do you think he's hiding something?"

"I have no idea. We're all new to this campus, and adjusting to new routines. There's no time to analyze our colleagues."

"Excuse me," a voice came from the doorway. A short stocky man in his 50s poked his head in and had a questioning expression on his face.

"Can we help you?" Ethan asked, standing, taking control of the situation.

Before the man could respond, Dr. Jordan spoke up and waved the newcomer in.

"Come in, Chad."

The gentleman walked cautiously into the room, looking from Ethan, to Caitlyn and then to Dr. Jordan.

"I should have mentioned that we also share office space with Dr. Chad Owens, a visiting marine biologist from the State University of New York at Stony Brook on Long Island. Chad, this is Sheriff Ethan Ewing and Caitlyn . . ."

"Jamison," Caitlyn added, shaking the man's hand.

"Chad is here to, well, you can explain," Dr. Jordan said, turning to Chad.

"As Brant said, the university offered me office space on the Riverview campus while I conduct studies on the health of the lakes. Hydrilla has appeared, as well as some other invasive species. I'll also be testing water quality, fish health, and things like that. Since Dr. Sullivan is here part time, I use his chair, and this little end table for a desk. I don't need much, as I am mostly working off-site."

Ethan and Caitlyn turned to where Dr. Owens pointed. In the corner there was indeed a small table on which two books, a pen and a lined paper pad were positioned. Not much of a workspace. They looked at each other, reading each other's thoughts.

Ethan addressed Dr. Owens

"We're here inquiring about Dr. Sullivan. He didn't show up for work today, and his whereabouts might be connected with a case we're working on."

"Sorry," Chad responded. "I've only seen him a couple of times."

Ethan decided he wasn't going to get any more information from either man, at least for today. He rose and said, "Thanks again, Dr. Jordan, and it was nice to meet you, Dr. Owens. Good luck with your work. Please understand that my visit here today is purely a preliminary inquiry. We hope Dr. Sullivan will return this evening. Here's my card. In the event Dr. Sullivan doesn't turn up, if you think of anything else that could help, please give me a call."

"Will do," Dr. Jordan said.

"Same here," replied Dr. Owens. "Nice to meet ya."

~ TWENTY-TWO ~

"What did you think of Drs. Jordan and Owens?"

Caitlyn fastened her seatbelt before pulling out her notebook. She jotted down another note, turned to Ethan and said, "I don't think Dr. Owens knows much at all. It appears the university has just granted him desk space and he doesn't have much else to do with the campus community. As for Dr. Jordan, other than the fact he was looking me over, I think he is curious about Steven Sullivan and suspects he might be more than a part-time lecturer. I believe Steven's life is compartmentalized and no one *really* knows him. He doesn't seem to allow anyone into his life. It would be worthwhile to check out his Boston colleagues to see what they have to say about him."

"I'm glad you're finally on board with the notion that there might be more to why Steven Sullivan is in Riverview. Unfortunately, we can't spend much time on this until it becomes official, and . . . I have a murder to solve."

"I don't want any part of your homicide investigation, but I can't help but be curious as to the whereabouts of our mysterious Uncle Steven," Caitlyn said.

~

Ethan watched Caitlyn drive away and then climbed the steps, two at a time, onto his office's veranda. He was on the fourth step when his phone vibrated. The caller ID indicated it was from headquarters. *What now?* Didn't he have enough on his plate without being bothered by trivia from downtown?

He answered, his tone terse, "Sheriff Ewing."

"Ethan, I want to see you in my office in thirty minutes," Captain Robertson said.

"But sir, I've got a suspicious death, plus several burglaries I'm investigating, and a possible missing person case. Is there something more pressing?" Ethan asked.

"I'll see you in thirty minutes," Robertson responded.

Ethan heard the phone click; call ended. What was going on? Was a situation developing that couldn't be communicated over the phone? Curiosity overcame his anger about being ordered back to Renwick. Maybe something big was brewing, and they needed *his* expertise. He checked his watch. The captain was aware it would take Ethan thirty minutes to get to headquarters.

Power play ran through his mind.

Ethan poked his head into the office and said, "Maddie, the captain has *requested* my presence in his office. Has Tom found anything out about our murder victim?"

"Yes he has," Maddie replied, nodding to Tom's desk where he was just finishing a phone call.

Ethan's commute time to Renwick was running out, but he decided to take the consequences in order to hear Tom's report.

"Boss," Tom's voice boomed with excitement. "We've got a problem."

"Fill me in. I'm supposed to be in Renwick in a few minutes."

"The victim is Richard Kent, Jr., son of state senate majority leader, Richard Kent, Sr.—the parents are divorced. Richard's father lives in Pound Ridge; his mother is a professor at the university in Renwick. Richard is a Ph.D. student. His record is clean. Not so much as a parking ticket."

"So, the questions are, why was this supposedly 'clean-cut' honors student, who was into drugs, murdered? What was he doing in this out-of-the-way place, and how does this tie in with Steven Sullivan?"

"Those are the questions, aren't they?" Tom replied. "I'm continuing to dive into Richard's past and doing web searches on his father. That might be the connection. If his dad has ties to the drug world or has worked *against* the drug cartels, maybe they got their revenge."

"It's how they operate. They know that it's more painful to harm loved ones than to harm the person," Ethan stated.

"How should I handle this?" Tom asked.

"Follow protocol. Contact the Renwick precinct and have them notify the parents, and offer to contact the university with a courtesy call," Ethan responded, while wondering if this situation could get any worse. "Continue to investigate Richard, Jr. If you need me, I'll be with the captain, and I'll fill him in on the details. This could be an explosive situation in more ways than one."

"Okay," Tom replied, getting started on his task.

~

Upon arrival at police headquarters Ethan was immediately directed to Captain Robertson's office. His boss didn't look up as he entered, but just waved to a chair in front of the desk.

"You're late."

"Sorry, sir. Tom had important information to share on this morning's . . ." he hesitated, finding the right word . . . "death before I left."

Ethan sat with his cap balanced on his knee and waited for the captain to state what was on his mind. The room's atmosphere was oppressive, and the list of reasons why he might be chastised scrolled through his head. He was not one to go by the book. He believed there were cases when personal judgment and common sense came into play. He bent the rules a few times, but for good reasons. But it took only one person to file a complaint, and only one with money and power to make waves, and the hammer would come down. So he waited. He'd share information about this morning's victim after the captain covered whatever was on his mind.

"I heard you've been spending time on the whereabouts of one of the college chaps, Steven Sullivan," Captain Robertson said, slowly putting down his pen and meeting Ethan eye to eye.

The statement took Ethan by surprise; it wasn't what he'd expected. How did the captain know that he'd been making inquiries and why would he care? These thoughts raced through his

101

mind in milliseconds. Ah, someone on campus must have made a call to headquarters. Why?

"Sir, I was only making initial inquiries in case it's tied to the overdose victim. I asked Tom to notify the precinct, but in case you didn't hear, the victim is Richard Kent, Jr., the son of Senator Richard Kent, Sr. I've got Tom getting as much information on the victim as fast as possible. We've notified the university so they can notify the parents. The mother is one of their professors. This is a delicate situation, and I wanted you to know as soon as possible."

Captain Robertson sat back with a start, placing his arms flat on the desk.

"*My God*, do you have any idea what this means? We'll have the state police, the press, and God knows who else, descending on us," Captain Robertson replied, shaking in anger.

"Captain, I'm not insensitive to the problems facing law enforcement, especially here in Renwick, and the importance of the mayor's task force, but due to present circumstances, I respectfully remind you of my responsibilities in Riverview. I've got a town filling up with college students, and we, too, are feeling the effects of the escalating drug traffic. Now we have a young overdose victim, who is no less than the son of an important legislator and a university professor. You question my inquiring about Steven Sullivan, but I think it's more than coincidental that the missing Steven Sullivan left his house near the time of the . . ."

"Did you not understand what I said?" Captain Robertson said, his voice rising.

"Yes, sir. I do," Ethan responded, knowing that the captain's rampage was about the success of the new drug task force, the incoming media attention, and his own job security. And now the additional stress of the latest drug overdose victim's family. He couldn't imagine what a zoo this precinct was going to turn into once the press learned about the senator's son.

Everyone was under pressure to get the drug problem under control. Local police departments were ill equipped to stem the tide of drug overdoses. No one knew what to do about the victims.

102

Police and paramedics called to overdose scenes did what they could to revive the victims, and then the same people would overdose again in a couple of weeks. Those were the "lucky" ones. Too many lives were lost. Families and entire communities suffered. Everyone was tired and frustrated. As these thoughts raced through his mind, he began to understand the captain's anger.

Captain Robertson cooled down and continued, "Back to the task force. It'll consist of a couple of my officers, an area businessman, a campus security officer, and of course Doc Morse. We needed a representative from the outlying towns. You were chosen because of your experience. As you know from this morning's briefing, crime is escalating. Addicts need money."

The captain took a breath before continuing, his voice rising with each word, "And that's why I can't have you wasting time on a 'missing' person who isn't officially missing."

"Yes, I'm aware of all that, but sir, . . ."

"No buts. You're dismissed, sheriff. The task force team leader will be in touch."

"And who will that be?" Ethan asked, exasperated at the turn of events, trying to keep his voice steady.

"I haven't assigned a leader yet, but it will probably be Brian Philips, a well-connected businessman in town. I'm meeting with him later today to decide a strategy."

Captain Robertson picked up his pen and went back to what he was working on prior to Ethan's arrival. In the captain's mind the meeting was over.

It was time to lay his bombshell at the captain's feet.

"Sir, there's something you need to know," he paused until the captain looked up. "I've ruled Richard Kent's death a homicide."

The captain's mouth dropped and he looked at Ethan in utter disbelief.

"What *the hell* are you thinking?" He roared. He stood up, leaned over, and planted his hands firmly on the desk.

Ethan was not going to be overruled. He raised himself up and stood his ground.

"Captain, I know this is highly unusual and will be controversial, but if law enforcement doesn't take a stand now, we'll continue to be overrun by the cartels." Ethan said firmly, making his case. Ethan hoped what he said made sense and that the idea was getting through.

Before the captain could respond his phone rang. Picking it up, he listened, and then hung up abruptly.

"I've got to attend to another matter. You and I are not finished. Change your ruling on Mr. Kent's death. Now, go," he instructed, waving Ethan from his office.

~ TWENTY-THREE ~

Ethan steamed all the way back to Riverview. The captain had no right to micromanage his decisions, but that was what was happening. He'd have a good long think about the situation and how best to handle it.

It was then he remembered the phone messages Maddie had placed on his desk. If there were going to be peace tomorrow, he'd better deal with the messages tonight. Dinner could wait. He'd go back to the office, return the calls that at this late hour would no doubt go to voicemail, and then he could honestly report to Maddie that he'd tried.

The games we play . . .

The office was unusually quiet. Tom and Maddie had left for the day and Jeff, the night dispatcher, was reading a book when he should have been tidying up or working on the endless paperwork. Ethan let it go. He'd had enough conflict for today.

He entered his office, sat down, and thumbed through the three messages. One was a local number, a complaint. The other two were from the same out of state number. He threw one of the duplicates in the trash, and dialed the number on the other. He had to answer several questions, and he was ready to hang up when a human voice came on the line.

"I'm glad you finally returned our call, Sheriff Ewing."

Ethan was surprised at that response, and short on temper. He had no time for games.

"And you are?" He demanded.

"Don Scott. I work for the DEA, and I manage cases assigned to Steven Sullivan."

Ethan took a deep breath, and sat back in his chair. He was right. There *was more* to Dr. Steven Sullivan, the part-time college lecturer.

"I'm aware of Dr. Sullivan's presence here, and that he may be missing. Does your call have to do with that?"

"Our intelligence tells us he is missing. He's working as a federal officer, which falls under our jurisdiction, *but* we have no desire to waste time fighting with the locals over jurisdiction, and so we hoped that you would help us out."

"You've got to be kidding! Do you have any idea what you're asking? The workload we're facing?" Ethan responded, aghast at what they were asking him to do.

Doing his best to keep his tone civil, Ethan added, "You're much better equipped to deal with a situation like this than a small town sheriff's office." He was not going to be pushed around with others deciding his priorities. "And if I decline?"

"Please, Sheriff. We know we're asking a lot, and if we had time, things would be different, but a man's life is at stake. We've reviewed your personnel file and you have the credentials to handle the assignment. We're sorry for the inconvenience to you and your department, but a man's life is at stake. We'll send the pertinent information about Sullivan by private courier. You'll have it first thing tomorrow. In that packet will be a number and a code word. Call that number, say the code word, and you will be provided another number on a secure line. Text updates to that number. We'd like daily reports on your progress. I believe you realize what a delicate situation this is, so it's extremely important that you do this without anyone else knowing. Do you understand?"

Ethan paused, letting Mr. Scott wonder what his response might be, although he knew there was no decision to be made. He had to help them out.

"What specifically is Sullivan doing here?"

"That information, Sheriff, will have to wait until you receive the packet. There is no more to be said. Please follow the instructions provided and stay in touch."

Frustrated and angry, Ethan responded, "I'll await your instructions."

The phone, still in Ethan's hand, went silent. He now faced conflicting marching orders, but at least the mystery surrounding why Steven Sullivan was in Riverview was solved, or would be once the packet arrived. Ethan sent up a silent prayer that Steven Sullivan would show up at his house this evening.

His gut told him that wasn't going to happen.

~ TWENTY-FOUR ~

The natural light faded as the afternoon hours slipped away. A cardboard box of family memorabilia remained at Verna's feet, serving as a silent sentinel of her past.

She took a sip of her chilled chardonnay before carefully placing the wineglass on the antique side table. She took pains to make sure it was centered on the coaster in order to prevent watermarks. She adjusted the lace doily, so that, too, was centered on the table.

Her attention turned to the lined yellow pad on her lap and she reviewed the notes she'd made about her family. As a result of that process, her eyes were tired and her head ached. She leaned back against the chair and tried to imagine what her brother's life had been like after his marriage, after she left the state. There wasn't a day now that she didn't think about him and wonder. Palle van der Molen's life remained a mystery; a mystery Verna was determined to solve as a way to assuage her guilt.

~

It wasn't by accident that she walked Old Mill Road every day. She was drawn there as if by a mystical force, and was it that same force that prompted her to come upon the body this morning? If it wasn't coincidence, was it fate? She was still shaken by the event, and couldn't help but wonder if the family homestead attracted evil. Verna shook her head. She didn't believe in spirits, evil or otherwise.

But what if . . .

The fact she didn't know whether her brother had died, or not, and if so, where he was buried, bothered her. Most of all, she didn't know a thing about his life after he married Edda. Her eyes closed and her mind transported her back in time.

The shrill ring of the doorbell jarred her back to the present

~

"Myra, what are you doing here at this hour?"

"I hope you don't mind my just stopping by, but I made a pot of soup today, and thought I'd share some with you. Did I come at a bad time?"

Verna shook herself, trying to dispel the thoughts that had seeped into her mind.

"No, no, please come in. I was just going through some old papers. Let me pour you a glass of wine and we can chat."

Myra glanced at her watch. She really needed to get back to put dinner on. But she also knew it was important to spend time with Verna, especially now.

"Sure, one glass won't hurt."

Myra sat on the couch and Verna settled back into her chair next to an old wooden box with papers spilling out.

"So, what have we here?" Myra asked.

"I've told you a little bit about my family, but now I am driven to find out what happened to my brother, Palle. He's two years younger than I, and up until the time he married, I mostly took care of him. Our mother was sickly and spent most of her time in bed, so I watched over Palle, did most of the housework, and fixed meals. Father was away much of the time, selling his produce, and trying to make a living by subsistence farming."

"So what happened?" Myra asked, and shifted forward to indicate her interest in the story.

"The family was not happy when Palle brought Edda home to meet them. Our parents warned Palle about marrying into the Villetta family, but Palle, carrying the inherent stubborn gene, married Edda anyway. Edda and I developed a mutual dislike, and she's the reason I accepted a teaching position in Florida. I wanted to be as far away from the newlyweds as possible. I dare say Palle's choice of a spouse was the reason our family was pulled apart. Communication ended. How silly it seems now."

"Families can be difficult," Myra said as she thought about the strained relationship with her sister.

"I tired of Florida, so after a few years, I took a position in New Jersey. Even though I was closer, I couldn't bring myself to be around Edda."

"But you got married at some point, didn't you?" Myra asked cautiously, trying to find a happier subject. Although they had been friends for a while, there were some subjects that were sensitive to broach. Verna never mentioned her husband and Myra was afraid to ask. But now seemed an appropriate time.

Verna put her head back and allowed happier memories to flood her mind.

"I met the love of my life, Ned Adams, in New Jersey. I was young and foolish then," Verna laughed.

"One evening after work a few of us teachers decided to go out and hunt for guys. We'd heard about a local bar where eligible men were ripe for the picking. Cheap liquor, music, and men was the recipe for fun in those days."

"I think it still is," Myra added with a smile, remembering her youthful days.

"I zeroed in on Ned as soon as he walked through the door that evening. It took all my wiles to engage him in conversation. Luckily I knew just enough about the building trades to hold my own with Ned and his buddies.

Ned worked at carpentry jobs for various big-name contractors, building huge houses on the Jersey shore for the rich folks coming out of New York City. Carpentry work was considered a blue-collar job, but he did well. He even had enough time and money to put a sunroom onto our suburban home. I was the one, however, with the secure position that provided us with the health insurance we desperately needed, especially when Ned fell ill. He was only fifty-three when cancer claimed him, and he was gone within nine months."

"Oh, Verna, I'm so sorry. I didn't know." Myra reached over and put a hand on Verna's arm.

"It was almost twenty years ago, but I still can't think about him without feeling empty and lost. You understand that pain. It gets better with time, but I'm sorry to say, it won't ever go completely away."

Thinking of her son's death, Myra wiped a tear off her cheek. Maybe she shouldn't have brought up this subject.

"When I retired, I faced two choices: move to a condo in Florida or back to Riverview. New Jersey was too crowded, as was Florida, so I decided Riverview would be like going home again. I should have taken Thomas Wolf's advice—*You can't go home again.* I don't like how the town is changing. I thought I was going to find solace coming back to my roots, but instead, I have become obsessed with the past."

The women sat in silence, both absorbed in their thoughts. Myra checked the time, and put her glass down.

"I have to get back to the house, Verna. I wish I could stay longer."

"Don't say another word," Verna said as she got up. "Sharing my thoughts and feelings has helped tremendously. And thanks to you I feel strong enough to tackle these family papers."

Verna showed Myra to the door, and then returned to her chair. She had saved two small boxes of family papers and photos that she had taken when she left for her job in Florida. When she returned to Renwick, she put the boxes in the attic, out of sight. One of those sat at her feet. She'd retrieve the other box tomorrow with the hope it held useful information. As for today, her energy was spent.

~ TWENTY-FIVE ~

There was no way Caitlyn could sneak into the house without Summit sensing her return; animals can do that. By the time she got out of the car she heard the dog at the door barking and scratching. When she reached the front porch she heard her uncle's baritone voice yelling for the dog to shut up. Caitlyn cringed. She didn't think her uncle would be home from Albany until the weekend. Her plan to spend time with Aunt Myra was thwarted.

She took a deep breath and turned the doorknob. Summit was all over her with a welcome jump onto her legs, and then he twirled into his happy dance. She laughed at the little dog's antics.

She hung her coat in the hall closet and wondered why she dreaded seeing her uncle. The answer was easy. He wasn't the easiest person with whom to get along—a typical hardnosed businessman and now a know-it-all politician. Those overbearing attributes sometimes carried over into his home life. How did her aunt stand it?

I wonder what the politicos in Albany are up to?

She doubted he'd share anything interesting with her.

Caitlyn placed a smile on her face, straightened her spine and walked down the hall into the kitchen where she found her aunt and uncle talking. Both seemed happy to see her, and the anxiety she'd felt melted away, at least for now.

They spent the next half hour with small talk, catching up on the minutia of their lives before the conversation turned to more serious subjects.

As they sat around the dinner table, Caitlyn asked, "Uncle Jerry, how serious is the drug addiction situation in New York State?

Upstate, I mean like here?" Subtlety was never one of her strong suits.

"Why do you ask?" Jerry responded with a question, putting another bite of medium rare prime rib into his mouth.

"Just curious. I know it's a problem in the big cities and in the mid-west. I'm curious to know if it's infiltrating New York's rural areas as well," Caitlyn responded, hoping he wouldn't catch on there was more to her inquiry.

"Well, unfortunately, it's a problem everywhere. In college towns like Renwick, there's the additional situation of a university. College age kids are always looking for a new high, or relief from the stress of their classes and exams. In fact, the senate recently set up a committee specifically to look at the upstate college towns."

He was starting to warm to the subject, and a chance to talk, or more likely brag, about his work in Albany.

"We're hoping to secure funding for treatment centers, like they have in Ireland. I believe they call them 'shooting galleries.'"

"What a horrible term! I hope the senators come up with better terminology," Caitlyn blurted out, not able to contain her shock over the unfortunate use of the term.

Jerry scowled. *Here she goes again, criticizing, causing trouble, trying to control everything.*

Caitlyn continued her questions, unaware or just not caring about her uncle's pained expression.

"Do you think there's a drug pipeline through this area?" Caitlyn asked, hoping she wasn't pushing the envelope, shutting him down from sharing information. Seeing his expression and how he concentrated on his food, she knew she'd crossed the line. She'd gone too far and her uncle was ready to end the conversation.

"That's nothing for you to worry about, my dear," he replied with a smile and condescending tone, making the point by waving his fork in the air. He put his napkin on the table and prepared to leave.

"Jerry, answer her," Myra demanded, finally joining the conversation.

"I did, Myra. And I have nothing more to say on the subject," Jerry said in a harsh tone as he rose from the table, picked up his plate and left the room.

"But I heard heroin use has become an epidemic," Myra said to her husband's retreating back. She wasn't going to be silenced.

You go girl! Caitlyn thought. Her aunt was becoming her own woman and was standing up to her overbearing husband.

Jerry stopped and turned to answer his wife.

"That's correct, but it isn't going to affect your life, now, is it?" He replied sarcastically, turning and walking into the kitchen. They heard his plate clank onto the counter where Jerry dropped it before heading to his home office.

The two women sat in silence as Jerry had, once again, successfully shut down the conversation.

They understood, only too well, the situation *would* affect them. Crime was on the increase. Addicts were always looking for ways to pay for their drugs. Breaking into houses and cars was only the beginning. The number of overdose deaths reported each day was staggering. Families, friends and colleagues suffered. Even if Myra stayed safe, it was only time before she or someone she knew was affected.

Caitlyn had other options for finding out what was going on. She thought about the articles in Steven Sullivan's office and wondered what part genetically modified organisms or GMOs played. What part did snack foods with high sugar content play if anything at all? As she cleared the table, she thought about the connection between food consumption and drug use. Was there a connection? It didn't make sense that every opioid user was previously on painkillers. The numbers were too staggering. There had to be another trigger. If that's true, then what was it? And would society be able to combat the large companies producing these products?

~

While their dinner dishes were being scrubbed by the dishwasher's warm sudsy water, Myra and Caitlyn washed the fragile items by hand. This chore provided Caitlyn an opportunity to talk with her aunt without the annoying interruption of her uncle who was now ensconced in his study.

Caitlyn gently dried the Waterford crystal wineglasses and dreamed that someday she, too, would be able to afford this glassware.

"How are you doing, Aunt Myra?" Caitlyn asked. A few months ago Myra's only child, Todd, was murdered. While they coped with that horrifying event, Jerry was appointed to fill a seat in the state senate where he now spent most of his time. Myra was left in Riverview to deal with her son's death, and to run the house, alone.

Caitlyn had tried to stay in touch with her aunt. She hoped her mother and Myra were able to bury the grudges between the two sisters and communicate again.

Myra took a few moments to respond to Caitlyn's question as she scrubbed the same fragile dish over and over. Caitlyn thought she might rub the delicate floral design right off. In hindsight, maybe the dish would've been safer in the dishwasher.

"I'm doing okay," Myra finally responded. "It's been tough going through Todd's things and deciding what to get rid of and what to save. It was tempting to keep his room as is, a shrine of sorts, but I knew that wasn't healthy and wouldn't allow me to move on. Over the summer I packed up mementoes to keep, and then redid the room. I donated the furniture, painted the walls, and hung new artwork. I use Todd's room for a craft room, and when I'm in there I feel his creative spirit channeling me. Does that sound silly?"

Caitlyn shook her head, understanding.

In a lowered voice, Myra stated, "It's actually easier with Jerry in Albany during the week. I had time to grieve on my own, in my own time, without him making me feel weak for doing so."

Myra hesitated, and then decided to be kinder to her husband. "You know how hard it is for men when women cry. I didn't want to put Jerry through that with all he has to do in Albany."

"Everyone has their way of grieving. Maybe Uncle Jerry's was to consume himself with work."

"Verna helped too," Myra continued as she nodded agreement. "We've become good friends over the last couple of months. We talk a lot. She has sadness and loss in her life as well. She and her brother lost touch many years ago, and now Verna is determined to find out what happened to him. She needs to know if he died, and if so, where he's buried. There was a wife and baby; a girl, I think. Obviously the family wasn't close. Seems to take a similar path to ours, doesn't it?"

Caitlyn didn't respond to the comment. She was as guilty as anyone. She never bothered to develop a relationship with her cousin, and now she couldn't find time to have a meaningful connection with her parents.

"What happened to them?" Caitlyn asked, bringing the conversation back to Verna's family.

"Verna doesn't know. That's what's bothering her, and that's the basis of her guilt," Myra said. "She's approached the age when she thinks about end of life. She needs to find the answers and come to peace with them."

"Verna doesn't look that old. Why would she be thinking about end of life?"

"Verna looks younger than she is. She also has health issues, though she refuses to talk about them," Myra responded.

"Did her brother live in this area?" Caitlyn asked, taking the overly scrubbed china dish from her aunt.

"Yes. Not too far from here, on Old Mill Road, the van der Molen place."

Caitlyn stopped wiping the dish in her hand and said, "That's strange. The sheriff mentioned the location of the body found this morning was by the van der Molen place."

"Really? Verna didn't mention that when she told me about finding the body," Myra said, dumping her dishwater into the sink. She grabbed a paper towel to dry her hands, and then turned to look at Caitlyn. "Now that I think about it, it's strange she didn't mention it. Or maybe she thought I'd figure it out, since she's told me some things about her family. At any rate, it's news to me."

"It is strange she didn't mention it, because I assume she'd know very well where she was," Caitlyn said. "Another mystery to be solved. Or maybe it's just a simple oversight. It must have been such a shock for her."

"I wish you could stay longer," Myra said wistfully, changing the subject.

Caitlyn noted the lonely expression on her aunt's face.

"I do, too, Aunt Myra. I do, too."

~

The phone vibrated against her hip as Caitlyn entered the guest room. She pulled it from her pocket and looked at the text.

Meet me @ Tony's Tavern @ 7. Urgent! Ethan

She was exhausted, and that was making her irritable. It had been a long and emotional day and she was going to crash. The last thing she wanted was to go out again. One drink and her head would be on the table. She certainly would be in no condition to drive. And what was this *urgent* about? If he was trying to be funny again, she wasn't laughing. The more she thought about it, the more annoyed she got.

Who does he think he is summoning me?

Her fingers hovered over the phone keys, her emotions in turmoil as to how to respond. Finally, she held down the button on the top of the phone, then swiped across to shut it down for the night.

Caitlyn brushed her teeth, gave her face a lick and a promise, lifted Summit onto the bed, and settled under the covers. Her head hit the pillow and she was sound asleep.

Unbeknownst to her, the phone continued to receive text messages for the next hour.

~ TWENTY-SIX ~

Ethan's frustration level was high. Caitlyn didn't answer his text messages and his calls went straight to voicemail, but he knew where to find her this morning.

Her car was parked off to the side of the winery's driveway. He didn't have time to admire the winery's prime location that featured breathtaking views in every direction. Nor did he have time to appreciate the grape vines populated with clusters of light green grapes.

As a result of his phone conversation with the DEA official who requested his help in locating Steven Sullivan, Ethan now had proof his murder victim and missing person were connected by more than just a credit card. It was imperative that Caitlyn wasn't involved. He was faced with the task of locating Sullivan without Captain Robertson, or anyone else, knowing while making progress on solving the murder of young Richard Kent. His day couldn't get any worse.

Walking along the rows of grapevines, Ethan heard Summit give a happy bark, and then Caitlyn's head appeared. Her camera was positioned so she could scan the vineyard for the perfect shot. She must have been bending down taking close-ups of grape clusters.

"Good morning," Ethan said before he reached her. He didn't want to break her concentration since she was intent on her job.

"Oh, you startled me," Caitlyn said, hand to her heart as she turned at the sound of his voice. "What're you doing here?"

He ignored the question and asked one of his own.

"Is there a reason you're not answering my texts?"

Caitlyn sighed. She still didn't know what to think about his *urgent* message from last night. Was she conflicted about Ethan's relationship with the new female medical examiner? Emotions were getting the better of her, and it was not something of which she was proud.

"Sorry, Ethan." Caitlyn sighed. "I was tired last night and turned my phone off. In fact," she pulled the phone from her pocket, "I guess I forgot to turn it on this morning. I had to get an early start today to photograph the dew-covered grapes and leaves." She stood up, looked him in the eye, and with a nod, stated, "And now you're interrupting my best opportunity."

She picked up her camera and continued to work.

"If that's the way it has to be, then I'll wait until the light *isn't right*, because we need to talk."

Caitlyn didn't know what to make of his tone or his stance. Whatever was on his mind, she understood that he wasn't kidding. Something serious was going on, and she was about to find out what. Maybe Abbie's uncle was found, hurt, or worse. Her stomach clenched, wondering what the news could be.

"Okay. Let me take a few more photos. Then we'll talk. There's a bench about three rows up. Wait for me there."

Ethan turned and walked in the direction she'd indicated. He waited impatiently, checking his watch every few minutes. He had to get back to the office for the overnight delivery.

Just as he was about to leave, Caitlyn joined him on the bench, placing her camera bag between them.

"Okay, what's so 'urgent' that you kept sending texts all evening?" Caitlyn asked.

Ethan didn't respond right away. He had to calm himself, and he accomplished that by looking out over the vineyards to the lake and the woods beyond. He chose his words carefully.

"Well, first, Captain Robertson told me to drop my inquiries regarding Steven Sullivan. Then he ordered me to change my ruling on Richard Kent's death. It's all about politics. He wants me to concentrate on the mayor's task force and my responsibilities in Riverview."

He paused, his conflicting emotions visible.

"So, what are you going to do about that? And what about Abbie's uncle? Don't you need to find out why his ID was found on the body?"

"Yes, but maybe the two events aren't connected," Ethan responded, hoping she didn't notice his white lie. He had to downplay the situation. Since his conversation with Sullivan's boss, there was no way she could be involved. It was just too dangerous.

"So Abbie's uncle hasn't returned?" Caitlyn pressed.

"That's correct. The captain said I shouldn't spend time chasing him down until a missing person's report is filed. The captain doesn't think one piece of evidence is enough to justify our time. It's possible the university is putting pressure on him to stop an investigation. That's the last thing they need the first semester on their new campus. Additionally, with resources at the limit, I have to do what I'm told."

He hoped this would put an end to the conversation. Before he could change the subject, Caitlyn asked, "What happens if Steven doesn't show up?"

"It isn't our concern. No missing person report has been filed. There's nothing we can do," Ethan replied more sternly than he intended.

Caitlyn turned and studied Ethan's face as he talked. She listened carefully to his words, searching for any hidden meaning. A slight twitch of his right eyelid spoke volumes. That small movement indicated stress, and that could be for any number of reasons. She knew him well enough to know it was because he was not being honest with her.

When he finished talking, she didn't respond, but instead turned to gaze out at the lake and let his words sink in. She wasn't buying his response, and even though they'd been together a short time, a close connection had formed, and she knew when he wasn't telling the truth. She had to find out why.

"Have you talked with his friend, Tracy?"

Damn! Why doesn't she let this go?

He knew very well why. Abbie was her friend; Steven was Abbie's uncle. And Caitlyn was, well, Caitlyn. Dog with a bone came to mind.

"I called Ms. Connor last night. Steven didn't come home, but she isn't worried. He's most likely doing research. You know how academics are."

Ethan glanced over to check Caitlyn's expression, hoping she was buying the story.

Caitlyn leaned back against the bench, arms folded across her chest. She'd have to take the lead on this. She turned to look at Ethan, "Maybe I'll stay around a few more days. This whole thing sounds suspicious."

Ethan shook his head in resignation. This conversation wasn't going the way he planned, but before he could come up with a response, Caitlyn continued.

"I'll talk to more of his colleagues. You can provide me with whatever details you need in order to locate Steven. Then you will be following the captain's orders, but still getting the information you need to find Abbie's uncle."

She turned to Ethan, waiting for his response. She was pushing the envelop with him big time. But it was the kind of push he needed if he were going to level with her.

He was trapped. Caitlyn was going to persevere and if he shut her down completely, she'd know something was awry. She'd talk to Abbie and Tim, and the three of them would go off half-cocked. Caitlyn could ruin his investigation, or worse, put herself in serious danger. He had to act fast in his response and decided it wouldn't hurt to have her do a little benign questioning. It would keep her busy, make her feel she was doing something, and he'd keep control of the situation.

Caitlyn continued her silence, mentally planning interview tactics.

Ethan was thinking as well. He couldn't discount the fact they made a good team. Last spring they'd solved her cousin's murder in record time. From what he understood about the circumstances of Steven Sullivan's disappearance, there were a lot of unanswered questions. If she could fill in his recent activity, that might be helpful. He'd know more about Steven's role when the packet arrived.

"I can stay a few more days and talk to anyone you think might have information. I want to help find Abbie's uncle," Caitlyn said with determination, not noticing Ethan's lack of enthusiasm.

He took a few minutes to think things through, and then said, "Let's be clear. Steven Sullivan hasn't officially disappeared. If you want to talk to a couple of his colleagues, okay, but that's all. Understand?"

Caitlyn nodded, a look of winning the battle spread across her face.

"I'll alert Tom and Maddie that you're helping out, but let me remind you, their workload is stretched to the limit. Tom has been tasked with digitizing cold case files on top of his regular duties. He is working ten to twelve hours a day in order to get the project finished."

"I didn't know. Thanks for telling me. I won't ask them to do anything unless it is absolutely necessary."

With that settled he still wondered why her attitude remained cool. Then he remembered. Carrie. To make up for his earlier treatment of the new medical examiner, he'd gone a bit overboard in his apology, implying an intimacy that wasn't there. Caitlyn must have misunderstood and assumed there was much more to their relationship. He needed to clear the air. He needed to explain his marital situation and the decision he'd made. But now was not the time. Knowing what was on his plate, would there be a time?

"When I arrived you seemed upset. Does it have anything to do with Carrie? Because if it does, you need to know there's nothing between us. In fact, I just met her and made an absolute fool of myself by my rudeness."

Caitlyn turned and looked at Ethan. She was ashamed of her jealous feelings, imagining his relationship with the new medical examiner as anything more than professional. She seemed adept at ruining her own personal relationships.

"Sorry I was so irritable, and yes, irrational. I'm just tired after the drive up following several weeks of intense jobs I had to get done in a short period of time. It will do me good to be away for a few more days."

Ethan breathed a sigh of relief. Relief that he was going to keep her out of harm's way with the investigation, and relief that maybe their relationship had a chance. That thought was overcome by a wave of sadness as reality hit him.

He was still married to Jennie, the woman who walked out of his life years ago, and a woman who wanted him back, but on her terms. Their marriage was in limbo. No one in Riverview knew about his failed marriage, and that his wife lived in Wisconsin.

Ethan decided it was time to end his marriage. He'd have to take that step if he wanted a relationship with Caitlyn, or anyone else. It was time he moved on with his life. He'd consult with an attorney next week. With that decision made, a weight was lifted. His professional life might be in chaos, but he was determined his personal life was going to improve.

~

Caitlyn watched Ethan's police car exit the winery's driveway and onto the main road below. She continued to sit on the bench and think about what had just transpired. Did she push him to investigate a possible missing person? What was she thinking?

She'd talked herself into helping learn the whereabouts of Abbie's uncle and she would see it through. She, too, hoped he was on a research trip. Abbie described Steven as elusive and not one to stay in touch, so what harm could come from talking to a few professors?

With a deep sigh, she packed up her camera and headed to the car. It looked like she'd be in Riverview a few more days than originally planned. That might work to her advantage, as she would have that many more days in which to take photos for the winery's brochure.

And visit with Aunt Myra.

~ TWENTY-SEVEN ~

Ethan raced up the steps leading to the sheriff's office, and then stopped at the top to catch his breath. He didn't want to raise suspicions with his office staff. When his heart rate returned to normal he entered.

The overnight package had arrived. He casually took it from Maddie and exchanged pleasantries with her and Tom as he headed to his office.

Once seated at his desk, he resisted the temptation to tear it open. Instead, he paused to look it over. There were no descriptive markings on the slim envelope showing from where it came from. He used caution when cutting the seal so as to not destroy whatever was inside. He slid out a piece of paper and read the instructions.

~

Caitlyn arrived at the sheriff's office a few minutes before eleven. Maddie was at the switchboard. Tom was at his computer surrounded by manila folders.

When Maddie finished her conversation, she turned to Caitlyn.

"You just missed the sheriff. He's headed into Renwick for a task force meeting."

"Did he mention that he asked me to help locate Steven Sullivan?"

Tom and Maddie nodded with hesitation as Caitlyn continued.

"I'm concerned because he is the uncle of my friend, Abbie Hetherington. Ethan explained that until a missing person's report is filed, nothing official can be done. With a little arm-twisting, he said I could ask around. He mentioned you might be willing to help?"

Maddie and Tom looked at each other, wondering how to respond. They were being put on the spot. They knew that Caitlyn had been invaluable in solving her cousin's murder last April, but they could get into big trouble—maybe lose their jobs if they were caught providing her with information. They also didn't have the time to go on a wild goose chase.

Caitlyn sensed their hesitation. She was asking them to go against department regulations. But there was more to this case than Ethan had shared, and she wanted to get to the bottom of it. She looked at Tom and hoped he'd get on board.

"Tom, I know you're working on the cold case files and you're facing a state-imposed deadline. And Maddie, I understand your workload as well."

Caitlyn paused to gauge their reaction with the hope she'd win them over. She looked from one to the other.

Breaking the silence, Tom sighed, "So what do you need?" Caitlyn wasn't going to give up, so they might as well give her a hand. He figured it wouldn't hurt to do a little preliminary checking.

Caitlyn looked at Maddie. "I'm not pressuring you to help. You have enough to do."

Maddie sighed. "Of course I want to help. It's just that I'm weighing the consequences. I can't afford to lose my job."

"I understand, and I promise you that this will be a short-lived assignment. Ethan thinks Steven Sullivan is doing research and will show up at some point, but I feel something isn't right. Abbie's worried, and I'm afraid the stress will reactivate her cancer cells. So, anything you can do would be helpful. I'll keep my requests to a minimum."

The arrangement was sealed with a nod.

"Ethan and I talked with two of Steven's officemates yesterday. I'd like to go back and talk with others in the department to see if they can tell me anything about Steven's comings and goings. Tom, can you get me any background information on the others in Steven's department? If he has in fact disappeared, maybe there's a connection. A long shot, I know, but better to cover the bases."

"Sure," Tom replied.

"I'll do some Internet searching as well. Maddie, do you have colleagues in the Boston area who would have information on Steven's life before Riverview? I believe he worked for the Boston PD, and was a forensic psychologist there. I'm curious to learn if there's another reason why he came to Riverview."

"Sure. I'll give a former colleague a call, but I think it's simply that the guy wants to retire, and this is his way of slowing down, changing lifestyles. After all, his niece lives in the area. Maybe he wanted to settle near family, and he's checking out the area, and just forgot what day it was," Maddie added.

"Good thought, Maddie, but Abbie mentioned her uncle wasn't close to the family. She gets a holiday card occasionally, but according to Abbie, he doesn't attend any of the family gatherings. Didn't you say you saw him in the neighborhood? What can you tell me about him?"

Maddie thought a minute and then responded, "He's a handsome guy, full head of brown hair with dreamy deep blue eyes."

Caitlyn could see Maddie was melting just at the thought of this guy.

"He's well built, not stocky, but solid, about six foot. I only met him once, but he's one of those people who, when you're talking with him, makes you feel like you're the only person in the world. I was glad that Tracy allowed him to rent from her. She has a small house off Elm Street, on a cul-de-sac called Greenway Drive, just down the street from me. Not too long after he moved in, I was out for a walk and they were out front discussing landscaping. I said, 'hi,' and then we were talking like old friends."

"Wait a minute," Tom said as he rushed over to his desk. He pawed through a box containing folders until he found the one he was searching for.

"Sorry to change the subject, but I came across this cold case the other day. It didn't mean anything at the time. You know, data entry, sometimes you're just inputting data and not thinking about it. But when we were called to the crime scene, something bothered me. That road name was familiar, but when I drove to it I was sure I'd never been on it. It's taken a while, but as we were talking, I remembered. I put that road into the database. The case file is in one of these boxes. A suspicious death . . ."

Tom was interrupted by a call through the switchboard. Maddie was in her chair with headphones on before the second ring.

"She's amazing," Caitlyn whispered to Tom.

"I agree. She seems to have a sixth sense about when the calls are coming in."

Caitlyn and Tom listened as Maddie calmly issued instructions to the caller while simultaneously letting the paramedics know the location of the emergency.

"What was that all about?" Caitlyn asked.

Tom hesitated before answering. "Drug use here is escalating. I don't know how much Ethan has told you about it . . ."

"Not much," Caitlyn responded.

"It's why the captain ordered Ethan to concentrate on the task force. It's because of his prior experience in the city."

"I guess I shouldn't be surprised," Caitlyn responded. "Drug use, especially heroin, has become a national epidemic from what I read."

"That's correct. And what we're learning is this area is a hub for the drug traffic flowing through the state," Tom explained. "You can image how unhappy that makes the town fathers. We have colleges here and a big tourism industry. The last thing we need is to be coined the 'drug hub.'"

"Oh, that's awful. I never want to connect this beautiful area with the drug trade. But if you consider the geographic location, it makes sense to go through here to get from one side of the state to the other," Caitlyn said.

"We're starting to see a fair amount of petty crime, and the new college campus doesn't help. Supposedly the task force is to figure out how to address the situation," Tom explained. "Now, you'd better get going if you want to catch the professors on campus."

"You're right," Caitlyn said as she glanced at the clock.

When she got to her car, she realized Tom never finished explaining the suspicious death in the cold case file and why it was relevant to their conversation.

~ TWENTY-EIGHT ~

Verna glanced at her watch. One o'clock. Where had the day gone? She blamed her belated schedule on the new route they'd taken for their morning walk. She couldn't bring herself to be on Old Mill Road again. Because of the unfamiliar terrain, Oliver stopped multiple times to research the new smells, which meant their walk took twice as long.

Due to a succession of nightmares she hadn't slept well. Each time she woke with a start just as a dead man's face appeared. Sometimes it was the man she came upon yesterday; other times it was Palle's face that appeared before her.

Were the nightmares the result of the shock of finding a dead man, or her obsession with Palle? Regardless, she was determined to solve the mystery of his whereabouts.

Her brother's marriage to Edda was in the fall of 1967. She remembered that much, because that was when she left the area. She'd heard a daughter had been born. Or was it a son?

Darn! My memory isn't like it used to be. Didn't they say when your memory starts to go you tend to remember what happened years ago, but don't remember what you ate for breakfast?

There were times when Verna couldn't remember either.

She thought about her family and decided it made sense to start with the house. That's where Palle was last. She'd look at land records, and those would be found at the town hall. Now what was the clerk's name? Penny something.

If she was going to get to the town hall before it closed, she needed to get a move on. She cleaned up her lunch dishes, put fresh water down for Oliver, grabbed her car keys and headed out the door.

130

~

The Riverview town clerk's office was located in one of the old Victorian homes that lined Main Street. Thankfully, the town fathers had the foresight to save these beautiful properties and utilize them for town offices. In Verna's opinion it was one of the things that made Riverview special, although she'd heard reports about the nasty town meetings when developers proposed tearing down the beautiful homes to build . . . who knows what. She was thankful the town board had won that battle.

Verna found a convenient place to park and walked the few steps to the clerk's office. Standing at the counter, she was overcome with feelings of inadequacy. She had no idea how to search property records, and if truth be told, she didn't even have a clue as to what questions to ask. The clerk was going to think she was a real dodo.

"Hello, can I help you?" came a voice from the back corner of the room.

Before Verna could cut and run a woman approached.

"I wonder if I could look at property records," Verna said, her tone uncertain. She looked at the nameplate on the counter. It read, "Penelope Mitchell," Town Clerk.

"Are you Penelope Mitchell?" Verna asked.

"Yes, I am. Everyone calls me Penny. And you are . . .?"

"Verna. Verna Adams. I'm related to Palle van der Molen. He might have died in the late 60s or early 70s. Actually, he disappeared. I'm not sure if he died or not. I might need your help. I've, well, I've never done property search before," she stammered.

Penny waited for Verna to share more information, but instead noticed the woman was confused and would need assistance. It was fortunate the clerk's office wasn't too busy at the moment.

"Not a problem. Come on back and I'll show you the ropes. By the time you leave, you'll be an expert."

Penny opened the gate to the back room that housed the town records, and led Verna over to a shelving unit that held oversized ledger books. With her finger touching the spines Penny finally stopped at the correct volume.

She slid the volume from the shelf and placed it on top of a slanted top cabinet. A narrow piece of wood nailed to the bottom edge kept the ledger from sliding off and provided a comfortable position for viewing. Penny slowly flipped through the pages, explaining the process at every step. When she got to van der Molen, she stopped and showed Verna what she found.

"This ledger is just an index of names. These numbers next to the name tell you in which volume and page the land record appears," Penny explained.

After jotting down the citations, Penny put the index volume back and proceeded to a set of rolling files. Again, she went down the aisle until she found the correct volume number. She lifted that oversized book onto the cabinet, and found the appropriate page.

"Don't be shy about asking for help. These volumes are heavy. I don't want you to hurt yourself," she said with a smile. "I'll leave you to look at the book. If you need more information, let me know."

Verna thanked her, pulled out her pad and pencil and immediately delved into the property description.

~

"How're you coming with your research?"

Verna jumped at the sound. She was so engrossed in the information she was reading she completely forgot where she was and even why she was there.

"Oh, fine, thanks," she replied. "There's lots of good stuff here. I had no idea. I'm afraid I got off subject and started reading about other properties."

"That's easy to do. I'm about to close for the day. Can you come back again?"

"I guess, but I'm not sure the answer to my question is here. I'm trying to figure out what happened to my brother. And this information is confusing," Verna said.

"I agree. Until you get used to the way the properties are listed and the jargon, it can be difficult. Why don't you have a talk with my husband? He's just retired and has taken over as town historian. He hasn't had time to go through all the boxes yet, but you can fill him in on what you are looking for, and if he comes across anything he can get in touch."

"That's a wonderful idea. Thank you," replied Verna, relieved to be able to hand off the research to someone more qualified.

Penny walked back to her desk and returned with a business card in hand.

"Here's his card. Give him a call and set up an appointment. You will be his first research project, and I know he'll be thrilled to help."

Verna took the card and nodded her thanks.

"I'll be going. Don't want to hold you up any longer."

"It was nice to meet you, Verna, and good luck."

Verna nodded again, and with conflicted feelings, she left the clerk's office.

~ TWENTY-NINE ~

Silence.

When Tracy moved back to Riverview, she had looked for a house that would provide her the privacy she craved. After weeks of looking she'd found one at the end of a cul-de-sac. And now, with Steven's arrival in her life, how quickly she'd adapted to the sounds of his presence.

Steven's unexpected arrival had altered her routines, and at first she regretted her decision to share the house with him. Although he was in the house, she remained determined his world would not intrude into hers. She'd worked hard to rid herself of the memories of their work together as well as of their relationship years ago.

She paced around the house as a million thoughts swirled through her head.

Where was he? Why didn't he come home last night? Was he dead or alive, and if alive, was he hurt? She shook off these thoughts. They were what she'd fought so long to dispel.

He'd left a number for her to call should something happen, but he'd also warned her not to call unless she was absolutely sure. If she acted too soon, it could ruin everything. Bottom line—she didn't know what to do. He could be working the case, which meant she had to continue the waiting game.

She forced herself to concentrate on her life. She was a professional businesswoman with a busy office to manage. She should get back to work. She couldn't camp out here waiting, but she also couldn't stop thoughts about what she'd do if he didn't come back.

~

She remembered well the day the elderly couple approached her to list their home on Greenway Drive. The couple wanted to move south, and leave snow shovels, and high heating bills behind. Tracy could tell they feared someone would buy their home, tear it down, and build a McMansion. When Tracy did a walk-through with them she realized the Cape's potential. She decided on the spot there wasn't anyone better suited to care for the home. She offered a fair asking price on the spot and saw relief wash over them. It was a good deal for both parties.

~

The sheriff had been at the house earlier and had given Steven's office a cursory search. But it was up to Tracy to scour the office, look at every piece of paper in every file. She'd go through Steven's nightstand, his closet, look in every pocket. She'd tear the outdoor shed apart to look for anything he might have put there, any clue as to his whereabouts. If he didn't reappear in a couple more days, she'd have to call it in. His boss would need every piece of information she could provide.

She had to find the answer, but frantic searching wouldn't help; she had to be methodical. And with that she took a deep breath and sorted through the papers on his desk.

Until her phone rang.

~ THIRTY ~

Tom was right. There was work to do. Caitlyn had to return to campus while the professors were still in their offices. And then she'd go back to the house to do some Internet research. There were too many pieces to this puzzle that just didn't add up.

The town appeared peaceful as she drove through. One would never suspect there was a dark undercurrent of illegal activity slowly creeping into this beautiful landscape. She hoped the task force could come up with a way to stop the criminals from further infiltrating Riverview and the surrounding towns.

Caitlyn drove around the campus looking for a convenient place to park. The second time around, she noticed a car backing out and she raced to claim the spot.

She grabbed her bag and made sure the steno pad and pen were tucked inside. She hurried into the building and tried to acclimate herself to where she and Ethan had entered. In her rush she'd passed the sign indicating down which hallway the science department was located. She'd also arrived at the exact time classes were letting out, so she had to fend off being jostled by the students as they left the building.

She backtracked and found an arrow pointing in the direction of the science wing. She hastened her step until she reached the office of the department secretary.

"Janie?" Caitlyn asked quietly so she wouldn't startle the woman.

Janie looked up from her computer and said, "Just a minute. Have to finish this email."

While Caitlyn waited she looked around the small office. She wondered if the room was its original size, or was it reconfigured during the building's renovation? She liked the way the interior brick walls added to the ambiance of the office space.

"How can I help you?" Janie asked.

"I was here yesterday with Sheriff Ewing," Caitlyn began.

"Yes, I remember. What can I help you with today?" Janie asked as she glanced back at her computer.

Caitlyn wondered if it was a work-related email that was so important or if Janie was in the middle of a computer game.

Stay calm and be polite.

Caitlyn took a breath and smiled.

"The sheriff asked me to talk to a few more professors about Dr. Steven Sullivan." She remembered to use the formal title. She was in an academic institution where there was sensitivity to titles.

"Oh, sure. Just walk down the hall," Janie said as she waved her hand to the hallway beyond, and doing her best to hide her annoyance at being interrupted. "Talk to anyone who's still here."

"Thanks. I will. Have a nice rest of your day."

~

Janie's instructions were easier said than done. Caitlyn was halfway down the hall before she realized she should have been more direct and asked if Janie knew who was still in their office. Most of the doors were closed. She knocked on each, waited to see if anyone responded before going to the next. She tried five doors before she found one that was open. A middle-aged woman sat at a desk that faced the window. Caitlyn noticed the woman's stylish haircut that appeared easy to manage, but yet was very striking.

Caitlyn knocked on the doorframe so she wouldn't startle the woman who appeared intent on her work.

"Come in," was the curt response. The woman didn't turn around. Her attention was focused on the computer screen.

"Excuse me, ma'am. I'm Caitlyn Jamison and I wonder if you could answer some questions about one of your colleagues, Dr. Steven Sullivan?"

The woman stopped typing and slowly turned around, giving Caitlyn the once over.

"Who?"

"Dr. Steven Sullivan, one of your colleagues in the science department," Caitlyn responded. Panic crept in. Did she wander into the wrong department? How embarrassing. She'd continue on as if she knew what she was doing.

"I'm working with the sheriff's office to gather information on Dr. Sullivan. He hasn't shown up for his classes, and we are making some initial inquires. The sheriff is unfortunately detained today, so he asked me to talk with Dr. Sullivan's colleagues. This is the science department, right?"

"Yes, but I don't know this Dr. Sullivan. If he's one of the new faculty," the woman replied as she turned back to her computer, "I haven't made his acquaintance."

Caitlyn pushed on, trying another tactic.

"Maybe you've heard about something he was working on, research that could have taken him away unexpectedly?"

The woman swiveled her chair back around to face Caitlyn.

"Did you say this person is missing?"

"Not officially," Caitlyn clarified, wondering what story she could come up with that would get this lady to talk. "He isn't at home and hasn't shown up on campus. His family is worried about him."

"Like I said, I don't socialize with the lecturers, even if they have doctorates," the woman replied in a haughty and dismissive tone. "And certainly not anyone working on pseudo-science research."

The woman paused, "But now that you mention him, I heard someone say one of our new hires was running in and out when they should have been spending time preparing for class. I really don't care. Now, if you don't mind, I have work to do."

Caitlyn was not going to be put off by this woman's holier-than-thou attitude. Before the woman could turn back to her computer, Caitlyn continued, "So you didn't know him or know anything he was working on? I know everyone is new to this campus. Oh, by the way, I'm Caitlyn Jamison, and you are?"

With a deep sigh signifying Caitlyn had overstayed her welcome, the woman replied, "I'm Dr. Deborah Kent."

"Oh, my, are you any relation to . . ." Caitlyn blurted out.

"If you are asking if I'm related to Richard, the answer is yes. Is that why you're here? Are you with the sheriff's department or with the press?" Dr. Kent replied angrily.

"No, I'm not. I mean I *am* with the sheriff's office," Caitlyn stammered.

"Richard's my nephew. My brother and sister-in-law are divorced. She works for the university in the English department. We aren't close, but she called to tell me about Richard. A real shame. Now if that's all," Dr. Kent said as she turned back to her computer.

"I had no idea. I'm so sorry for your loss," Caitlyn responded, not knowing how to save this awkward situation. She also wondered how this woman could be so cold and uncaring about the death of her nephew, but people grieve in different ways.

This place gets stranger by the minute.

"Let me try again. It's nice to meet you, Dr. Kent. I'm sorry to bother you, especially now since I know you're Richard's aunt. The sheriff is also trying to learn what Dr. Sullivan was working on that might have taken him away from Riverview and his responsibilities." She didn't want to mention that Ethan suspected a connection between Steven Sullivan and Richard Kent.

Deborah Kent paused before responding. "Our family is under a lot of stress right now, and the way I deal with that is to work. Let me be clear that the fact this Dr. Sullivan may be missing is not something I care anything about. You're correct that we're all new on this campus. Most of us have been with the university for years. With some of our courses located at this rural campus, our routines have been seriously disrupted. I'll leave it at that."

Caitlyn thought she understood what was bothering this woman. It was an insult to be assigned to a rural satellite campus.

What administrator had she crossed to be assigned to this outpost?

139

"Maybe some of my colleagues went out of their way to make this new person feel welcome. That's not the case with me. I'm a loner. I come in, do my job, and leave. I don't socialize."

"Did any of your colleagues mention what Dr. Sullivan might have been working on, regarding articles, or working with anyone outside the classroom?"

Dr. Kent hesitated before responding.

"There are always rumors on a campus. I don't know or care what my colleagues are working on. Besides, this GMO mumbo gumbo is just that. Check with Dr. Jordan. He might be able to give you more information."

"The sheriff talked with Dr. Jordan yesterday."

"Then I guess I can't give you any more information," Deborah said, her tone ending the conversation. "If you don't mind, I have a syllabus to finish by this afternoon."

"Sure, and thanks for talking with me. If you think of anything else, please call the sheriff's office and leave a message with the dispatcher. Again, please accept my condolences."

When Caitlyn reached the doorway, she hesitated.

"One more thing, Professor Kent. Do you know what your nephew might have been into?"

Not looking up from her laptop, Dr. Kent replied, "Have you considered the dark web?"

Shivers worked their way down Caitlyn's spine. She'd heard of the dark web and wanted nothing to do with it.

What have I gotten myself into?

~ THIRTY-ONE ~

Penny Mitchell put the last of the chopped fruit and vegetables into the green salad she was making for their dinner. Before she left for work that morning she'd taken out a pan of lasagna she'd prepared on the weekend. She liked to cook ahead so that her work nights weren't taken up with meal preparation. She didn't want to think about dinner at seven thirty in the morning. Doug was starting to watch his weight, so she wouldn't offer garlic bread. The store-bought salad dressing selection in her refrigerator would remain there as she whipped up a simple olive oil and raspberry vinegar dressing. She wanted to help Doug with his weight loss program as much as she could, and looking down at herself, she, too, was experiencing the start of a wheat belly. It was going to take work to change their habits. The lasagna wasn't helping, but one step at a time. There was something to be said for convenience.

Doug finished setting the table. It was nice to have him home and willing to do chores around the house. She was also relieved he was getting right into his town historian role.

When they were seated and had taken their first forkful of lasagna, Penny asked, "Did you have a good day?"

"I did. I met with the president of the historical society and we figured out a way to work together. I didn't realize there were silos in this town regarding safeguarding its history. Everyone's protecting their turf and they don't share information or help one another. Ethel, the woman I met with today, was reluctant at first to meet with me. I had to sweet talk her," Doug replied.

Penny smiled at his choice of words. Her husband's smile could melt any heart.

"It sounds like your sweet talk and agreeable personality won the day with the locals."

"We'll see. The jury is still out on whether they'll be willing to work with me."

They sat and dug into the steaming hot lasagna.

"Ah, comfort food," Doug said between bites.

"Hold that thought. With your new diet, this type of dinner will become a distant memory."

Doug frowned and continued to enjoy his meal. "Why do I feel like this is the last supper?"

"Not to change the subject, but a woman come into the clerk's office this afternoon. Her name is Verna Adams. She was looking at a property on Old Mill Road, the van der Molen place. You know, that run down house."

Doug continued to enjoy his meal, nodding to acknowledge that he heard and she should continue.

"That's where they found the body this morning," Penny said.

"Right. There was a lot of talk at the historical society about that, but I was so focused on winning over my new best friend Ethel, I didn't pay much attention," Doug replied as he continued chewing.

"There's more to her inquiry than just searching the property record. She's trying to find out what happened to her brother. I guess he died or disappeared a number of years ago. Verna is determined to learn what happened. I don't know why she waited this long, but I guess that isn't any of my business. I suggested she contact you for help. You do have a way with the older women," Penny said with a grin.

Doug put his fork down, having done his best by the lasagna and salad. He looked longingly at the casserole dish, desperately wanting seconds, but he shouldn't, and besides, Penny wouldn't allow it. Wiping his mouth with the paper napkin, he could now join the conversation with more than just a nod.

"I'd love to meet Verna and help her in any way I can. I hope you told her the condition of the files, or the non-condition of them, papers stuffed into boxes. It's going to take me years to sort through all that material. That's why I went to the historical society today. I hoped to enlist a volunteer."

"And that didn't happen?"

"Not yet, but I'm not giving up. I'll talk with them again, but in the meantime, this new assignment will be the incentive to get busy on those boxes."

"And maybe keep you out of the refrigerator?" Penny added as she got up to clear the table.

~ THIRTY-TWO ~

Caitlyn concluded that Steven Sullivan's colleagues sensed there was more to him than being a part-time lecturer. They just didn't know what. To their credit they'd only been working together a few weeks, and they were still getting used to the new campus and a new student population. There was also the learning curve of the online courses.

Dr. Jordan mentioned Steven kept running out for "appointments." Why, and who was he meeting and where? It'd be helpful to search his home office and for that she'd need Ethan's help.

Right now she'd get back to the house and see if there were any emails from her clients. She couldn't get so caught up in this new mystery that her business suffered.

~

As soon as she walked in the front door, Summit was there to greet her with his usual happy dance, and then ran to get his favorite toy. As he circled around her, she tried to give him the attention he needed while she made progress into the kitchen from which mouth-watering smells emanated.

"Aunt Myra, I'm back," Caitlyn yelled, as if her aunt wouldn't know from the dog's loud welcome.

"In the kitchen," Myra shouted.

"Dinner smells delicious," Caitlyn said as she entered the room. Her aunt beamed at the compliment.

"I put a pork roast in the Crockpot this morning. What you smell is the meat slowly cooking in whole berry cranberry sauce topped with a scattering of herbs," Myra responded.

Caitlyn's phone vibrated against her hip. "Excuse me, Aunt Myra, I'd better take this call," she said as she left the kitchen.

To Caitlyn's retreating back, Myra yelled, "We're entertaining guests for dinner tomorrow evening. Make sure you're back here by five."

Caitlyn nodded to her aunt as she held the phone to her ear. She really didn't want to be included in her aunt and uncle's dinner parties. Spending the evening listening to her uncle pontificate about his Albany connections was more than she could handle right now. She had too much on her plate, like what happened to Steven Sullivan, and keeping up with her clients' needs. But as their houseguest, she'd do what was expected.

~

Summit followed Caitlyn up the stairs and into the guest room. She quietly closed the door and they both settled onto the bed, Summit for his nap, and Caitlyn with her laptop. The call was from a client, but was nothing urgent. Thankfully there were no other urgent messages, so she decided to learn more about Steven Sullivan and what he was really doing in Riverview. She didn't believe for a moment that he was out doing research. He seemed to have a varied career and it didn't add up. He was a trained forensic psychologist, and then took police training, and was now a college lecturer in Riverview. For her, these dots didn't connect. There had to be a key. If only she could find it.

She read over her interview notes, and brought to mind the exact words that were said, and *how* they were said. Tone of voice and body language tell a lot. If a voice starts to quaver, it means the person's stress level is rising, which means they may not be telling the truth, or they are hiding something. She was also good at reading faces and expressions. She closed her eyes and concentrated on what she had observed with each person they had interviewed. She made additional notes on each individual with the hope that something would pop out at her.

She brought up *Google*, her go-to search engine and tried a number of search terms in order to educate herself on every aspect she knew of Steven Sullivan's life.

"Ah ha!" She finally came upon something relevant. An older article in the *Boston Globe* explained how a special-forces unit was being trained. These men would be available to agencies for assignments in need of 'unique skills.'

I bet Steven was chosen for this special unit. But what is he doing in Riverview?

She made a list of criminal activities that would bring someone like him to the area.

"I have one more thing to check," Caitlyn said to the snoring dog. "The Dark Web."

Her hands wavered over the keyboard, uncertain as to whether she wanted to enter that space through the browser *Tor*. She knew her computer would be routed through several computers and layers of encryption. Should she take the chance? Just as her finger pointed to the T, her cell rang.

Saved by a client.

~

It wasn't a client calling; it was Ethan.

She took a deep breath, mentally changed gears, and shook off the feeling of what she was about to do.

"Hi. How was your day?" Caitlyn asked, hoping to sound normal.

"It was a day, and yours?"

Caitlyn paused, deciding how much she should tell him. Definitely *not* the fact she had almost entered the *Dark Web*. Instead she mentioned some of her clients' work, and that a couple of projects were due soon.

"I talked with Maddie and Tom. They're willing to help me gather information on Steven. I went to the campus and talked with Professor Deborah Kent. She says she doesn't know or care about Steven Sullivan, or anyone else for that matter. She's a recluse, and a definite snob. Apparently she comes to campus to teach her courses and do research. She isn't interested in getting to know her colleagues. She said she doesn't socialize with 'lecturers,' indicating they were of a lower class. What is it with academics?"

"I think you'll find that kind of attitude in almost any big business."

"I guess you're right," Caitlyn added, thinking back to her time working in the large ad agency in New York City. "Oh, and, guess what?"

Ethan had no patience for guessing games. Instead of responding he took a deep breath.

Caitlyn didn't catch on to his impatience, so she continued in a slower than normal tone.

"Deborah Kent just happens to be Richard Kent's aunt!"

Ethan's attitude changed. "Now that *is* interesting. I'll catch up with you later. Call coming in. Gotta go. Let's meet at seven tomorrow morning at the park, on the bench."

"Sure," Caitlyn responded.

Again she was left with an abrupt end to the conversation. *Story of my life.*

~ THIRTY-THREE ~

Caitlyn loved early mornings in the park where she could enjoy the sun's rays as they danced across the water. She shuffled her feet in the small stones while the mature willow tree to her back provided privacy. The draw of the lake remained in her psyche, and she wondered why she hadn't found a place like this in Virginia. Such spots existed; she just had to find them.

The morning's solitude would soon be broken when the morning dog walkers and joggers arrived. But for now, the entire property was hers with the only sound coming from the gentle lap of waves onto the shore.

~

She tensed. Someone was walking towards her. She'd always felt safe here, but times had changed. Our society had become more violent. Caitlyn sat still and rounded her shoulders into a defensive position. She took short shallow breaths, and hoped the person would walk on. The footsteps stopped behind her and Caitlyn's fight or flight instinct took hold.

"Mind if I join you?"

A long exhale. She recognized the voice with that Long Island twang, and immediately breathed a sigh of relief. It was Dr. Chad Owens, the marine biologist they'd met in Steven Sullivan's office. She turned to face him, and with relief in her voice, she said, "Sure."

Caitlyn motioned for him to join her on the bench, which he did, choosing the opposite end so as not to violate her space. He had noted her body language upon his approach.

"What brings you to the park this early in the morning? Work?" She asked.

"Yes. I'm down here at different times of day, taking samples. There's an algae bloom issue, and I'm also working on two other lakes in the area. Makes for long days. The sooner I can get the tests done, and things under control, the sooner I can get back to Long Island and to my family."

"Do you have children?" Although she had much on her mind, like the murder of Richard Kent and the disappearance of Steven Sullivan, Caitlyn wanted to get to know a little more about this man, as she was intrigued by his work.

"My wife and I have two teenage boys. They are in the local high school and one will graduate next year. We are looking forward to being empty nesters. Maybe travel. I'd love to bring her up here. It's a beautiful area."

"It is," Caitlyn replied as she looked at the colorful hills beyond.

"Have you located our missing office mate?"

"He hasn't returned that I know of," Caitlyn responded. An alarm went off in her head. It wasn't what he said, but how he said it. She had conflicted feelings about this man. She couldn't put her finger on it. A simple question, but . . . she saw him stand and peer down at her.

"Good-bye for now. I'm sure we will meet again," Chad said, as he turned and walked swiftly away.

~

Ethan arrived and plopped down next to her on the wooden park bench. "Love this view."

"I do, too. Very peaceful," she replied. "So, is this meeting social or business?"

"A little of both. I hoped to see you while you're in town, and not just to talk business, but since you brought it up . . ."

Caitlyn laughed. Not much had changed in their relationship. They were foremost about the business at hand.

"Who was that you were talking to? I only saw him as he quickly escaped."

"That was Dr. Chad Owens, the guy sharing the office with Steven Sullivan and Brant Jordan."

"Ah, I thought there was something familiar about him, but couldn't place it. I should have recognized the stocky build and his signature brush cut. What did he want?"

"Not sure. At first it was just small talk, you know, pretty area, stuff like that. Then he started to question me about whether or not we found Steven. It wasn't so much his words, but how he said them. Maybe I'm just being too sensitive, because other than that little oddity, he's a likable guy. He said he is working on several of the lakes around here."

"I'll have Tom check him out, just in case. In the meantime, I have a task force meeting this afternoon."

"I thought you went to a meeting the other day," Caitlyn replied.

"I did," Ethan explained. "The captain gathered a few of us to brainstorm what the meetings should cover before the entire group gets together. I'm not sure we accomplished much, but maybe the discussion will get him headed in the right direction. The mayor is pushing his agenda hard, and the captain is likely to cave in just to keep political peace. The captain also has a tendency to gather people and then do what he wants anyway."

Caitlyn nodded in acknowledgment. She'd been in similar situations. Too often meetings were frustrating and a complete waste of time; another reason she left the New York City ad agency.

"I'll meet the team and assess how well everyone will work together. I don't know the city police officers assigned, or the businessmen, so I asked Tom to gather information. One businessman is a pharmacist, the other runs a big distribution center to the south of Renwick."

"Sounds like an interesting mix, and it makes sense to have people from the community involved. It shows the group is serious about getting results. It's good there's a pharmacist, because maybe he can provide information on the root cause," Caitlyn said. "This supply and demand thing is bothering me."

"Identifying the root causes would be nice, but so far the discussion centers around how to deal with the result of overdoses rather than how to halt drug use before it begins and gets out of control. I'll let you know after this afternoon's meeting how they plan to proceed. In the meantime, any info on Steven Sullivan?"

"Not much more than what I told you yesterday."

"Other than the fact the victim's mother works at the university, and the father is a legislator, I don't know much about the rest of the family, but I appreciate the information about the aunt," Ethan replied. "I'll ask Tom to do a little more research. Maybe it'll shed light on why this young man was into drugs, which could lead us to his supplier."

"So the aunt, Professor Deborah Kent, didn't know anything about Steven. Just rumors, and even at that, I'm not sure how much attention she gave them," Caitlyn added.

Ethan could tell Caitlyn was getting right into this investigation. He had to pull her back.

"Don't put too much more time into it. I'm sure he'll show up, and I know you have your clients and the winery's brochure to work on."

She ignored his comment and said, "I think we should talk with Tracy Connor. Maybe she'd let me go through his files," Caitlyn replied, her creative juices flowing.

"That'll be tricky. I'd be going against the captain's directive."

Ethan could see that Caitlyn wasn't going to let go, and if he couldn't dissuade her, he'd have to go with her. Sensing she was zeroing in on this request, he sighed, "Maybe we can fashion it as a social visit. I'll give her a call and see if we can stop by."

"Okay, I'll wait for your text to see if we're on," Caitlyn responded.

Ethan thought he could tell her that Tracy declined a visit, but the lies were piling up. He'd be trapped in them at some point and then all trust would be lost. He couldn't afford that. His phone buzzed and he pulled it from the holder. He scowled.

"Disturbance on campus. The state police are supposed to help cover the new campus, but so far that ain't working out so well. I'm going to call the state budget office myself to see what's holding up the request for more staffing. I'm tired of the run-around I'm getting from the Renwick precinct."

Ethan got up to go, took a last look at the calm lake, sighed, and turned to face Caitlyn.

"We need to take time for ourselves while you're here. We need to talk. I have something I want to . . ."

He hesitated, not knowing how to phrase what he needed to tell her.

"Yes?" Caitlyn asked, wondering what was troubling him.

His phone buzzed again and he checked the display.

"Another time. I've got to go," Ethan sighed, turned and raced to his car.

Caitlyn watched him drive away. Their conversation was so abrupt she didn't have time to ask him about his investigation into Richard Kent's murder.

~ THIRTY-FOUR ~

Verna believed there was no time like the present. She never considered that she might not be welcome at Doug Mitchell's home office at any time of day.

She checked her watch. Ten o'clock. He should be up by now. Time was of the essence. She walked around to the side of the house until she came to the door that indicated it was the office of the town historian.

She knocked and waited.

When the door opened, she introduced herself and blurted out the reason she was there.

"I'm Verna Adams. I met your wife yesterday and she suggested I talk to you about my family."

Doug was glad Penny filled him in on Mrs. Adams, so he wasn't caught completely off guard by her unannounced presence. He was also glad he had already showered and shaved this morning.

He could tell the woman was nervous, so he'd do his best to make her visit as comfortable as possible.

"Come in Mrs. Adams. I'm pleased to meet you. Penny mentioned you were in the clerk's office yesterday and looking at land records. Am I correct?"

"Yes, that's right, but I didn't find anything to answer my questions," Verna replied. "It was all very confusing."

"I hope I can help you sort that out, and in the meantime, please excuse the mess. I'm just getting organized, and as you can see, there are many boxes yet to unpack."

Verna surveyed the room with disgust. She didn't realize there would be so many dusty boxes. She hoped her allergies weren't going to act up.

"No problem," she replied, not meaning it, and looking around for an empty chair.

Doug scurried to clear two chairs so they could sit and talk.

"Penny said you were interested in learning about your family."

"My brother, Palle, to be exact," Verna replied.

"Tell me about him," Doug said, sitting back in his chair. He grabbed a pad and pen for note taking.

Now that she was here, Verna wasn't sure where to begin.

"Growing up, Palle and I were close. In fact I raised him. When he was eighteen, he met Edda Villetta. They fell in love, but the family didn't approve."

"Why not?" Doug asked.

Verna hesitated. "There was a story passed down through the generations that her ancestors poisoned people." Verna noticed Doug's eyebrow rise a bit. To answer his disbelief, she continued, "I've looked it up. If grain, like wheat and rye is not dried properly, it grows a mold toxin called fusarium that makes it poisonous. And that was what was handed down about the Villettas."

"Why didn't more people succumb to this kind of death so we may have learned about it?" Doug asked.

"The wealthy people avoided rye, so they remained healthy. It was the poor who could only afford this grain, and of course it was most prominent during times when conditions were wet," Verna explained.

"And so what makes you think your sister-in-law would harm your brother? I don't see the connection," Doug said softly. He was getting confused. Her story didn't make any sense. Was his first research assignment going to be nothing but a wild goose chase? Was he destined to work with people this confused about their past?

"It's just that the rumor followed the family down through the years and we were afraid that she might do something to Palle," Verna explained. "Like history might repeat itself and that the behavior was inbred into that family. Palle worked in the mill, and the family knew, though no one said anything, that he was stealing small amounts of grain." Verna was flustered as she realized how ridiculous her explanations sounded. And she never should have told Palle's secret.

"Tell me what else you know," Doug said, deciding to veer away from the topic of what he thought was close to an accusation of witchcraft.

"I believe there's a child, a daughter, I think. I'd like to find her," Verna explained. "I think Palle might have died, sometime about 1970, but I'm not sure. I've not been able to track Edda, the child, or if and where Palle might be buried. I wasted many years being upset with him, busy with my own life. For that I will never forgive myself."

Verna wiped a tear from her eye. She took a breath, composing herself.

Doug made careful notes as Verna talked. He captured names, relationships, possible dates, and locations as Verna haphazardly wove her way through her family history. His adrenalin raced as he started to place each piece of her family puzzle in his mind. This was the kind of work he longed to do. He couldn't wait for the Boston University course materials to arrive so he could get started on his professional genealogist certification.

". . . and that's about all I can tell you at the moment," Verna said, grabbing her purse in preparation for leaving.

Doug was embarrassed. He'd been so preoccupied with his future plans that he missed the last few sentences.

"That's great, Mrs. Adams," Doug replied, noting her readiness to leave. "You've given me a lot of information with which to get started. I'll work on this, and if you give me your phone number, I'll call when I have some answers."

As anxious as she was to meet with Doug Mitchell, Verna was now anxious to leave. Sharing her family's history for the first time with a stranger was more upsetting than she realized. She was emotionally drained.

"I look forward to hearing from you," was all Verna could utter as she headed for the door.

~ THIRTY-FIVE ~

The campus police had the situation under control by the time Ethan arrived.

"What happened? Why was I called?" Ethan asked, annoyed at the waste of his time.

The campus security officer in charge answered, "Another break-in. There's been several over the last couple of weeks. Kids think there's money in the faculty offices. When they can't find cash, they take small electronics, anything that can easily be hocked. We thought they might still be in the building and we feared weapons might be involved. We thought we had better have backup."

Ethan calmed down once the rationale was explained. He believed in the adage better to be safe than sorry.

"What's behind this sudden rash of burglaries, and why do you think it's kids?" He needed to know if something other than drug abuse was going on in the academic world.

"It's the rise in drug use. We don't use the word 'epidemic,' since it isn't good for the university's image, student recruitment efforts, or fundraising. But that's what we're seeing. Lots of middle of the night calls for overdose cases and many trips to the campus health center. We're thinking maybe it wasn't such a good idea to put student housing at this location. But then who would have guessed this would become such an issue?"

Ethan thanked the officer and said, "I've been assigned to the new task force in Renwick. We meet this afternoon." He checked his watch. "Better get going. Is one of the campus officers included in that group?"

"Yes, Officer West has been assigned."

156

"Great. I look forward to meeting him."

"Actually, Pamela West is very much a female," the officer stated with a laugh.

~

The campus situation was under control, so Ethan headed to his car and planned his next step in the Richard Kent murder investigation. His phone buzzed and he was surprised at the caller ID.

"Sheriff?" A female voice asked.

"This is Deborah Kent, a professor at the college. Your colleague of sorts, Caitlyn Jamison, came by yesterday asking questions about one of the faculty."

"Yes. I hope you didn't mind. Caitlyn is capable and has been a great help in the past." God, he hoped this woman wasn't going to file a compliant. From what Caitlyn told him about their conversation, this woman was obnoxious.

"So, Professor Kent, what can I do for you?"

"It's what I can do for you, actually," she replied. "I'm in my office with Richard's mother, Veronica. She would like to talk with you about Richard."

Ethan glanced at his watch. It was only a short time before the task force meeting in Renwick, but talking to the victim's mother was more important.

"Actually, Professor Kent, I'm just outside your building now. If you don't mind, I'll be right up."

~

Ethan approached Deborah Kent's office door and wished Caitlyn were with him. She was good at noting body language and reading between the lines. He valued her insights after interviewing subjects, but he wouldn't have that luxury today.

He knocked lightly, and hearing an affirmative murmur from inside, he let himself in. The women sat apart, their relationship status obvious. Caitlyn had told him the aunt and sister-in-law weren't close, so this situation must be especially awkward.

157

The woman who had been seated at the desk rose, but did not come forward, nor did she offer her hand.

"I'm Dr. Deborah Kent." She turned and nodded to the woman who remained seated. "This is Richard's mother, Veronica."

The woman Deborah pointed out looked too young to be the mother of a college student, except for the graying hair she had pulled back into a bun. Her vivid blue eyes were awash with tears. Ethan's heart broke, understanding the loss she now suffered. He nodded to each woman, and then walked over to Richard's mother, took her hand, and gave her his condolences.

"Please, be seated, sheriff," Deborah stated firmly, as she reclaimed her desk chair, establishing the power base in the room.

Ethan suspected that Deborah Kent was not comfortable with his attention to her sister-in-law. Caitlyn was correct about this woman. Deborah Kent was cold and controlling.

"Mrs. Kent . . ." Ethan started, turning to address Richard's mother.

"Please call me Ronnie. Although my name is Veronica, my friends call me Ronnie." Ethan noticed she glanced at her sister-in-law who had just used the more formal name during the introduction.

"Okay, 'Ronnie.' Again, I am very sorry for your loss."

"Thank you," Ronnie responded, wiping a tear.

"I also want you to know that since the medical examiner's preliminary examination ruled his death a drug overdose, I've declared your son's death a homicide. I believe it's time we take a firm stance on the drug trade and label these dealers for what they are—murderers."

Deborah's head jerked up. She started to comment, then thought better of it.

Ethan noted her reaction, paused to let her comment, but when she didn't, he continued, "That means I need to know everything about your son, who he was as a person, who he hung around with, anything you can tell me that will help us figure out why he was killed. You may be forced to share things that are very personal."

Veronica wiped her eyes, her hands wringing a handkerchief into wads. She took a deep breath and cleared her throat. The woman's suffering was obvious.

"I believe his drug problem began two years ago. He was skiing in the Adirondacks with friends. Richard fell and broke his leg. It was a bad break. His friends tried to help him off the mountain, but in doing that they exacerbated the injury. The doctor at the small hospital there didn't set the leg correctly, and by the time Richard got home, his pain was unbearable. The doctors put him on strong pain medication. I'm not sure what it was, but I'm sure it was an opioid."

Ethan nodded.

Same old story.

"Are you sure he wasn't into drugs before that?" Deborah interrupted.

Veronica glared at her ex-sister-in-law.

If looks could kill, Ethan thought.

"Richard recovered at home, went to his PT, and continued his coursework. We were both so busy," Veronica's voice trailed off. Taking another deep breath, she stated, "I should have been more aware of what was going on with him. I never thought he would continue to take the painkillers. How would he have gotten them? He was such a good boy." She turned to Ethan, "You must think I'm bad mother."

"I don't think that. Richard was a grown man. He was responsible for weaning himself off the medication, and if he couldn't he needed to get help. As for how he got the drugs, there are a number of ways."

Ethan noted Deborah didn't add anything more to the conversation, but she wore a smug expression that he so wanted to wipe off her face. She seemed to take pleasure in seeing her ex-sister-in-law suffer.

Veronica further explained, "Even though Richard was attending the same university in which I was teaching, we didn't see each other that often. He had his own apartment in town. He was working on his doctorate in anthropology; I teach in the English department."

Veronica turned to Deborah in an accusing tone, "You work in the science department. Why couldn't you have taken more interest in Richard? Whatever you think of me, Richard was your brother's son."

"He's your son, not mine," Deborah responded angrily. "Don't lay your failures at my door."

The meeting was turning confrontational. If Ethan didn't change the conversation, the two women would be at each other's throats.

"What about Richard's father? Did they have much contact?"

"Richard's father and I divorced ten years ago. If they were in contact, Richard never mentioned it to me. I didn't care to know so I never asked."

She gave Deborah a questioning look. Deborah shrugged her shoulders, and then replied, "My brother called to say he was coming soon, but he didn't say exactly when. And, no, we're not in regular contact."

Ethan couldn't believe this family. A young man, a good student, caught up in the abyss of drugs, and his father and aunt seemed uncaring. Only the mother seemed distraught. That could be an act as well. Look to the family first. He made a mental note.

"Can you tell me who his friends were?" Ethan asked.

Veronica handed Ethan a piece of paper.

"I spent yesterday writing down everything I thought might be helpful."

Deborah was getting antsy, indicating she was losing patience and wanting the meeting to end. She just couldn't contain herself.

"As a scientist, I've done research on addiction," Deborah added.

"And?" Ethan asked.

"Rutgers University has been awarded grants from the National Institute on Drug Abuse for genetic research on addiction. They've found susceptibility to addiction created by environmental triggers, though many scientists agree that addiction is partly hereditary. They are looking at that as well as environmental, socio-economic, education, a whole host of factors," Deborah stated.

Ethan wished Deborah had stayed silent. In essence, she was blaming her brother and sister-in-law for Richard's addiction.

Nice job, Deborah, pouring on the guilt. What is it with these people?

He couldn't stand being around these two women any longer. If he had further questions, he'd see them individually.

As Ethan rose, the office door opened, and Dr. Brant Jordan casually walked in.

"Oh, I'm sorry," Dr. Jordan mumbled, giving Deborah a furtive glance. He was obviously surprised and uncomfortable at seeing Ethan.

What are these two up to?

"I was just leaving," Ethan said, as he turned his attention back to the two women.

"That's all the questions I have at the moment. Here's my card. If you think of anything else that might help, please be in touch."

"One more thing," Veronica stated, her eyes looking off into the distance as if that would make Richard come back. "The morning he died, well, he called and left a message on my home phone. He said he'd done a bad thing, but he was going to make it right. He was meeting someone; someone who could help."

Veronica paused, thought, and then turned to her ex-sister-in-law, "He said he was going to give you a call as well."

~ THIRTY-SIX ~

Ethan pulled into the Renwick police station with only seconds to spare. He'd stopped at a fast food drive thru to grab a quick burger. He finished eating it in the parking lot. No wonder he suffered from indigestion.

He parked next to the university's patrol car that told him Officer Pamela West had arrived. He looked forward to meeting her. He had been so busy getting to know Riverview and its residents he hadn't taken the time to visit neighboring towns or the university to meet their law enforcement officials.

He resented his monthly meetings with the captain, and consequently didn't hang around to meet and chat with the officers. He also didn't like being assigned to this task force, but had to admit it would provide him the opportunity to meet fellow officers. He'd also learn whom he could call on in time of need.

The Drug Enforcement Task Force meeting was to be held in the basement of the old precinct building. The small street level windows let in light, but not as much as Ethan would have liked. The cars parked alongside the building further deterred any natural light from entering the room. He chose a seat facing the windowed wall just so he wouldn't feel so closed in.

Was this room chosen to set the tone?

When everyone had gathered, most greeting each other like long lost friends, the captain arrived followed by the mayor. They took seats at the head of the table. The captain rose, calling the meeting to order.

"Good afternoon everyone. I hope you don't mind meeting this afternoon. With everyone having a different schedule, we couldn't find any other time to gather. I've asked Mayor Goodrich to join us because he has developed a plan for dealing with the drug problem here in Renwick."

Everyone looked to the mayor, who sported a satisfied smile.

Warning bells went off in Ethan's head. There was no "plan" proposed at the pre-meeting. He didn't like the fact there was already a plan before the first full task force meeting began. If this were the case then he was out of here. He wasn't going to waste his time being a rubber stamp.

The captain continued his introduction, but Ethan caught just the last part. ". . .the table and introduce ourselves."

There were two officers from the Renwick PD, then Pamela West. Ethan was impressed with her introduction as well as her looks. She was tall, with short black hair. Her clear complexion and facial features reminded him more of a model than a police officer. But that was sexist. He could tell she was educated from her use of language.

The older gentleman sitting next to Pamela was the local pharmacist, Harold Johansson. He talked at length about his family ties to the area, and how important a family business was to the local economy. Blah, blah. Next to him was a gentleman Ethan suspected was in his forties. Ethan wondered why this guy was on this task force, but he didn't have to wonder for long.

"I'm Brian Philips. I know most of you already, and am glad to meet the others," he nodded to Ethan and Pamela. "I own and operate one of the largest food distribution centers in New York. We are centrally located, and our trucks deliver all over the state. Right now we handle food products and most of the popular snack items that fill the vending machines. With the growth of the state's wine industry, we've applied for an alcohol license. As you can imagine, that will take a while to get through the state agencies," he added with a laugh. "On behalf of the company I want to say we're proud to be part of the Renwick business community and a part of this task force."

Ethan didn't realize there was such a large distribution center in the area. He should get more familiar with the towns in the county.

He suspected the center provided a good number of jobs, and that's why the guy was on the task force. But there was something about the guy that said, 'sleaze.'

After Ethan introduced himself, keeping his bio as brief as possible, it was the mayor's turn.

"I don't have to introduce myself to you, do I?" He said with a laugh.

The group chuckled if for no other reason than to be polite.

"I want to add my thanks to the captain's for taking time out of your busy schedules to attend this important meeting. As Captain Robertson mentioned, I've developed a plan, a draft plan that I want to present to you today."

The mayor looked around the table to make sure everyone was listening.

"People of all ages, all walks of life, are suffering, dying, leaving families devastated. Homes and businesses are being broken into on an almost daily basis. Drug users are desperate for the next fix, and when they're caught, we throw them in jail. That's not the answer."

Everyone around the table nodded in agreement. It hadn't taken long for those in law enforcement to understand the government's drug policy was a failure, but until laws changed, there was nothing they could do. Faced with an actual "epidemic" would force a change, at least on the local level.

While the mayor was talking, Ethan slipped the phone from his pocket. Keeping it on his lap, and making sure he kept looking up and nodding his head at every point the mayor made, Ethan sent a text to Tom.

Need more bkgrnd on H Johansson and B Philips.

Ethan needed to know everything he could about the players and what was in it for them. His job had made him cynical, and he'd be surprised if these two businessmen were serving on the task force purely out of generosity. The economy wasn't so great that they could afford to be away from their businesses. With his text sent, he slipped the phone back into his pocket and gave the mayor his full attention.

With another nod to those sitting around the table, Mayor Goodrich continued his diatribe. "I'm proposing something different. I want to set up a number of clinics in the area, one in each town. Overdose victims will be taken to the closest clinic that has available space. I'll be asking each town to donate space and volunteers to staff the locations. We'll ask the town supervisors in each location to set aside funds for simple furnishings, and at this time I want to thank Brian Philips for his generous donation of space for our first clinic."

Ethan joined in the half-hearted applause.

"Mr. Johansson will give us, for a short time, a reduced price on naloxone that's used to counteract the heroin overdose. We'll start out this way until other funding sources can be obtained. Eventually there will be a paid doctor and nurse at each location, or maybe a nurse and paramedic. Those details will be ironed out. Everyone treated will remain in the clinic for twenty-four hours for observation and counseling."

"And then they go back out and overdose again," stated one of the city cops, arms folded across his chest, defying anyone to disagree. "We're enabling 'em."

The mayor sighed. "You may be right, but we *have* to take action. Until we get adequate funding, this is the best first step. This will give us a better handle on how many people are out there that need services. We need solid statistics to make our case. In the meantime, we can be proud to be on the cutting edge of dealing with this situation. It will be called 'The Renwick Model.'"

"I think the mayor has a great idea, and I'm all for it," Captain Robertson exclaimed.

Sure he does, thought Ethan. *He wants to keep his job.*

"Excuse me, sir," Ethan said, raising his hand.

"Ah, yes, and what's your question?" Mayor Goodrich asked.

"Your plan is a good one for treating overdose victims, but I thought we were gathered here today to talk about how to stop the flood of drugs into and through Central New York."

Captain Robertson cleared his throat and answered for the mayor.

"That's certainly an item for discussion, but we'll save it for our next meeting. Now, if all are in favor, let's go ahead with the mayor's plan.

"One more question," Ethan said, raising his hand again.

Captain Robertson looked annoyed, but responded to Ethan's question.

"Yes, what is it now, Sheriff Ewing?"

"I thought Doc Morse was supposed to be on this task force."

"Originally he was. But we thought Mr. Johansson would be a better choice. Now, if you don't have any more questions, let's finish this meeting and get back to work."

The captain looked around the table to make sure everyone was on board. Silence. No one was willing to speak up.

"The next order of business is a chairperson for this committee. Unfortunately, I won't be able to attend every meeting, so I've asked Brian Philips to chair the group and he's agreed. I'll let him set the meeting dates and times. He'll check his calendar and let you all know. So, if there's nothing more, this task force meeting is adjourned. Thank you for coming."

Ethan couldn't believe what just happened. They were railroaded into not only accepting the mayor's plan, but they weren't even allowed to choose their own chairperson. He would have nominated Pamela, as she seemed to be the most capable person in the room. As his anger flared, his cell phone vibrated against his hip. He tipped it up to see the screen.

Hve info you requested.

Ethan picked up his folder of material and left the room. He didn't want his anger to show, and he needed to call Tom.

"Excuse me, wait!"

Ethan turned around to see Pamela running towards him.

~

"So what did you think about the meeting?" Pamela West asked as they walked to their cars.

Ethan wasn't sure how to answer. He didn't know her or what allegiances she might have, and he didn't want to come off as being a negative person.

"There's no doubt something has to be done and quickly. I just had an alert that deaths due to opioids rose 49% for counties outside New York City, with our county outpacing many others in the use of naloxone. The statistics are staggering."

"I agree. The university is running all sorts of preventative programs, but whether they will work, we just don't know yet. In the meantime, we have additional officers assigned to the dorms. More nurses have been hired at the campus health center. I don't see an end to this anytime soon," Pamela stated.

Their attention turned at the smell of cigarette smoke.

"He's got a lot of nerve lighting up as soon as he left the building," Pamela said. "I think it's rude."

"Our new fearless leader, Brian Philips. Do you know anything about him?" Ethan asked, as they moved away from the offensive smell.

"Only that he has a big warehouse business and has pushed his way into the more elite organizations in town. I heard he was raised in a commune."

"If that's so, then he probably has the right personality to manage a warehouse and truckers," Ethan said with a laugh.

"From his looks during the meeting, I think he took an immediate dislike of you and all your questions," Pamela commented with a smile.

"I should be so lucky," Ethan responded.

~ THIRTY-SEVEN ~

Caitlyn heard the doorbell ring promptly at six o'clock. As requested, she was back at the house by five, changed and ready to meet her aunt and uncle's dinner guests.

~

Upon her return she'd checked emails, and then took Summit for a walk. On their way back to the house Caitlyn checked out the barn, a place where so much happened just six months before. She knew the answer to her question, but she had to see for herself. Using all her might, she slid the heavy barn door open. The barn was empty except for a few hay bales left to rot in the loft. Absent were the fresh earthy smells of new hay, oats, and horse.

Aunt Myra assured Caitlyn that Todd's horse, Rudy, had been placed in a good home with a family in Cattaraugus County, near the Allegany State Park. Rudy was now on a farm with other horses.

The barn that once held so much life and promise was now stagnant. Caitlyn wondered if her uncle had any plans, like renting the space—anything to bring life back to the property.

~

Caitlyn dreaded spending the evening with her aunt and uncle's dinner guests. She was too tired to make small talk, and knowing her uncle, politics as well.

And she couldn't stop thinking about Abbie. They hadn't had any more time together and Abbie must be worried about her uncle.

Caitlyn pulled out her phone and sent a quick text.

How about a walk early tomorrow. Show me that place you mentioned. The one I missed because we'd moved.

A text came right back. *Sure. Tomorrow early works. Hve to be back by noon.*

Another text arrived, this one from Ethan sharing his uneasy feelings about the task force.

Is he becoming paranoid?

She had to stop thinking about Ethan, the task force, and Steven Sullivan and get ready to meet her aunt's dinner guests.

With Summit settled, Caitlyn checked her outfit once more in the full-length mirror before she put on a smile and headed down the stairs.

~

"Here she is," Aunt Myra exclaimed as Caitlyn entered the room.

"Caitlyn, let me introduce you to Harold and Doris Johansson," Myra said.

"It's very nice to meet you," Caitlyn replied with her sweetest smile. How ironic that this was one of the task force members Ethan mentioned. Maybe this evening would be interesting after all.

"Come sit down," Myra instructed. She went to the credenza to pour Caitlyn a glass of wine. Caitlyn noted that Myra refilled her glass from the nearby bottle of Perrier mineral water. It must be difficult for her aunt to entertain with alcohol always present. Myra's life had not been easy, and she had turned to alcohol as a release. Caitlyn admired her aunt's strength and hoped she was still attending AA meetings.

"Harold was just telling us about Mayor Goodrich's new drug task force," Myra said.

Caitlyn was all ears, hoping she could pick up information that Ethan could use. Before she could get seated, he continued.

"Well, I was just saying," Harold began, puffing up his chest, "I'm pleased as punch to be included in the task force. I've been a pharmacist in Renwick for over twenty-five years and, if I say so myself, I've got the knowledge, experience and contacts to make a real difference."

169

Caitlyn couldn't believe this guy was so blatant in tooting his own horn. She glanced at Mrs. Johansson to see how she was taking her husband's bragging, and saw only admiration in her eyes. Caitlyn changed the subject.

"Mrs. Johansson, do you have children?" Caitlyn asked.

"Yes, three. Two boys and a girl. They are all grown now. Our boys are in college, one at Harvard, and the other at Yale. Our daughter is married and our first grandchild is on its way," she replied, happy to be included in the conversation.

Caitlyn could kick herself. That was a stupid question to ask in front of her aunt, who had just lost her only son. To recover, she muttered, "That's nice," and then to cover her faux pas, she asked, "Where's Uncle Jerry?"

"He's in his office taking an important call," Myra responded. "He'll join us in a minute."

To continue the conversation, Caitlyn turned back to Mr. Johansson and asked, "This task force. How bad do you think the illegal drug situation is in Central New York? It can't be as bad as in the big cities."

"You'd be surprised," Harold responded. "The task force is charged with treating these victims. Now, this is confidential, but I think I can trust everyone in this room," Harold Johansson laughed. "The mayor wants to set up clinics. Instead of arresting abusers, they'd be taken to the nearest clinic for treatment. I'm proud to say that my pharmacy is one of the first in the area to carry naloxone, and I'm offering special large order pricing for our first responders. I don't like to sell it to individuals, because there are serious side effects. But on occasion ..."

At that moment Jerry Tilton entered the room, greeting his guests and apologizing for not being able to join them sooner.

"Sorry to be delayed, but we've got several important bills moving through the senate that need our immediate attention, so even when I'm home, I'm working," Jerry said with a self-gratifying expression.

After welcoming his guests, he poured himself a drink and joined the group, taking a chair that was obviously left empty for him.

"I was just telling your niece about the mayor's new task force and what we're doing to deal with the situation. Being from the south, she doesn't think crime and drugs can infiltrate the rural areas. I have been disavowing her of that notion," Harold stated with a sly laugh.

Caitlyn didn't like the way Mr. Johansson was making her out to be an uninformed country bumpkin. *Country Mouse and City Mouse* immediately came to mind and she smiled to herself. Interesting to note that he had no idea she lived just outside Washington, D.C., and served clients who were on the cutting edge of their industries. This was going to be an interesting evening, though she'd have to temper her comments for her aunt's sake. Caitlyn didn't want to ruin the dinner party with snide remarks. She found Mr. Johansson to be an interesting, if obnoxious, character. She looked forward to hearing what Ethan thought about this guy. Everyone has a story. She sat back with her glass of wine, content to let the conversation flow around her.

~ THIRTY-EIGHT ~

Abbie was only too happy for a get-away and eager to accompany Caitlyn on their mystery field trip. It was Saturday and Tim was home. He could manage the winery for a few hours.

While Abbie fastened her seat belt, Summit raced from one back seat window to the other unable to rein in his excitement. He sensed they were going to a new place, which meant different smells. There was so much doggie research to do.

Seat belt fastened, Abbie turned to Caitlyn and asked, "Any word on Uncle Steven?"

"No, not yet, but Ethan's not too concerned. He's talked to the woman your uncle's renting from, and she thinks he's doing research." Caitlyn wanted to put her friend at ease, because there wasn't anything she could share at this point.

"So, let's get started, shall we? You'll have to navigate. I've no idea where this place is," Caitlyn instructed.

"That's right, you weren't here long enough in high school to get in trouble for trespassing, were you?" Abbie teased. "Senior year that was the thing to do. Go to the closed World War II Army Depot and find a way through the fence. It was a rite of passage."

Caitlyn gave her a sideways glance that dripped sarcasm. "Yeah, right. Sounds like *a lot* of fun."

"It was! It was a daring thing to do, and we got a big kick out of who would try it and who would be too scared and back out."

"So, is there a big fence? Are there guards? What's the story?"

"One question at a time. You have this annoying habit, Caitlyn. Your mind races and I can't keep up," Abbie replied.

"Sorry. Take one question at a time."

"Before I do, don't drive too fast. When you get to the road that goes along the lake, go north for about five miles, and I'll look for the turnoff."

"Okay," Caitlyn said, checking her rearview mirror for any cars that might be impatient about her slower speed. She didn't mind slowing down when she reached the lake road. The expanse of lake shimmered as the morning's sun bounced off the gentle waves. She rolled down her window, even though the late September temperature hadn't yet reached sixty degrees. The fresh lake air invigorated her.

"There's barbed wire. That was the challenge. There were guards when the depot first closed, but not anymore. It's an abandoned property. There was a real uproar years ago when word got out that the depot had been used for storing nuclear weapons." Abbie said.

"Nuclear weapons? You've got to be kidding! Where would they put them?"

"In storage areas called silos. That's what's exciting about sneaking into the area. During World War II, the government took over about 11,000 acres, displacing families, farms, whatever was there."

"They did the same thing to build Quantico in Virginia," Caitlyn added. "In one section residents had several weeks to move out. In another section, the government gave the families only a day or two to vacate their property. Not only did people have to leave their homes, they left their farms, and their livelihood. We don't understand or appreciate the sacrifices people made during that time. Nowadays, our society gets upset over the slightest inconvenience."

"I agree," Abbie responded. "One of the first things they did on this property was build 500 concrete igloos and silos to store munitions used on planes guarding the Atlantic Coast. The igloos were covered with dirt and seeded with grass so they weren't seen from the air. A clever disguise, unless you're on ground level walking between them. They're real creepy, and that was the

173

challenge for us crazy teens. Get in, locate the igloos, and break into one if we could."

"You guys *were* crazy!" Caitlyn exclaimed.

Abbie jerked her head to the rear, checking for traffic. "Turn here, *now*," she exclaimed.

As they traveled north, Caitlyn had scanned the road looking for an intersection that might lead to this mysterious depot site. At Abbie's outburst, Caitlyn checked her rear view mirror, as well as what was coming at her. The turn off was on a curve, which made it easy to miss. A driver's attention was on traffic coming around the curve, not on an abandoned dirt road.

With no traffic in sight, Caitlyn turned onto the road and slowed to a crawl. "This can't be it," Caitlyn said as she drove down the rutted dirt pathway.

Summit pushed his nose past her head as he, too, couldn't get enough of the smells coming from the woods.

"This isn't the main road. What fun would that be?" Abbie said. "This is the back way we used as kids. We'll see if the small hole under the fence is still there."

Caitlyn stopped the car and couldn't help but laugh. After all Abbie had been through last spring with her chemo treatments, today she looked and acted like a kid again. If nothing else, Caitlyn had brought lightness to Abbie's life.

"Okay, I'm game. Let's see if the hole still exists," Caitlyn said as she inched her car forward through the ruts and weeds.

She stopped the car at the turnaround point. Something wasn't right. The abandoned road showed signs of use. She noticed tire tracks that crushed the weeds.

"Abbie, did you notice it looks like there's been a car through here?"

"No. I'm too busy looking for the place in the fence we used to gain access."

"Well, get out and look back down the road. We aren't the only ones who know about this dirt road."

"You worry too much, Caitlyn. Look, over there. That's the spot," Abbie said as she took off through the weeds. "Besides, don't you realize this is the perfect place for romantic encounters?"

The women exited the car, and Caitlyn followed Abbie with Summit on leash. She didn't want to lose him should he chase the wildlife that populated the enclosure. She'd heard about the white deer and wondered if the albino deer resulted from nuclear material being stored at this site. Or was it a genetic trait started elsewhere and the deer had been trapped in the enclosure.

The three explorers made their way through the small hole in the fence that surrounded the former Seneca Ordnance Depot. The base closed sixteen years ago, but it appeared to have been abandoned much longer.

As they made their way through the thick brush and weeds, Caitlyn brought up the subject of Steven Sullivan.

"Abbie, I've talked with your uncle's colleagues, and they know little about him, but they mentioned he seemed distracted."

"What do you mean?" Abbie replied, holding a branch back so it wouldn't snap into Caitlyn's face.

"Well, like he rushed out of the office a lot. There were articles on his desk about things not normally associated with his coursework."

"He could have been working on some sort of research, couldn't he?"

"Yes, but I hoped this information might jar your memory."

Abbie stopped, turned and said, "I'm sorry, Caitlyn, but I can't be of any help. As I told you the other day, he's a recluse as far as our family is concerned. He's always been a sore point, so we didn't talk about Uncle Steven at all."

Caitlyn sighed. Her ploy to jar Abbie's memory about her uncle didn't work, at least for now. But maybe a seed was planted that she would remember later. At least this adventure got them out in the fresh air for a couple hours.

Abbie pointed to a series of hummocks. "Those are the igloos that are made of concrete, because they needed the steel for the war effort."

"Ah, I see. Let's not get too close. I'm getting an eerie feeling about this place," Caitlyn said.

The two women stood and surveyed the area while Summit pulled on his leash, trying to get to all the new smells.

"Do you hear that?" Caitlyn asked.

"It's just the wind blowing through the trees. Don't get spooked. Nobody's here," Abbie replied.

"Well, it gives me a creepy feeling. Maybe the ghosts of the war," Caitlyn responded.

"Maybe," sighed Abbie. "Not a place you'd want to have a picnic. Let's head back."

When they were almost back to the fence, Abbie turned and pointed to the tree line.

"See the white deer?"

Caitlyn turned, following Abbie's finger.

"Oh, how cool is that?" Caitlyn said.

As they climbed back through the hole in the fence, Abbie said, "I think it's interesting that a place such as this, associated with war and hard times, would have white deer. I learned that a Lenape Indian oral tradition states, '. . . *there would come a time when a white male and female deer would be seen together, and that this would be a sign to the people to come together.*' So far that hasn't come true for our world."

There was nothing Caitlyn could add to that statement, except a long sigh. This trip into no man's land, as she liked to think of it, did not yield the results she wanted. She lifted Summit back into the car, took off his leash, leaving the world of the past and prepared to face the world of the present.

~ THIRTY-NINE ~

Tracy locked the doors and windows, and then pulled the window blinds tight before she made her way to the desk. She sat down, twirled back and forth in the chair scanning the room. It was time to look through Steven's office.

Where could he be?

Tracy knew too well what might have happened.

She stopped the chair mid-swivel to face the desk and hesitated before she pulled the extra desk key from her pocket. She put the key in the lock, turned it until she heard the familiar click. She had taken a quick look through the center drawer the other day, but today she'd do a more thorough job.

Steven had made it clear that no matter what, she was to act normal. Go about her daily business so if anyone was watching they would not suspect her. To the outside world they were to remain as homeowner and renter. He didn't understand how hard that was. Meeting clients and showing houses was pure torture right now— poor choice of words. No matter how far she'd run, memories of her previous life had caught up with her.

She tried the side drawer where papers were stashed. In the back were several small notebooks. She'd need time to go through them to see if they'd provide a hint of Steven's activities. If and when she made the call, they'd need to know everything. She was about to close the drawer, when her hand touched something cold and hard. The drawer had stuck at first, but opened after she gave it a yank. As it teetered on the edge, she realized it was where Steven placed his phone, gun, and wallet. She pulled out the wallet to find his license and a Boston library card.

The fact he left these belongings behind confused her. Why did he go out unarmed? Unless he had another weapon.

She placed the items back in the drawer, and covered them with the papers. She continued to look through the other drawers, but found nothing of note. She piled the small notebooks on top of the desk, locked it, and placed the key in her pocket.

Tracy glanced at her watch. She'd scheduled a showing this afternoon, but until then she'd pour through the notebooks to see if they held anything useful. Steven instructed her to wait a week. She doubted she could wait that long. If he didn't show by Monday, she'd make the call.

~ FORTY ~

The body Verna Adams found on Old Mill Road several days ago had precipitated an avalanche of emotions. Since she'd moved back to Riverview, a day hadn't passed that Verna didn't think about her brother, her parents and grandparents, but truth be told, she was afraid of what she might learn.

In talking with the town historian, she had broken through that first barrier. He would help her learn what happened to her brother and then she'd be able to put the past to rest.

She thought she'd told Doug Mitchell everything about her family, but he assigned her homework. He wanted a list of every family member, a description of each, and any stories she remembered. She was to add as many dates as she could and geographic locations. If she wasn't sure, she should put "abt" next to the date. She should use the words "I think" next to any fact she wasn't sure about.

Verna had worked diligently on this assignment. Her head hurt, her fingers were numb, and she was exhausted. She understood why he was asking her to do this, because the more she brought up those distant, hurtful memories, the more she'd remember. Any tidbit of information would help him find the answers she desired. But in her current state of exhaustion a thought crossed her mind.

Maybe I should call Doug and cancel my request.

Her hands ached with arthritis, the result, she was sure, of so much writing. With slow deliberation she reached for Oliver's leash. She had to get out of the house, clear her head. Oliver was always ready for a walk, but today wouldn't be just a walk. Today they would tramp through the weeds near the crime scene, but staying as far away from that area as possible. They would approach the abandoned farmhouse from the side. She didn't care if there were no trespassing signs posted. It was her family's house and she had every right to be there.

~

Verna parked in her usual spot on Old Mill Road. She got out and made sure Oliver's leash was secure.

Chills ran down her spine as she walked past the place where she'd come across the body, but they continued on until she noticed a difference in soil content. She stopped, studied the spot, moving the weeds around with her foot. This must have been the old driveway. She hesitated as she noticed vehicle tracks.

Was someone still here?

She decided to proceed cautiously and kept an eye out. She pushed the weeds aside and made her way towards the house. The broken windows and warped roof screamed abandonment.

The back door wasn't shut tight, and as she reached for the door handle childhood memories flooded her mind. How many times had she and Palle rushed through this door into the kitchen with its sweet yeasty smells of freshly baked bread, cookies, and fragrant berry pies—before their mother became ill?

Verna opened the rusted door and cringed at its creaking cry. She stopped to listen, but Oliver pushed ahead as his curiosity had no bounds. She entered and noticed not much had changed from the last time she was in there. Palle and Edda had made no improvements, but how could they? The same old metal kitchen table, same old kitchen sink, both stained by years of use and then neglect.

She walked around, looking for what, she didn't know, except maybe a clue as to what happened here.

It was then she noticed a small bag stashed in a far corner of the kitchen counter. She picked it up and poured the grain onto the table. It looked like rye, molded and disgusting. Could it have been here all this time? Why hadn't the rats gotten into it? Or did they know better? Could the rumors about Edda's family be true?

~ FORTY-ONE ~

Ethan was asking a lot of Tom, maybe too much, but there wasn't anyone else he could ask to research the backgrounds of the task force members. Heavy on his mind this morning was whether Tom would give notice and move on. Ethan couldn't afford to lose his valuable partner.

Tom was at his desk clicking away at his keyboard. Ethan approached and pulled up a chair.

"Tom, we need to talk . . .," Ethan began.

"Not now, boss. I know what you're going to say, and it can wait. Right now we have higher priority issues to deal with," Tom replied. He put a manila folder aside and looked Ethan in the eye.

"Okay, but let's not let our talk wait too long. You and Maddie are valuable to the team and I can't afford to lose either of you. Working six or seven days a week for months doesn't help."

"I know. When we get extra help, then we can take comp time," Tom said. "I bet you're here to learn about your task force members."

"You read my mind," Ethan replied with a smile. "I'm all ears."

"Harold Johansson has been a pharmacist in Renwick for about thirty years. He and his wife Doris live in a nice house at the end of South Street. They've got three kids, two attending Ivy League universities. Ouch. That has to be a big financial burden for them, but they don't seem to be hurting. Besides the house, they both drive new high-end cars." To make his point, Tom checked his notes and continued, "Let's see, he drives a Mercedes; she has the Lexus."

Ethan absorbed the information and nodded for Tom to continue.

Tom hoped his boss was reading between the lines, but just in case, he editorialized. "From what I can tell, Mr. Johansson's pharmacy is a 'mom and pop' operation, and I can't see where he'd have enough sales to support their current lifestyle."

Ethan nodded, making a mental note to visit the Johansson pharmacy on his next trip to Renwick.

"Brian Philips is another interesting personality. Apparently, his father was from a wealthy family, but Brian was brought up in a commune."

"Pamela mentioned that as well. Have you checked on a present address?"

"I haven't been able to find a home address for Brian yet, but I'm working on it."

"Anything else?"

Tom checked his notes, flipping through to make sure he covered everything.

"Brian is quite the entrepreneur," Tom continued. "He started with nothing, and somehow got enough funds together to start a warehouse business, which has grown over the last five years. There are several newspaper articles about this business."

"What does his warehouse carry?" Ethan asked, making his own notes.

"He's the middleman for snack foods and high-fructose cereals and stuff like that," Tom replied with a sneer.

Ethan took Tom's overly health-conscious editorial expression in stride.

"He recently applied for an alcohol license to ship beer and wine," Tom continued.

This information coincided with what Brian had said to the task force and Ethan sat quietly absorbing the information as he mentally pushed the puzzle pieces around to see where they fit. Ethan didn't believe in coincidences, and so he would look further into the activities of his task force colleagues.

Ethan got up, then stopped and turned toward Tom.

Tom waited, wondering what his boss was thinking. Something was going on in his head, and Tom knew it was best to wait.

"Tom, do me a favor and get information about Mr. and Mrs. Kent," Ethan said. "And include the victim's aunt, Deborah Kent. That family's dynamics bothers me."

Tom tried not to show his surprise. Then he remembered that no one was above suspicion. He wondered what brought Ethan to this conclusion. Best not to ask too many questions at this point.

"Sure, boss. No problem."

~ FORTY-TWO ~

When Doug didn't respond to her call that lunch was ready, Penny walked down the hall, tapped on his office door, and entered.

Doug sat on the floor surrounded by boxes; many were slit open with papers scattered all around.

"Didn't you hear me say lunch was ready?"

"I did. Sorry, honey. It's just that there's so much neat stuff here. You won't believe what I found," Doug explained.

"Can you tell me over lunch?"

"Sure," Doug said as he rose.

Penny put out a hand to help him up.

"It's hell getting old," Doug said, rubbing his back and rear end.

"Sitting on the hard wood floor doesn't help. Come on. Lunch will make you feel better."

Doug took a big bite of the ham and cheese sandwich, as a look of satisfaction and relief spread across his face.

"This is delicious. Thanks for making my this today."

Penny placed her hand on his, indicating he was most welcome.

"Now, tell me what was so interesting in those boxes that kept you from your favorite sandwich?"

"You know the woman who came to see me the other day?"

"Verna Adams? Yes, I remember."

"Well, I came across old newspaper clippings about a commune in this area in the 1960s and into the 70s," Doug said.

"I remember hearing about a commune, but it's been a while. So what did the article say?"

"It talked about how it came to be. A Chicago newspaper tycoon's son came here with a bunch of his friends to be 'free.' I

184

guess his daddy was glad to be rid of him, so he kept sending the kid money."

"Interesting, but what does this have to do with Verna?"

"I was getting to that. Keep in mind I haven't had time to go through everything, but from the few articles I read, an Edda van der Molen lived there."

"You're kidding! In what respect?" She now knew why her husband didn't respond when called to lunch.

"The article mentioned a marriage between this Edda van der Molen and one of the original commune residents, Jon Philips," Doug explained, taking another bite of his sandwich, then wiping the mayonnaise from his cheeks.

"I'll be darned. When do you meet with Verna again?"

"I'll call her when I have more information, but I'm sure that this person is related. We didn't set a time, because I just started to unpack boxes and organize files. There's so much there I don't know if I'll ever get through it all," Doug sighed.

"It's Saturday and I'm off work, so I'll help you unpack. We'll do one box at a time. You make piles and I'll make up the folders."

"You'd do that? I thought you and the girls were going out," Doug said.

"This is more important. I didn't want to see that movie anyway. If the two of us work at unpacking the boxes, we might be able to answer Verna's question sooner."

They nodded agreement and dug into the warm apple pie Penny made that morning. Diets be damned.

~ FORTY-THREE ~

Gentle waves lapped onto the shore just a few feet below where Caitlyn sat. The patio seating area built out over the lakeshore was a unique idea, though a bit unsettling at first. Caitlyn wondered how much of the deck would be covered with water after the spring thaw or when heavy rains brought the lake's level up over the boards. She needn't worry about that this evening. The water level was perfect.

The lake air exhilarated her, and she took a deep breath. She looked across the table at Ethan and thanked him for suggesting this quaint waterfront restaurant. It was a lovely Saturday evening at the end of September, warm enough to enjoy their dinner outside. The setting couldn't be more peaceful.

"How did you find this out-of-the-way place?" Caitlyn asked.

"I didn't. Someone told me about it and I figured we needed time away. I drove around until I found the back road that came down to the lake," Ethan replied. "I bet you didn't notice we were lost most of the time."

Caitlyn laughed. "You're right. I didn't notice, because I loved the drive. I haven't been on these back roads in a long time. I'm glad you found it. The menu options look inviting and I'm hungry."

"I guess I should take a look," Ethan said with a smile. He tore his gaze away from Caitlyn and opened the menu placed in front of him.

Would this be the evening when he would tell her how he felt? How could he explain his disastrous marital situation?

Ethan shook his head at the thought. He'd wait and see how things went. He didn't want to ruin their short time together. Instead, he picked up the menu and studied the choices.

Caitlyn noticed his expression. "Anything wrong?"

"No, nothing, just trying to decipher this menu," Ethan responded with a smile.

Their waitress arrived and took their drink orders. After she left, Ethan leaned toward Caitlyn and said, "I don't want this to be a business evening, but it might be a good time to share what we both learned."

"You're right." Caitlyn looked around. "Except for that family at the other end of the deck, with the three small children all talking at once, we're the only ones out here, so I guess we can talk without the fear of someone listening. How did the task force meeting go?"

Ethan waited to respond until the waitress served their drinks. He picked up his beer glass and proposed a toast, "Here's to better days."

They took a sip of their beverages, and then he continued.

"It was . . . interesting. It was nice to meet the other police officers, and to get a read on the town's power base."

"What do you mean by that?" Caitlyn asked.

"The drug task force is comprised of two officers from Renwick, one related to the captain, Officer Pamela West from the campus safety division, Harold Johansson, a pharmacist, Brian Philips, who runs a food distribution center, Mayor Goodrich, Captain Robertson, and me, representing the outlying districts. I asked why Doc Morse wasn't on the task force, and didn't get a good answer. Seems decisions were made before the group assembled, and we weren't encouraged to ask questions. An ominous start."

"Why a warehouse distributor?" Caitlyn asked, confused.

"I think it's because he's a long-time resident and well known in the community. He sits on several boards. I suspect the plan is to tap him for the funding needed for the clinics."

"There's always more to these selections than meets the eye. There's always a back story," Caitlyn replied with a sigh.

"You're right. Politics and money come into play. I haven't figured out how everyone fits into this picture, but I'm sure I will after a few more meetings. Tom did a background check on Johansson and Philips, and came up with interesting information on the guys. I've been trying to figure out if or how they fit into the puzzle. We can talk about those later. How are your campus interviews going?"

"Maddie got background on Steven Sullivan, but it's pretty vague."

Caitlyn paused. "We came up with several scenarios . . ."

Ethan didn't want to talk about Steven Sullivan, so his attention went to the menu.

"The steak looks like a great choice for this evening."

Caitlyn signed. *Men and their meat.*

She returned to their discussion, hurt that Ethan wasn't interested in her part of the investigation. She'd keep him talking about the task force, and then try to work in her questions about Steven Sullivan.

"Did you ask Maddie about the two businessmen? She knows everybody. She'd know about Mr. Johansson, and she might even know about Brian Philips if he owns a distribution center. Oh, I met Mr. Johansson last night. He and his wife were dinner guests of my aunt and uncle. I thought he was quite a pompous individual."

"That's the same sense I got from him. Interesting that your uncle knows him."

"I think it was my aunt who's friends with Mrs. Johansson," Caitlyn explained.

"I'll ask Maddie what she knows about these folks. You know, I've been here a year and I've never taken the time to actually get to know Maddie. We're so busy that personal time is just that. She goes home; I go home. When the mill renovations began we got crazy busy, and so we crave our private time more than ever. It's about time the three of us went for a drink after work."

"I understand," Caitlyn said, staring off into space. She, too, was thinking about how she had so little time to herself, working from home, being available to clients day and night. That was even more the case upon her return to Virginia last spring when she took on a client from California, and another from England. She envisioned her body spread across the globe in order to keep both clients happy. That silly thought brought a smile to her face.

"Penny for your thoughts," Ethan said, noticing her faraway look.

"Oh, it's nothing. Just thinking about work, my clients and their time zones."

"So what did Maddie tell you?" Ethan asked, knowing the subject would be on the table until she could tell all.

"Maddie has a friend in Boston and learned that Steven Sullivan worked for the Boston PD for years as a forensic psychologist. He also saw clients on the side. About ten years ago his history becomes sketchy. Maddie's contact suspected Steven trained for special undercover work and went underground. It was her friend's educated guess that he worked for some government agency, but which one is a guarded secret."

Caitlyn was getting too close to the truth and Ethan had to divert her attention.

"That's interesting, but might not be true. Sullivan could be just as he presents himself, a fifty-something wanting to reinvent himself and looking for a place to retire," Ethan said.

The waitress approached to take their order, which ended their conversation about Steven Sullivan.

They decided to share an appetizer of bruschetta, and although Ethan had eyed the steak, they both ordered the wild caught salmon topped with peach salsa, with a side of risotto and the fall vegetable medley.

When the waitress was out of earshot, Caitlyn asked, "When's your next task force meeting?"

Before he could answer, Chad Owens, the marine biologist they had met in Steven Sullivan's office, approached their table.

"Hello there! Nice to see you two out enjoying the evening."

Caitlyn looked at Ethan indicating he should respond.

"So, how's the investigation going?" Chad asked. "I told my co-workers on Long Island about this place, a murder and missing person all in one day. Almost like living in New York City."

This guy was starting to get on Caitlyn's nerves. She looked at Ethan to do something. He took the hint.

"Thanks for stopping by, Dr. Owens. I've nothing to report on the investigations, but thanks for asking. Have a nice evening. I think the waitress is bringing our appetizer."

Chad Owens got the hint, nodded to both, and rejoined his colleagues at the inside bar.

The waitress placed the bruschetta on the table between them. The fresh tomatoes and basil gave off a mouth-watering aroma. On her first bite, Caitlyn savored the sweet-tart flavor of the balsamic vinaigrette reduction. She closed her eyes as the flavor combination made her think this was pretty close to heaven.

Ethan continued his report.

"Captain Robertson asked Brian Philips to chair the task force. The entire task force would normally vote on that position after we've gotten to know one another. At least that's the democratic way of doing things. Instead, the captain announced it as a done deal. Pamela, the university safety division officer, caught me after the meeting and asked what I thought. She, too, was surprised and disappointed. I think she wanted a chance to lead the group."

"Did you observe any other reactions to the announcement?"

"Yes, a few, though I was mostly so taken aback I didn't react fast enough to look around the table. One of the Renwick officers who sat directly opposite me had a funny look on his face. I noticed that, and wondered."

Just as they were finishing their meal, Ethan noted a couple being seated several tables from them.

"Let's sit at the bar awhile," Ethan suggested, picking up the check, and nodding to Caitlyn to follow.

"So what's the hurry?" Caitlyn asked, annoyed at losing their spot next to the water.

"The couple that just arrived. That's Brian Philips, a member of the task force. I don't have a good feeling about the guy, and I don't want to get into a conversation with him, especially not tonight."

Caitlyn stole a look at the couple, especially taking note of Brian, and shook her head. Would Ethan's job follow him everywhere?

~ FORTY-FOUR ~

Doug Mitchell couldn't sleep. He checked the bedside clock through the three o'clock hour and until it reached four. There was no hope. His mind was racing with all the possibilities of Verna Adams's family.

He rose quietly so as to not wake Penny. She needed to sleep. They were up late unpacking and sorting the boxes piled in his office. During that process, it was all he could do to not stop and read the documents and clippings contained therein. It was good she was there to keep him on task.

Those boxes represented a goldmine of information on the original residents of Riverview, and it was now his responsibility to put all that information into researchable format. Once accomplished, he'd digitize it and use his paltry town historian stipend to develop a website and pay for a reliable hosting service.

He swore under his breath as the wood stairs creaked under his weight. Once downstairs, he went to his office and shut the door. He turned on his computer, and looked around for his file on the van der Molens.

Darn. Did it get mixed in with all the unpacked material?

If that were the case, he wouldn't find it for a while.

Ah, there you are!

Doug logged onto his computer and checked a website with the hope that Verna's brother might appear. He didn't know why he didn't think of it before—well, he'd been so darn busy unpacking, sorting, trying to make sense of what he found, and then setting up files, and he didn't want to check this particular website while Verna was sitting with him. At this early hour and alone in his office, he typed in www.Findagrave.com.

Clicking on New York and then the county, Doug typed in the name.

No results.

He tried just the last name, and then variations of the name, and then searching just New York State. He typed in just the first name and came up with several Palles—who knew there would be so many?

How could it be that Palle van der Molen wasn't listed? Well, it is a volunteer site and maybe the cemetery he's in, assuming he died, isn't listed on the Findagrave site. Or, if he didn't have a marker, or . . .

The next try was the county's Genweb site, scrolling down until he located the first area cemetery. He put in Palle's name and again, no result. He got the same result with the other area cemeteries. He was about to click out of this site, discouraged, when he noticed a small rural cemetery at the bottom of the list. It was worth a try. He clicked on the Old Mill Road Family Cemetery and scrolled down through the list, making note of the names as he did. There, halfway down was Mollen, Palle. His date of death was 31 January 1969. Doug noted another lesson learned. When researching, try *every* variation of how the name *might* be spelled.

Doug sat back in his chair staring at the name and the information attached to it. Palle was buried in a family plot. Edda was not mentioned. Was she still alive or buried elsewhere, and under a different name? Now, there is a challenge.

Why did he feel as though he'd opened a can of worms?

It was four thirty in the morning. He needed a cup of coffee. Quickly.

~ FORTY-FIVE ~

Caitlyn woke with a start, gasping for breath, heart racing from her nightmare about drowning. As she brought herself out of the deep sleep she realized she wasn't anywhere near water, but instead in a warm bed. The wetness she felt upon waking was Summit licking her face. He'd sensed her anxiety and wanted her to wake up.

She stretched, allowing herself time to recover from the nightmare, and tried to capture everything it entailed. Why did she dream about drowning? Was it her subconscious telling her she was over her head in the investigation? Did it signify trouble ahead? She glanced over at the clock.

Oh my God! It was nine o'clock. She never slept this late. No wonder the dog needed her to wake up. She raised herself to a sitting position pumping her knees to get the synovial fluid moving.

As her head acclimated to an upright position, she thought about last night. Neither she nor Ethan wanted the evening to end, so with their dinner finished they moved inside the restaurant to the bar area and continued to talk. She ordered more wine, but noticed Ethan went for the non-alcoholic beer. Caitlyn didn't have the foggiest idea what time she arrived back at the house, but it must have been late.

Caitlyn hoped her aunt and uncle had gone about their day and not waited breakfast for her. She pulled on a pair of sweat pants and sweatshirt, slipped into her shoes, grabbed Summit's leash, and headed for the front door. She hoped the little dog didn't want to go for a long walk, because she needed coffee.

~

Summit *was* ready for a long walk. He'd felt neglected yesterday since she was gone for such a long time and returned late. He'd make her pay.

When they finally arrived back at the house, Caitlyn rushed to the kitchen.

"You're up!" Myra said, sitting at the kitchen table. "There's fresh water in the coffee maker. Help yourself."

"Oh, thanks," Caitlyn replied, choosing a robust French roast. "Summit needed his walk this morning and I didn't have time to grab a cup."

"We figured you needed to sleep in and so we ate breakfast without you," Myra said. "And we don't expect you to attend church with us," she added.

"Thanks. I needed to catch up," Caitlyn replied, not mentioning her late night with Ethan.

"So you're still working as hard as ever?" Myra asked with a wink, taking another sip of her coffee.

"My clients are as demanding as ever," Caitlyn responded, avoiding eye contact. "I think I'm finished with the winery's photo shoot. The brochure is done and sent to the printer for a proof. If Abbie and Tim have no more additions or corrections, they'll have their new brochures in less than a week."

Myra nodded, knowing Caitlyn wasn't going to share anything about her Saturday night.

"Jerry should be down in a minute. I know he'll be glad to visit with you."

Caitlyn doubted that very much, but it was the polite thing for her aunt to say.

"When does Uncle Jerry go back?"

"This evening. He likes to get a full weekend here before he goes back to Albany," Myra replied.

"Good morning," Jerry Tilton said as he walked into the kitchen. He gave Caitlyn a superficial hug and headed for the coffee pot.

A chill ran through her at his touch, but for her aunt's benefit, she forced a smile.

Once seated, and small talk about Caitlyn's life in Washington over, Caitlyn was eager to continue the conversation about the state's response to the war on drugs.

"Uncle Jerry, sorry we got off on the wrong foot the other day. I didn't mean to be critical of what the state is doing to address the drug problem. I've seen lots of articles on what's happening, especially the escalation of heroin use. What is New York doing to stop the dealers?"

Jerry sighed. Caitlyn was persistent. Once she had a cause, she went headlong into it whether she was right or not. He'd keep his answers short and maybe she'd get the message—just do what she came to do and go home.

"I was appointed to the senate's Drug Enforcement Task Force," Jerry replied. "We've been holding weekly meetings and have developed plans for recovery centers. I believe I mentioned that the other day. To respond to your comment, I agree with you that the term 'Shooting Galleries' is distasteful terminology for a recovery/treatment center, and I'll do my best to convince my colleagues to adopt a more positive term."

"Is any money being spent to stem the tide, to cut it off at the root?" Caitlyn countered.

"The short answer is no. Again, you have a point, but it's not that easy. The immediate need is to help those who are trapped in drug abuse, and to keep them from relapsing. If we can do that, crime will lessen and our population will be safer."

Ah, the government will protect you scenario.

Caitlyn appreciated the fact her uncle was taking time to share what the state was doing, but she wasn't satisfied. She could tell her uncle was losing patience. She wouldn't let this go, but right now there was another problem to solve—the disappearance of Steven Sullivan and the feeling Ethan was trying to steer her away from the investigation.

Why?

~ FORTY-SIX ~

Ethan swung the patrol car into the Tilton's driveway at eleven a.m. sharp. He'd asked Caitlyn to accompany him and take notes when he met with Carrie Young.

Caitlyn was waiting on the porch, not understanding what the emergency on a Sunday morning could be. Ethan had called and said to be ready in fifteen minutes. As soon as the car came to a stop, she climbed in.

"So, what's the big hurry?" She asked, fastening her seat belt.

"Carrie called. She needs to talk. I said I'd be right over. I want you there to take notes, okay?"

"Sure, but on a Sunday?"

"I think, under the current circumstances, she and Doc are working straight through."

When they reached the morgue Ethan said, "Carrie will explain things, and it might mean the corpse will be in full view. Are you prepared for that, or would you prefer to stand a distance away, but close enough to capture notes? I guess the other question is, will you be able to tolerate the morgue at all?"

Caitlyn swallowed hard. It was a good question. Was she ready to be in a morgue with the indescribable sickening odor of decay? She wasn't sure. She loved to watch shows that relied on forensic evidence, but was she ready for real life? The lifeless discolored forms in front of her, the smell, the instruments.

"I'll try," was all she could say.

Entering the foyer, Ethan flashed his badge at the receptionist as they hurried past her and headed down the long hallway. At the morgue doors, Ethan hesitated and looked at Caitlyn.

197

"Here goes."

Carrie Young was at the other end of the room cleaning instruments and counter tops. She turned as they entered.

"Thanks for coming," she said. "I know it's Sunday, but around here it's just another work day."

Ethan scanned the room. "Is Doc around?"

"No, he's not. Last night at the Hudson River State College police went to a frat house for a suspicious death. What they found were three young men dead of suspected drug overdoses. The campus is in a small rural community not unlike Riverview. They called here for help. We objected, but those objections were overruled and he left early this morning to assist with the autopsies."

Carrie pointed to the wall of coolers, "We're full. We can't keep up with the number of deaths. We can't get more help. There aren't even enough trained medical examiners in the state to cover the drug epidemic plus what we call 'normal' autopsies."

Carrie walked to a table that held a covered body.

"This is what I wanted you to see. I heard you're on the drug task force, and so I thought you might be interested in our newest arrival."

She pulled the sheet back to expose the top half of a male in which tattoos covered the torso, head, and neck.

Caitlyn gulped at the horror. "How can . . ." She couldn't finish the sentence.

"Let me explain what you are seeing. Most tattoos have significance. Some have a butterfly signifying that person escaped an abusive relationship, but these tattoos signify cartel membership. In case you didn't know, cartels have their member's bodies completely tattooed. It is similar to branding. What you see is the brand of a Mexican cartel I assume is working this area. The tattoos make it impossible for the person to change cartels, and it gives the cartel power over its members."

"I never thought about it that way. Actually I never thought about it at all," Caitlyn said. "But it makes sense. The cartels are run by unscrupulous people so it makes sense they'd enslave their own."

While Carrie was talking, Ethan leaned closer and studied the various tattoos. "I recognize a few of these. My department encountered cartels in the city."

"Let me have your magnifying glass," he said. "Several of these have the number 13, which signifies he was a member of the Mexican mafia."

Carrie took the magnifying glass and looked at what Ethan pointed out.

"You're right. They're faint, but they're there."

"It confirms this particular cartel is operating in the area," Ethan said. "What area of the county did this body come from?"

"The northwest corner." Carried responded, pulling the sheet back over the body.

"That's what I was afraid of. The cartels are infiltrating the rural areas. This guy is dead because he was a user or had violated their rules. The cartel is strict. I suspect this guy stepped over the line and was murdered by his own people."

Carrie nodded.

Caitlyn stood back and listened to the conversation cringing at the thought that these men allowed tattoos to be put all over their body. She understood it was only part of the initiation process of an organization whose only purpose was to cause harm. On this beautiful Sunday morning she was face to face with the ugly side of life.

~

"You know the saying it's easier to ask forgiveness than ask permission," Carrie continued. "Since Doc is having a difficult time giving up being head of this department, I'm trying to be understanding, but . . . there's new equipment and new tests available that he doesn't know about or utilize or spend money on. Without him knowing, I've been utilizing those new tests in order to get a better turnaround for results."

199

Ethan nodded his understanding. "We also know he's been overwhelmed with work. It doesn't give him much time for continuing ed courses, does it?"

"Point taken," Carrie responded.

"So back to Richard Kent. I called in a favor from a lab where I used to work. They did additional blood tests and he had heroin and carfentanil in his system. Carfentanil is used to sedate elephants. As you know, heroin is being cut with synthetic opioids like carfentanil and fentanyl that are many times more potent than the heroin. If the combination is sold as pure heroin, on the street it is called garbage dope."

"Oh, dear lord," Ethan exclaimed. "This could be disastrous. We could become like that West Virginia town where they experienced twenty-six opioid-related deaths within hours."

Up to this point Caitlyn had been able to cope, but she now felt faint. The body laced with tattoos, the worsening news about drug-related deaths, and the smells. She held her arm up over her nose to help, but it was becoming too much. She swayed, but caught herself before either Ethan or Carrie noticed.

Ethan took one last look at the body.

"Thanks, Carrie, for sharing this information with us. I don't know if this death is tied to our missing Steven Sullivan, but it confirms the cartels are infiltrating the rural areas. What a mess."

Ethan thanked Carrie as he and Caitlyn headed towards the door. "You'll call as soon as you get any more information?" Ethan stated.

"Of course," Carrie said with a wink.

Caitlyn turned to wave good-bye and noticed Carrie's response.

~ FORTY-SEVEN ~

"We need to talk with Tracy Connor again," Ethan said as they got back in the car.

"I thought you were told not to spend time on that case and it's why you asked me to help," Caitlyn responded. "What if the captain finds out?"

Ethan ignored her question as he turned toward her.

"Let's talk this through. The two cases are linked. I'm sure of it. Sullivan left his house early Wednesday morning without telling Tracy. A body is found about a mile away with Sullivan's credit card in a pocket. Sullivan is missing. A university student is dead. Those things prove a connection. It could be a drug deal gone bad and Sullivan left town, or Kent knew too much about Sullivan and was murdered."

"I don't like the way your scenarios are pointing," Caitlyn said with arms crossed. She didn't know why she needed to defend Abbie's uncle, but that was the answer. He *was* Abbie's uncle.

"Or, if you let me finish . . . Sullivan was there for another reason." Ethan chose his words carefully so he didn't share more information than he should. "So he is either being held somewhere or he's been murdered."

Caitlyn cringed. Up to this point she thought of her search for Abbie's uncle more like a game, a challenge to figure out what he might be doing. She didn't project what the outcome might be.

Ethan shared these scenarios with Caitlyn without giving up the real reason Steven Sullivan was in Riverview. He'd be walking a tightrope, but he'd done it before. He needed more information on Steven, and that information might be in Tracy's house.

"That's why we need to talk with Tracy again. From what Carrie told us about Kent's death, we now have more information that might jar her memory. Maybe she heard Steven mention Richard Kent."

"Okay, but shouldn't we call first?" Caitlyn said, glancing at her watch, knowing Tracy was a real estate agent and could be anywhere in the county showing houses or running errands on her day off.

"We'll take our chances. If she's not home, we'll figure out a way to meet her at a convenient location. I can't be seen going into her office downtown," Ethan responded.

"We could always request an appointment for a house showing," Caitlyn joked. "That would give us privacy."

Ethan gave her a sidelong glance and a wry smile.

Don't tempt me.

He turned the car onto the main road and headed north towards Riverview.

Tracy's house was at the end of a cul de sac, a lazy street lined with mature oak trees. In different circumstances the street would appear peaceful, but not today.

Ethan slowed his cruiser and pulled into the driveway. "Damn! No car," he said. He put his hand on the back of the seat as he twisted in preparation for backing up.

"Wait!" Caitlyn said. "Her car might be in the garage."

"But her car was parked outside when I arrived the other day. I assumed Steven's car was parked inside and the second bay is full of stuff."

"You assume too much," Caitlyn said as she jumped out of the car and ran to the house. She rang the doorbell just as Ethan joined her.

The top half of the front door was beveled glass that allowed light to filter in. By training, Ethan stepped back away from the line of sight of the door, and motioned for Caitlyn to do the same. When there was no response, Ethan pushed the doorbell again, this time leaving his finger on it for a lingering second.

The door opened, and Tracy Connor stood before them, hairbrush in hand.

"Oh, it's you. What do you want? I have a showing in thirty minutes."

"We have a few questions, Ms. Connor. May we come in?" Ethan asked.

She emitted a loud sigh in response, opened the door, and walked back into the house. They followed, and Caitlyn quietly closed the door. Tracy turned to face them, her face flushed in frustration. "I told you everything I could the other day. Steven's a renter, not family."

"I'm just trying to help, putting puzzle pieces together without the benefit of the end pieces if you follow my thinking. Remind me, how did you two come to be in Riverview?" Ethan asked.

"I went through this the other day so I'll repeat," Tracy responded, not hiding her anger. "We met in Boston. We worked for the Boston PD, different departments, but were assigned cases together. At the time we had a relationship and you can read into that what you want. Neither of us was married, so no one was hurt. But then I had had enough of Boston, enough of the job. Steven stayed there. We lost touch. Now I think he's trying to figure out the rest of his life. It was a coincidence he ended up here," Tracy said, hoping Ethan was buying her story.

Ethan nodded, not believing her, but urged her to continue. The more he could keep her talking, the more likely she'd slip up.

"It might surprise you, but I grew up here. When I decided to leave Boston, I came 'home.' I got my real estate license, was hired by one of the large firms, and started an office in Renwick. I've built up the business in a short time, and now the satellite campus is bringing a lot of people into the area, and business is booming."

Tracy paused, hoping she hadn't gone too far with her explanation.

"As for Steven, he accepted a teaching opportunity and we met when he arrived at my office looking for a rental. We were both surprised. I'm renting him a room until a better option comes along," Tracy explained.

"Thank you, Ms. Connor. It's helpful to have that background," Ethan said, trying to sound convincing.

"I looked through the office, but found no clue as to what he was working on," she continued, hoping to get rid of the two unwelcome guests.

"May we take another look?" Ethan asked.

Tracy froze, her mind racing as to what she might have missed or accidently left on Steven's desk. She knew the little notebooks were upstairs in her bedroom.

"Sure. I don't think I missed much, and you've already looked around, so I don't know what you think you'll find. You know where the office is. Help yourself and if you'll excuse me I'll finish getting ready for work."

They watched Tracy run up the stairs before they headed down the hallway leading to the room Steven used as his office. The door stood open, and Ethan noticed evidence of Tracy's search. He figured she'd have been thorough, but so was he. At least he liked to think so. There had to be a clue somewhere as to Steven's whereabouts. Was he meeting Richard Kent on Wednesday morning, or was he simply in the wrong place at the wrong time?

Ethan sat at the desk and tried the drawer. Locked. Whatever Steven had in there, Tracy was making sure no one would get to it.

Caitlyn walked around the office. She had to figure out a methodical way to search the space in a limited amount of time, and so she headed for the filing cabinets. She opened the top drawer and let her fingers walk over the manila folders before she stopped at one that didn't seem to fit. She took the folder to a nearby chair and sat down to study its contents.

"Remember the article on food we found in his campus office?"

"Yes," Ethan replied, busy looking through files in another cabinet.

"I found a folder labeled 'food.' I thought it might contain grocery receipts, but instead there's articles on food additives, sugar content, stuff like that. Just scanning through them I'm picking up words in the articles and handwritten notes about how sugary foods and carbohydrates change the body's metabolism. Further down it talks about the body's magnetic and electrical systems. Some of these articles look intriguing."

Caitlyn sat down in one of the straight-backed chairs that lined the wall, as she further scanned the articles.

"One of these articles states opioid drugs like heroin compensate for the biochemical imbalance caused by eating too much of these kinds of foods, what we refer to as junk food, and that may be one of the root causes for drug addiction. A reason so many people, not just those on pain medications, are getting addicted."

"That's the first time I've heard anything about food driving people to drugs," Ethan responded. "Don't you think that's far fetched? And, does it really have anything to do with our case?"

"It might. It makes sense in a way. There has to be a reason so many people from different walks of life are resorting to heroin. A poor diet lowers a person's serotonin levels. Here's an article that states that low serotonin levels have been linked to mental illness, drug-taking and violent crime. Down here at the bottom it states foods that are high in sugar and fat make for a sense of euphoria that conditions children and adults for the drug experience. But why would a forensic psychologist be interested in food interactions?" Caitlyn asked.

"Because he's a scientist," Ethan uttered with impatience, as he frantically looked through the bottom drawer of the filing cabinet he was searching. But her comments started him thinking of new scenarios.

Ethan closed his file drawer and went to see what Caitlyn found. Before he reached her, Tracy appeared at the door. She looked at the two, Caitlyn sitting with a manila folder open on her lap, and Ethan on his way over to her.

"What've you found?" Tracy asked, her voice stressed, looking from one to the other.

Caitlyn waited for Ethan to respond. It wasn't her place to share what they were discussing.

"Not sure," Ethan replied. "Caitlyn was looking through the files and found some interesting articles in a folder, similar to ones we saw in his campus office. I was going to take a look and determine whether they are relevant."

Tracy walked over, reached down and took the folder, quickly leafing through the articles.

"I don't think these are important. This is a topic Steve was interested in several weeks ago. He asked that if I came across an article about high fructose corn syrup and GMO foods, to clip them. I think he's done with that project now. Anyway, I'm late for my showing, and that could lose me the sale. So if you don't mind . . ." She held out her hand to take the folder from Caitlyn, which dashed Ethan's hopes of going through the articles.

"Thanks, Ms. Connor, for letting us look through the office, and please don't let anyone know we've been here," Ethan said.

"Sure. Don't worry. I know the drill," Tracy replied. She now had leverage if the sheriff continued his uninvited visits.

When they heard the front door close behind them, Ethan asked, "Do you think she's right? Those were just old articles?"

"No. The dates are recent. There are articles other than about corn syrup and GMOs. There are pages of handwritten notes that would take time to go through. She didn't want us to have that information. Something's screwy here," Caitlyn responded, hesitated and turned. "Ethan, it's starting to make sense. Was Steven Sullivan looking for the root cause? Setting up treatment centers is fine, but wouldn't it be better to locate the root cause and stop the abuse before treatment's needed? Would be a lot less expensive. And most important, if there's no demand, it would stop the widespread drug use, which would hurt the suppliers, which means losing money," Caitlyn stated, then stopped.

"It's not that simple," Ethan replied. "And . . ."

"Follow the money," they said simultaneously.

"Seems like I've been saying that to myself a lot lately," Ethan remarked.

Caitlyn turned and faced Ethan. "Seeing those articles made me think of a worst case scenario. What if there's multiple root causes to the drug problem? And what if cartels are competing for customers? Ethan, do you think Steven Sullivan is involved in the drug trade? Or, did he learn who the 'money men' and the suppliers are? We've *got* to keep looking. He *had* to leave a trail," Caitlyn pleaded.

"Slow down. I think we're in way over our head. We only got through a few of his papers and we've worn out our welcome with Tracy," Ethan responded with frustration. He had to discourage Caitlyn from going any further with the investigation.

Not to be deterred, Caitlyn responded, "We now have a better idea of what we're up against. Let's stop talking and get busy!"

~ FORTY-EIGHT ~

On their way back to the sheriff's office, Ethan's phone rang.

"Yes, Tom, what's up? Okay. We'll be right in."

"What's going on?"

"Tom's found something and he'd prefer to tell us when we get back to the office."

~

Tom jumped up from his desk when Ethan and Caitlyn walked in.

"Okay, what's so important?" Ethan asked. "And why are you here on Sunday?"

"I've been working through these cold case files," Tom replied as he pointed to the stack of folders on the corner of his desk. "I want to get them finished so we can focus on the more important things."

"Okay, so what have you found?" Ethan replied.

"I came across a file listed as a suspicious death on Old Mill Road in 1969," Tom replied, waiting for the light to go on in Ethan's eyes. When it did, Tom continued. "The name was van der Molen. That abandoned house near where the body was found this morning is called the van der Molen place."

Ethan pulled up two chairs and placed them in front of Tom's desk, as it sounded like a long story.

"Okay, I'm confused. What does this have to do with our case?" Ethan said.

"According to the article, Palle and Edda van der Molen lived there, though the property was in someone else's name. The husband, Palle, died of unknown causes, though from what I read in these case files, the cause of death was suspicious."

"What makes you think there is anything untoward about the man's death or that the incident is relevant now?" Ethan asked.

"Because I think it was a perfect storm of inability bordering on incompetence. Remember, forensic tests in the '60s weren't as sophisticated as they are today. Riverview was a small rural community. Well, it still is, but we've come a long way. The file reveals the medical examiner was the local GP, going on eighty. Not one to make waves. The sheriff wasn't inclined to work too hard. He didn't pursue leads. Palle's wife was good looking, and apparently from these notes, she had left her husband. They didn't have close neighbors, but his fellow workers at the mill mentioned he hadn't been feeling well for a period of time. He'd developed tremors, and exhibited strange behavior that made it difficult for him to work. They noticed changes in him, but then guys don't talk about that much. When these cases were originally filed, someone thought this case was suspicious and it ended up in the cold case box."

"Do you think he was being poisoned?" Caitlyn asked.

"Something was going on with him. I've done research on the mill. It ground grain brought in from local farms, so they were grinding wheat and rye. Sounds innocent enough until I checked the weather for that summer. It was cold and rainy, which means the grains brought to the mill were likely damp. I Googled what would happen if grains got wet. There were a number of interesting articles, as well as a book online that stated cold and damp conditions were ripe for mold," Tom explained. "And certain molds could have caused this guy's symptoms and eventually death."

Ethan and Caitlyn were enthralled with the scenario, and before they could ask questions, Tom continued, excited by the research he had done.

"If Palle were taking grain from the mill, and if it were ground and not allowed to dry like maybe in a low temperature oven, the mold toxins known as fusarium, would be poisonous. His wife could have been poisoning him without knowing. But, if she didn't know, why didn't she get sick as well? So maybe she poisoned him deliberately?"

"That's an interesting scenario and it would be wonderful to solve a cold case, but how could we find out now whether the grain was dried or not? And another detail is when did the wife leave? If she left him and he had to fend for himself, he may have eaten the poisonous grain without knowing."

"I've thought of that," Tom replied, "so I talked with Doug Mitchell, the new town historian. I asked him to keep the name van der Molen in mind as he goes through his boxes. I've asked him to develop a timeline that I can add to what we have in the case files."

"Good job, Tom, and I hope your search yields a result."

"Oh, did I forget to mention that in my discussion with Doug, he said he was already researching that family line? The woman who found the body, Verna Adams, met with him. She says she's related to Palle van der Molen. She claims to be his sister. Doug also mentioned that Edda might still be alive."

"Whoa, worlds colliding," Ethan laughed.

"Yes, and what's more, Mrs. Adams wants to know what happened to her brother. If he's dead, which I now know he is, she wants to know where's he buried," Tom replied.

"Keep on this, Tom. But for now, let's keep this cold case information to ourselves. It's possible these things are connected, but I want time to sort it all out."

~ FORTY-NINE ~

He estimated it was four, maybe five days since he was, for lack of a better term, kidnapped. Steven Sullivan wasn't sure what day it was, but when he woke he had a stabbing pain in his head. His head still throbbed, and it was difficult to focus.

He was thankful the blindfold was off so he could better tell day from night. He had become accustomed to the rhythm of the place. Workers arrived at daybreak to add or remove the inventory stored along the far wall behind him. He didn't know what was being stored and moved, but he had a good idea.

The musty-smelling cavernous structure was dark when the workers were not on site. When his eyes finally acclimated to the darkness he was able to survey the large empty space. The walls were made of concrete blocks; the floor was poured concrete that invited the cold to seep up his legs. To keep his blood circulating and to exercise his stomach muscles, he'd pull his legs up and down several times a day. But his arms, tied behind his back, cramped after the first day. The only time he could shake them out was when he was allowed a quick meal and bathroom break, which came only three times during the day.

He knew when his captors were arriving because the creaking door broke the nighttime silence. The sound was accompanied by a slit of bright light that blinded him so he couldn't see who approached. They positioned themselves to his rear so he was unable to see their faces. They'd been gentle in their interrogation tactics so far in their attempt to learn what other agents were working the area. At some point their patience would run out. He wasn't going to give them what they wanted, and he would become a liability. He knew what happened to liabilities.

Their apparent inattention was because they were too busy moving inventory in and out of this storage facility. He knew this was the perfect place to store drugs or illegal firearms for distribution around the state.

What would his next move be? The operation perplexed him, because it didn't fit with how the cartels usually worked. This was different and that difference set off alarms in his head. It must be a competitor. What organization was strong enough to go up against a cartel?

So far he hadn't figured out an escape route. After feeding and bathroom privileges were extended, he was tied back into his chair. Sleeping in this position was difficult, even painful, but when he was tired enough, he slept.

Damn!

He was so close! One mistake was all it took. He never should have agreed to meet in that remote location. He was too quick to trust and his instincts were failing him. He was too anxious to get the information his contact was going to provide. Where was that person now?

There was no time for regrets. He had to figure a way out. Tied to a chair with his hands securely fastened behind his back would make it a challenge. When alone, he rocked back and forth in an attempt to loosen his restraints. So far he had made little progress.

~

It was time Ethan told his staff what was going on. He owed them that much. They were a team, and no one was going to force a wedge into that relationship.

He poked his head out his office door to make sure no one else was there. "Tom, come into my office; Maddie, you stand in the doorway to keep an eye on the switchboard and the front door. What I'm about to tell you is for your ears only. I have been sworn to secrecy, but I'm tired of being manipulated by outside agencies and I need your support. Do not utter a word of what I am about to tell you. Understand?"

They nodded, dreading what Ethan had to say.

"I received a package the other day . . ."

Maddie nodded, remembering the delivery. She leaned forward so as not to miss a word. Tom's expression perked up. This was going to be interesting.

"The package was from the DEA. It confirmed Steven Sullivan is one of their agents. He's working undercover posing as a part-time lecturer to work his way into the drug network in this area. The DEA doesn't have jurisdiction over the local police departments, except if there is a kidnapping of a federal agent. Steven Sullivan is here as a federal agent, and they think he may have been kidnapped. I got the impression they want to be cautious about jurisdictional disputes, so they *asked* if I could help them locate Sullivan."

Stunned, Tom and Maddie were silent in order to process what Ethan said and how this information was going to impact their lives. It was Tom who broke the silence.

"What will you do about Captain Robertson?"

"That's my problem. I'm reading you into this situation, because we're a team, and I'll need you to cover for me."

"So what's the plan?" Tom asked as he continued to figure out what this meant for him, the office, and his future.

Maddie wasn't quite so discreet.

"How the hell do they think we can do that with everything else on our plate?"

"Excellent question," Ethan responded. "I've got leads to follow-up. In the meantime, you two go about business as usual. Just know I have an extra assignment that may take me out of the office, and I'll depend on you to give the captain a believable story if he asks."

"That we can do," replied Maddie looking forward to handling the captain.

"Our job is to find out who murdered Richard Kent, and I, alone, will work on the whereabouts of Steven Sullivan."

"Sheriff, do you think he can be found?" Maddie asked, knowing full well what would happen to the man if drug lords were involved. She shivered at the thought.

"We hope he can be found. I certainly don't want the alterative," was all Ethan could say in response. "Now, let's get back to work!"

~

After listening to the information Tom found in the cold case files, Caitlyn headed back to her aunt's house. She needed to clear her head and decide what she would do about her part of the investigation. When she drove into the driveway, she noticed a familiar car parked by the front steps.

"Hello?" Caitlyn yelled as she entered the house.

"Caitlyn, we're in the kitchen. Come on back," Aunt Myra responded.

Caitlyn made her way to the kitchen where she found her aunt and Verna Adams sitting at the table near the bow window that looked out onto the back yard.

"Would you like to join us for lunch?" Myra asked.

"No, thanks. You two go ahead. I'll grab something after I've done some work." Eyeing the fresh berries on the counter, Caitlyn added, "When it's time for dessert, let me know and I'll join you."

Once settled on the bed with her laptop, instead of logging into her client's project, she instead thought about Matt Miller, the reporter she had contacted last spring. She wondered if he'd have any information on the current drug problem. She poised her fingers over the keyboard and drafted what to say.

Matt: You may not remember me, but we corresponded last spring when the hydraulic fracturing bill was working its way through the state senate. The current issue I am concerned about is regarding the flood of illegal drugs into Central New York. Crime is on the increase. Peoples' lives are being destroyed. What's the state's response? I've heard one idea is to set up treatment centers. Is there any talk of putting resources towards stopping drugs from entering the state and addressing the root cause? It seems a vicious cycle as many of those going through the centers return to drug use. Is there something I'm missing?

Her phrasing was awkward, but she hoped Matt would get the idea.

It took a lot of emotional energy to compose the note to Matt Miller, so instead of getting back to her client's annual report her attention turned to the thought of the sweet tart combination of a raspberry shortcake that awaited her in the kitchen. It must be near the time her aunt would serve dessert.

Her phone vibrated against the bedspread. She picked it up, seeing it was her friend Abbie calling.

"Hi, Abbie, what's up?"

"One of our seasonal workers just collapsed. We've called the paramedics. Please come."

~ FIFTY ~

The paramedics were gone by the time Caitlyn arrived at the winery. She hadn't passed them on the road, so they must have worked fast getting the person into the ambulance and rushed to the hospital. There was nothing for Caitlyn to do except to calm Abbie, and she suspected that was the only reason she was called.

Abbie ran towards her as she walked into the processing area where the grape harvest was automatically being dumped into huge vats, ready for crushing. The works milled around, upset by the events.

"What happened?" Caitlyn asked.

"Oh, it's so horrible. Poor girl. And Tim's on campus today," Abbie sobbed.

Caitlyn put her arm around Abbie and walked her towards the tasting room. When she looked back, she noticed the foreman talking with the workers, easing them back to their jobs.

"Who collapsed?" Caitlyn asked, trying to get Abbie under control.

"It's Lizzie. Lizzie Bradley. She's a college student. Working here part-time," Abbie responded between gasps.

"I remember her. She poked her head in to speak to you the day I arrived. You said she was doing well with recovery. Are you sure it's drug related?"

"I wasn't. Not until I heard the paramedics talking. They were saying they were out of naloxone, and were discussing how they should handle the situation. Apparently, when drug use became widespread, the pharmaceutical companies raised the price of the naloxone. The price increase is taking a huge chunk out of the local

216

budget, so fewer doses are ordered. By the end of the month they don't have that lifesaving option. What's our world coming to?"

"I'm so sorry. I didn't know. Why would the drug companies do such a thing?" Caitlyn asked.

Abbie gave her a look.

"Yeah, I know. Money," Caitlyn replied. "Irresponsible, unethical actions of big pharma. I hope Lizzie makes it."

"So do I," Abbie said, her sobs subsiding.

~

The task force members were annoyed because they were asked to attend a meeting on Monday as well as Friday. They agreed the task force's charge was critical, but they had jobs to do, businesses to run, and couldn't afford the time away.

They were getting impatient with the chitchat while waiting for the meeting to be called to order. Neither the captain nor Brian Philips had shown up yet.

Ethan's phone vibrated, so he pulled it out, held it down against his hip and saw it was a text from Caitlyn. He read her note with interest and alarm. A worker at the winery overdosed. He wondered how that could have happened. Wasn't there oversight, a foreman? Though he supposed the person could have gone into the bathroom to take a hit. This whole business was so out of control.

He heard a stir, and realized the meeting had started with Brian Philips's arrival.

"I thank everyone for being patient, and I apologize for the late start. I had to take an important call. Captain Robertson's niece was taken to the hospital. Suspected drug overdose. That information is for your ears only. He has gone to the hospital, so he won't be attending today. He asked that we get on with business; our task has taken on a new level of urgency."

Unless there was another overdose victim, and these days it could be, Ethan knew who had overdosed at the winery. The crisis now hit one of their own, and members of the task force would be pressured into making decisions before due diligence was done. This would be an even more difficult situation than he thought.

~

Caitlyn returned to her aunt's house and asked Summit if he was ready for a walk. She had helped Abbie regain control of her emotions, and was taking charge. Caitlyn left when Abbie headed to the pressing room to talk with the foreman. He was a good guy, and would make sure that Abbie and her employees were okay. Production would continue.

Summit met her at the door, with Aunt Myra close behind.

"Caitlyn, I looked all over for you when we were ready for our raspberry shortcakes," Myra said.

"Sorry, Aunt Myra. There was a medical emergency at the winery. Tim is teaching today, so Abbie needed moral support. I'm disappointed about missing out on those delicious looking shortcakes," Caitlyn responded.

"No problem. I saved one for you. Come into the kitchen and tell me about what's happening at the winery," Myra said, taking Caitlyn's arm.

Summit looked on. She had said w-a-l-k, but she didn't mean it. He plopped down on the floor by the front door, head on his outstretched paws and waited. He'd do his best to make her feel guilty.

~

The meeting was finally coming to a close after a number of ideas had been shared. Ethan wondered if the willingness to talk was because the captain was not in attendance. His attention was drawn back to the meeting as Pamela took the floor.

"In case you don't remember, I'm Pamela West, and I work as a campus safety office at the university. In that position I've had the opportunity to meet and talk with a number of our professors. The topic of the day, of course, is student drug use. I recently read an article by one of our professors that I want to share with you. In that article he states that we have become a lonely society. If a person doesn't have connections, or what he terms healthy relationships, then they are more likely to turn to drugs. He suggests we need to decriminalize drugs, and focus on helping these people

218

have purpose, like jobs. I want this task force to include that portion in the plans for addiction recovery."

Ethan nodded agreement. Pamela made sense. But, again, it all came down to funding and trained personnel to turn these lives around. Ethan looked around the table to see if anyone else had anything to add. Otherwise, the meeting should be over. A clerk came in and handed Brian a note.

"Before we adjourn, I have to tell you that Lizzie Bradley died moments ago from a drug overdose. She wasn't able to get the naloxone in time to save her life."

~ FIFTY-ONE ~

Her sweet tooth satisfied, and the dog walked, Caitlyn turned her attention to her workload. Two messages from clients awaited her, and the deadline loomed for an annual report. Pressure was building. She had to spend more time on her clients and less time trying to make things right in Riverview.

She tried to concentrate on her client's annual report, but her thoughts kept returning to Steven Sullivan. What happened to him? Was he still alive? She shuddered. She *had* to do something. A light bulb went off. She'd type up the notes she took when they talked with Dr. Jordan, Tracy Connor, and Deborah Kent. There must be something in those conversations to give her a clue. The process of writing always showed you what you were missing. She'd also include her thoughts and observations of when she and Ethan had searched Steven's office.

Caitlyn forced her attention back to the annual report when a red number 1 appeared over her laptop's email icon. An email arrived; she hoped it wasn't another anxious client asking for a progress report.

Her hand hovered over the mouse as she debated whether to open the email, or to ignore it for now. Maybe better to keep working on the current project than taking time to communicate with another client. However, curiosity got the better of her. She clicked on the icon, and was relieved to see the note was from Matt Miller, the reported she had emailed.

~

Caitlyn: I do remember you. It was your intervention that helped save the Catskills from a disastrous situation. Because of my articles on that situation I was asked to take over as the editor of Watchdog, *an online newsletter.*

220

You're correct about the drug epidemic. The stats are coming in from every state, and my staff is having a difficult time keeping up with the latest information. The governor tasked the state senate to develop a plan. Whether that can be done without party politics getting in the way is the question. This issue has so many tentacles I don't think the senate has any idea how to stop or even slow down the infiltration. You understand the control the money interests have.

Your idea of getting at the root cause, other than those who were prescribed pain relief and then became addicted, is interesting. I'll put a staff member on that.

In closing, I view the drug situation as one person standing on the railroad tracks facing a huge locomotive bearing down. That person ends up as a spot on the rails. My warning to you is to not be that spot. – Matt

~

Matt's email ended with the ominous warning. She was good at reading between the lines, so she read his note again. He was telling her that although she had played a role in derailing the plans of unethical Wall Street bankers and certain state congressmen, she was lucky she wasn't harmed. This situation was one in which she should stay clear. He was telling her it was too dangerous.

Caitlyn sat back on her bed where she'd been cross-legged working on her laptop. She put the laptop aside, straightened and shook her legs to get the circulation going again, and rested her back against the pile of decorative pillows. This case was getting complicated: A corpse with a deadly amount of synthetic heroin in his system; Abbie's uncle gone missing, and now Matt Miller issuing a serious warning.

Her phone buzzed again. She saw it was Abbie.

"Caitlyn, Lizzie died."

~ FIFTY-TWO ~

Caitlyn was devastated to learn the news of Lizzie Bradley's death. She asked if Abbie needed her to come over, but since Tim had come home, Abbie just wanted to be alone with him.

Caitlyn suggested a late afternoon walk along the gorge that she felt would help Abbie with her grieving process. Abbie agreed that it would be good to get away for a while.

~

As soon as Abbie got in the car, Caitlyn said, "I'm so sorry to hear about Lizzie's death. You did everything you could for her, you know."

Abbie wiped a tear.

"Yes, I keep telling myself that, but it's just not right. She was such a wonderful person."

Caitlyn put her hand on Abbie's arm, giving her permission to cry and she need not to say anything more.

"So, where are you taking me?" Abbie asked, needing to change the subject.

"We're going to the state park to walk one my favorite trails," Caitlyn replied. "The walk will give us time to clear our heads. We don't need to talk if you don't want to," Caitlyn said.

She pulled into the park and followed the winding road to an out of the way parking lot where a few pick-up trucks were clustered at one end.

Have others found this trail, or are fishermen taking advantage of every last minute of fishing season?

Grabbing jackets, Caitlyn said, "The most beautiful glen is a short walk away. When I was a teenager I found solace walking these pine needle covered paths. I love being surrounded by nature, by the quiet, and watching the water. Not many people know about this part of the trail. It was cut off from the main trail years ago," Caitlyn explained. "I know Summit will love it!"

Abbie looked unconvinced.

"Okay, if you say so," Abbie said as she unhooked her seat belt. "Are you sure we won't get in trouble?"

Caitlyn gave her a sideways glance.

"You, who have no qualms about breaking into a closed federal facility are anxious about a closed state park trail?"

"Point taken," Abbie responded as she zipped her fleece jacket right up to her neck, though she didn't look convinced.

As usual, Summit continued to pace back and forth on the back seat, looking out one window, then the one opposite. He was going to experience new and exciting smells again today.

Caitlyn placed Summit on the well-worn path that led to the glen. She noted the sign stating dogs were to be on leash. Even though the trail was closed, she obeyed the sign, just in case. She attached the leash to his collar, for now.

"Sorry, fella. I forgot there might be leash laws in the park. Maybe as we get further into the glen and don't run into anyone, I can let you off leash," Caitlyn explained.

Summit seemed to understand as he stood still while she attached his leash. Or maybe he didn't care whether he was leashed or not. Just being in a new place with all the new smells might be enough.

It didn't take long for Caitlyn's stress to lift. The soft pine covered path that wound through the rocky glen worked its magic once again. They walked on in silence, each with her own thoughts, stopping occasionally to wait as Summit did his research.

A half-mile down one of the paths, Caitlyn stumbled when she realized Summit halted. A low growl came from his throat. Abbie sensed the lack of movement, stopped and turned with a questioning look on her face. Summit didn't usually growl, so this interruption in the silence gave them a start.

Caitlyn's internal warning system was activated. She trusted Summit's instincts. Something was awry, though she didn't know if the danger were human or animal. She stood still and for the first time noticed the surroundings. She had been so into her thoughts with head down, watching the path so she didn't trip, she didn't realize how far they had traveled into the glen. Up ahead, to the right, appeared to be a small building. It was one of the park's storage sheds. Why was Summit upset about that? Then she heard voices.

"Where are we?" Abbie whispered as she looked around. "Do you believe we were both so intent on our own thoughts we have no idea where we are?"

"We know where we are," Caitlyn whispered back, though not convinced of that. "We're still on one of the park's trails, so all we have to do is turn around and head back."

Despite Caitlyn's sage advice, they knew it wasn't true. They'd meandered onto trails that branched off the main one.

They listened to the voices coming from the shed. They were not park employees discussing maintenance issues. Against their better judgment, they stayed and listened, and then they heard words that frightened them.

~

Caitlyn debated what to do. She picked Summit up and tucked him under her coat, holding him close to silence his growl. She prayed he wouldn't bark. He could be vocal when the situation warranted.

Without thinking, she decided to find out what was going on in that building. She waved Abbie back, a motion Abbie was only too happy to obey.

"Where are you going?" Abbie whispered. "We need to get out of here!"

Caitlyn put her finger over her mouth signaling Abbie to be quiet. She continued to hold Summit under her coat so he couldn't see, with one hand around his muzzle. She prayed he'd understand;

that he'd know it was important to stay quiet, even in this dangerous situation.

She crept closer to the cabin, staying low so she wouldn't be seen or heard. She was finally in a position where she could hear at least some of what was being said.

~

Harvey Davis felt confident this meeting would go as planned. He surveyed the mangy looking crew that sat before him in the park's abandoned storage shed, and he didn't trust a one.

Harvey was sent to this location to manage the drug traffic between New York City and Buffalo. The route up the Hudson, then west on the Erie Canal served the major cities along the way, but now the company wanted to control the inland route, servicing the small towns through the central part of the state. To pave the way, the cartel controlling that route had to be run out. The men sitting in front of him would make that happen.

Harvey cleared his throat to get their attention.

"Glad ya'all could make it here, and find this place. Wasn't easy, was it," he laughed.

The men sat with arms crossed. They weren't in the mood for jokes. They were here to discuss business and to get out.

"This abandoned state park building was chosen for its isolation, so relax."

You know why you were chosen for this meeting. Not all drivers have the delivery options you enjoy." He let that sink in. They understood. Play by the rules and the rewards would come.

The men stole glances around the room, verifying what Harvey was telling them. They still looked uncomfortable, so Harvey got down to business.

"Our products travel the waterways between New York and Buffalo, and that has served us well getting to major cities along the way, as well as into Canada. But we have to stay alert. We can't let our guard down. We can't have a repeat of the bust a few years ago when thirty of our guys from the Bronx were taken by surprise and arrested in a small town north of Albany. That situation can't be

225

repeated. Our job is to disrupt and then destroy the Suarez cartel that's shipping product through the center of the state."

The men stirred in their seats. They were impatient. Meetings weren't their thing. Action and violence were. Harvey needed to keep their attention for a few more minutes.

"There are federal agents assigned to this area."

He got their attention. They liked nothing better than to take out government agents. This was such an important point he repeated it. He hoped they were listening because he had specific instructions.

"Federal agents are being sent to this area. We need to ferret them out and learn what they know about the cartels operating in the state."

Harvey spread out a map on the table next to him. The men approached, and when all were gathered around, Harvey explained the details of the attack while pointing to the geographic areas on the map. He wasn't dealing with mental giants, and he was sure they had no idea what New York State look liked. They needed visuals.

"Okay, men, you know your targets. Let's meet back here in three days, six p.m. sharp."

With nothing more to say, the men left the building.

When Harvey was sure the men were well down the path, he took out his cell phone and called her.

"Mission accomplished ma'am."

~

Caitlyn couldn't believe what she overheard. Was this happening or was it preparation for a movie? The meeting ended, and she heard the rustle of the men as they prepared to leave. She knew she couldn't get away without them seeing her and Abbie. And what to do with Summit? She knew she wouldn't be able to control him once the men came out the door.

Her heart pounded as she backed further into the bushes and tried to figure out how to make herself and her dog invisible, and how to get word to Abbie.

~

The men left the small outbuilding in a rush, without saying a word. With instructions in hand, their passion for blood was difficult to control. They were intent on getting out of this wilderness, so they didn't take notice of anyone else on the path. They only stopped when the path ended and the parking lot began. Their pick-up trucks were where they left them, but now there was another car, a light green Prius. They looked at each other. They'd not met anyone on the trail, and so where was the owner of this car? At that point they heard voices coming from a trail that ran off to the south. The owners of the car were on another trail and were heading back. The men hurried to their vehicles and drove out of the parking lot before the hikers saw them.

~

Caitlyn held Summit tight as she watched the last person exit the building. She assumed he was the leader as he was busy talking on his cell phone. She wished she could hear the conversation.

When he passed by a safe distance, Caitlyn untangled herself from the bushes and motioned for Abbie to do the same.

"What was that all about?" Abbie asked.

"I'm not sure, but I know it isn't good," Caitlyn replied. "I think these guys are part of a drug cartel that's planning some kind of confrontation with another one." She pulled out her phone and touched Ethan's number.

"Voicemail. Darn!" She sent a text. If Ethan's phone was on vibrate, it'd catch his attention. Then she remembered. He was probably in his meeting.

~ FIFTY-THREE ~

Caitlyn woke, uncertain of the day or time. Sweat had drenched her nightgown. She glanced at the clock—one o'clock. She sat up in bed, took deep breaths in order to keep her heart from exploding through her chest. As she brought her body back from the brink of a full-blown anxiety attack, she attempted to capture every detail of the nightmare. She remembered being trapped in a dark place, but the nature of dreams doesn't always allow you to know how you got there and usually ends before you get yourself safely out. Someone was with her, not someone she was afraid of, but danger lurked in the darkness.

She tried to make sense of it. She was sure this nightmare came from her scare in the gorge, and then the fact she and Abbie had explored the abandoned military depot. Those two experiences, besides the anxiety over the disappearance of Abbie's uncle, had clashed into one humongous nightmare.

~

Ethan had answered her text about what she had overheard in the gorge. He chastised her for walking on a closed trail—it was closed for a reason, yada, yada, and then he went on about what a dangerous situation she had put herself and Abbie into and when will she learn to stay in safer environments. After he vented, he thanked her for the information and said he would report this to the task force. She didn't hear from him again and that was okay. She didn't need to be beaten around the head and shoulders any more.

~

Putting Ethan's admonition aside, she now thought, *what if*. What if her dream held the key? Was Steven Sullivan trapped in a place *like* one of those igloos? And if so, why? If the drug cartel was responsible, why would they keep him alive? She didn't have an answer—except for her dream, and she was sure her subconscious was trying to tell her something.

Caitlyn slipped out of bed, careful not to wake Summit. She didn't want him along. It was too dangerous. She pulled on a pair of jeans, her navy blue turtleneck, and a dark blue sweatshirt. With socks and shoes in hand, she opened the door and made her way downstairs. She had to find out if this **strong** feeling was true, and if not, she'd be back in bed within an hour, and no one the wiser. She was thankful once again for her Prius that would start without a sound. Her aunt wouldn't hear a thing.

In the car, Caitlyn had second thoughts. If her instincts were right, it would be a dangerous situation. She hated to admit it, but she needed to include Ethan. She pulled out her cell, touched his number, and prayed she could talk him into her crazy scheme.

"Hello," a groggy voice answered.

"Ethan, it's Caitlyn," she whispered. "I think I know where Steven Sullivan is. I'm going there now, but I need you to come with me. It's dangerous, but if I'm right . . ."

Ethan sat up in bed and shook himself awake. "Are you crazy? It's the middle of the night!" He yelled.

"I know," sighed Caitlyn. "Please humor me. If I'm wrong, you can be back asleep within the hour. But if I'm right, we could save Steven's life."

The pause was so long, Caitlyn thought he had hung up.

"Okay. Stop by here. I'll be on the front porch waiting," Ethan said without enthusiasm.

"Thanks, Ethan," Caitlyn responded as she touched the disconnect icon before he changed his mind.

She picked him up a few minutes later and they drove towards the lake in silence. At the intersection she turned north along the lake road and drove for another few miles.

229

"So how mad at me are you?" Caitlyn asked, breaking the silence.

"I'll let you know tomorrow," Ethan replied as he sipped his bottled water. He was not in the mood for chitchat.

Caitlyn got the message and drove on, hoping she'd remember how to find the turnoff in the dark. On her previous trip Abbie had given directions, and since they were talking all the way, Caitlyn hadn't paid close attention.

She recognized the road as she went by it, so she drove into the next driveway to turn around. There wasn't much traffic this time of night, and for that she was thankful. She turned down the dirt road and passed by a chain link fence with "No Trespassing" signs posted every few feet. The place looked even creepier in the dark, and she felt the first inkling of fear.

Once on the dirt road, the only sound she heard was that of tall weeds scratching the car's undercarriage. It must have rained earlier, because her tires were slipping in the soft earth. She prayed she wouldn't get stuck. When she reached the parking area where she and Abbie had accessed the property. Caitlyn had second thoughts. Ethan was right. It was crazy to be here in the middle of the night.

She turned to look at Ethan and hoped he wouldn't confirm what she was thinking and talk her out of going any further. If he did, was she determined enough to follow her instincts? Would she wander around this property in the dark, trying to find her way back to the igloos? The answer was no, and her dream of searching for and possibly finding Steven Sullivan would be dashed.

She'd done it again. Gone off on a lark because she was so damned determined to do things her way. This little venture might get them killed and no one would find them. Ever.

What kept her resolve was if she *was* right, they'd find Steven Sullivan, and just maybe they'd save his life—assuming they didn't lose theirs first.

~ FIFTY-FOUR ~

Ethan hadn't spoken the entire ride.

"This is where Abbie brought me the other day. We walked the path to where some of the igloos are. The igloos were from . . ."

"I know what the igloos are and I know what this property is. And, there's a *No Trespassing* sign over there. This is private property, you know," Ethan said, annoyed. Not only had Caitlyn dragged him out into the middle of nowhere in the middle of the night, because she had a 'feeling,' but now she wanted him, a law enforcement officer, to trespass.

"I know, and I'm sorry, but my intuition tells me Steven Sullivan might be in one of those igloos. It's been several days since he's gone missing. Time is running out if he's still alive," Caitlyn responded. She realized she was begging, and her reasoning was weak, but she didn't care. The feeling was so strong she couldn't ignore it. She gathered her bag that held a flashlight, bottled water, and some bandages.

"I'll go with you, but you realize, don't you, that we don't have time to search the entire property. This place is 11,000 acres. Do you see how futile this search will be?"

Caitlyn stared ahead at the fence she planned to breach. Ethan was right. By the time they reached the igloos, they wouldn't have much time at all before daybreak, and Ethan would be expected back at work. And if Steven were in there, it'd be by luck he'd be in one of the first ones they searched. But they were here; they had to try.

"Let's check the first few, and if nothing, then we'll return and we can talk about another plan of attack, deal?" Caitlyn asked.

"Deal," Ethan said as he climbed out of the car and looked for the flap in the fence to allow them entry onto the Seneca Ordnance.

Ethan and Caitlyn looked at each other, and without saying what they were thinking, both thought *here goes.*

With the help of their flashlights, they found the tear in the fence and folded the flap over. She pulled a twist tie from her pocket to keep the flap open.

Caitlyn went through the fence first, with Ethan following. They were careful not to tear their clothes on the barbed ends. Once onto the property, Caitlyn oriented herself to the direction she and Abbie had taken. She remembered a path, so she waved the flashlight back and forth along the ground until she saw a remnant.

It seemed to Caitlyn as though they'd been walking forever, but looking at her watch, it was only fifteen minutes.

Those buildings should be close.

The igloos were covered with earth and grass, so they didn't stand out from the landscape. They'd have to look carefully or they'd walk right past them.

A glint from the quarter moon hit the concrete blocks, which warned Caitlyn they were close. She remembered something Abbie said as they walked. There were five hundred of these buildings. If Steven Sullivan *were* here, finding him would be like finding a needle in a haystack. If he *were* here *and* still alive, this time of night he'd be asleep. He wouldn't hear them if they walked through the property calling his name. And if he *were* here, he'd be under guard or dead. If under guard, the guard would have weapons. Her plan was futile.

She turned to Ethan to voice her concern, but noticed he had walked ahead of her. He was walking along the structures one row at a time, listening at each one, and then knocking to see if anyone responded.

Caitlyn took the opposite side, doing the same. An hour passed. She lost count of the number of igloos they checked. There was no sign of life. She looked at her watch; they should head back soon.

As she turned to head back to the car, hoping she was going in the right direction, she tripped over an outcropping. She went down hard.

"Ow!" Caitlyn cried out. She pushed herself up, and then bent over to dust off the front of her jeans. She focused the flashlight first on her hand, and then her right leg as she checked for scratches. She noticed a small cut, but it wasn't bleeding too much. She'd put a Band-Aid on it later.

It was then she heard a sound.

Ethan heard it too. He rushed over to help steady her.

"Did you hear something?" He asked.

"Yes," Caitlyn responded. "What do you think?"

"Shush. Let's listen," Ethan whispered.

A scrapping noise came from the igloo on Caitlyn's side.

"Stay here," Ethan directed. He walked around the building, shining his flashlight up and down the sides to attract the least amount of attention.

~

Unusual for Caitlyn, she did as she was told. She was sure the sound they heard was not from nature, not raccoons scavenging in the night. It definitely was a scrapping noise. Both fear and hope clenched her heart.

When the sound came again she focused on it. It came from the metal structure on her left. She couldn't wait any longer. She picked up her flashlight that had remained on after hitting the ground, so it was easy to locate. She swung the flashlight around and faced the igloo. She joined Ethan as he made his way back to the front.

The large doors looked formidable, so they walked around the side and found a personnel door. She kept the flashlight pointed to the ground to ensure their footing as they approached.

Ethan placed his hand on the knob, turned it, and pushed, hard. It opened. By putting his hand out, he cautioned her to stand back while he checked the inside. She was wary of entering knowing the structure could be ridden with vermin, human or otherwise.

She took a deep breath. They'd come this far, and she was not going to let fear take control. This was her idea and she was not going to back out now.

Cautiously entering the building, with her light shining on the floor, she didn't notice that Ethan had stopped and she ran right into him. Before she could chastise him for not moving, she heard him exclaim.

Caitlyn caught her breath and prepared herself for the worst. She wasn't used to seeing dead bodies, and didn't want to see one now in the dark recesses of this abandoned munitions warehouse. With her eyes closed tightly, she felt Ethan move forward. She grabbed his shirt, and then heard shuffling and Ethan talking softly. She opened her eyes and before her, about twenty feet away, in the middle of the vast space was a man tied to a chair. His mouth was taped, his hands behind his back. He was looking at them with pleading eyes. Ethan hesitated only a second before rushing forward, pulling a knife from its Zermatt holder.

While Ethan worked at the restraints, Caitlyn asked, "Steven? Steven Sullivan?" The man nodded, then answered as Ethan ripped the tape from his mouth.

"Yes, I'm Steven Sullivan. Who are you?" He asked as he surveyed the two of them.

"I'm Caitlyn Jamison, a friend of your niece, Abbie. She's worried about you. And this is Sheriff Ethan Ewing."

Ethan finished cutting the ropes that bound Steven's hands and feet.

"What are you two doing here? Never mind. Hurry, they'll be back at daylight."

~ FIFTY-FIVE ~

They rushed out of the igloo and found the path back to the car.

"We'll use only one flashlight to keep our presence at a minimum, so walk slowly and close together," Ethan instructed. "I'll go first, Caitlyn, you follow, and then Steven, you take up the rear. If your captors are coming back, they'll come from the other direction."

"Can you walk okay?"

"I'm fine," Steven responded. "I'm lame from being tied up for so long, and from some previous injuries, but I'll make it. Let's get moving. We don't have much time before the thugs return."

At first, Caitlyn could feel Steven's presence close behind her. But then she knew he was lagging, and she suspected it was a struggle for him to keep up.

"Do you want to take my arm?" She whispered. "The ground is very rough, and I don't want you to fall."

"No, keep moving. I'm fine," he replied, his tone sharp.

Caitlyn picked up on this and replied, "You have to trust us. We're here to help."

Steven didn't respond as they continued their trek through the brush.

Caitlyn gave up trying to make him understand.

~

For the second time this evening Caitlyn was thankful for her Prius. It started without a sound, and moved down through the weed-strewn roadway with the minimum of noise. Steven sat in the front seat, Ethan in the back.

Before they got into the car, Ethan whispered to Caitlyn to take them to his house. He would question Steven there and then determine the next step.

~

Steven was silent during the drive, not sure who these two were and how they came to locate him in that remote location. He didn't trust them and didn't know for sure whether the guy was a sheriff, or someone hired from a cartel or . . .

~

Caitlyn pulled up to Ethan's house, and when stopped, Ethan opened the car door for Steven, and motioned for him to climb the steps onto the front porch.

When they were safely inside, Caitlyn said, "I can make coffee."

Ethan pointed to where she would find the kitchen, keeping his eye on Steven.

"Coffee pot is on the counter. Coffee is in the fridge. Everything is close by. I'm sure you can find what you need," he said as he ushered Steven into the living room, but before they sat down, Ethan said, "I'm sorry, I'm sure you would like to wash up first, and then we can attend to those wounds. You've had a rough few days."

"Thank you. I'm the worst for wear as you can see. I'll need to clean these wounds before infection sets in. And yes, we need to talk," Steven replied, still wary of Ethan.

~

When Steven entered the living room, Caitlyn and Ethan were sitting on the couch, the table before them laden with a coffee carafe, cups and accompaniments. Caitlyn grabbed a cup and poured one for Steven. As she handed the cup to him, she noticed some of his wounds were deep.

"Ethan, do you have any bandages?" Caitlyn asked.

"Yes. I'll get them," he replied as he headed down the hallway.

"Some of your wounds are deep. You need to get to a doctor, or the ER," Caitlyn said softly.

"That's not going to happen," Steven replied, taking the coffee cup from her and relishing the first sip.

"But . . ."

"No," Steven replied, his tone still sharp. "You bandage what you can, and then we have to move . . .fast!"

They sat in silence waiting for Ethan's return with bandages and antiseptic cream.

Caitlyn cleaned and bandaged Steven's wounds as best she could. She wished she had taken a first aid course. When done, she returned to her seat and they waited for Steven to set the tone and explain why he was tied up in that secluded place.

"First, thank you for rescuing me. I'm still not sure who you are, or if I can trust you, but it sure feels good to be out of that dreadful building."

"I am the sheriff of Riverview. My name is Ethan Ewing, and once I'm sure you are Steven Sullivan, then we can talk more specifics," Ethan responded, showing Steven his identification. "And this is Caitlyn Jamison whom you can thank for your rescue. It was her 'intuition' that took us out in the middle of the night, against my better judgment I might add."

Steven looked at Caitlyn and said, "I've never been rescued by a lovely lady before, so this is a memorable first. Thank you."

Caitlyn was pleased that Ethan gave her credit. All she could do was nod an acknowledgement to Steven. There was too much serious business to discuss and they shouldn't be wasting time on pleasantries.

~

Steven shifted in his seat. Just because this guy was a sheriff, it was no proof he wasn't controlled by a cartel.

Ethan sensed Steven's hesitation, and to stop the game playing Ethan started.

"I had a call from Don Scott of the DEA. I believe he is your boss? He sent me an overnight package that gave details of your assignment and instructions I was to locate you, dead or alive," Ethan began.

Steven sat up, his senses kicking in. Relief. He *could* trust these people.

Caitlyn, on the other hand, was shocked. She turned and stared at Ethan. He hadn't told her anything about the package. But things now made sense, the way he tried to discourage her from investigating Steven's disappearance. It was a dangerous game and he didn't want her involved. She remembered Matt Miller's admonition.

Steven took a deep breath and started, "Okay, I'll tell you what you need to know and what we need to do."

~ FIFTY-SIX ~

The sheer curtains covering Ethan's living room windows filtered the early morning sunlight. Ethan and Caitlyn sat in silence while they absorbed the information Steven Sullivan shared and knowing he was telling them only a fraction of the situation.

Caitlyn had no idea how he could be successful in stemming the drug traffic through Central New York. She never realized the depth of this business. Exhausted, she fought her body's need for rest.

"How are we going to find these criminals?" Caitlyn asked with a yawn.

"*We* will not do anything," Steven responded. "Ethan will continue his duties as sheriff, and I will work on a plan to complete my assignment."

Caitlyn was not about to be pushed aside. The fear that had almost paralyzed her a few hours before was a distant memory and her adrenalin had kicked in. She had ideas on to how to deal with the drug problem.

"I was thinking . . . I read an article that suggested addiction was tied to diet and the body's magnetism. Those deficient in folic acid, zinc, thiamin, and some other minerals I can't remember, are more susceptible to addiction. Drugs serve as a compensatory mechanism for this imbalance. Foods high in sugar and carbohydrates give people, especially in children, a feeling of euphoria, which conditions them to want to continue that feeling. Some seek it in food, with noticeable weight gain and health problems, others turn to drugs," Caitlyn explained.

"And your point?" Steven asked. They were all showing signs of fatigue, with patience and tempers running short.

239

"My point is, while you are hunting down the head of the hydra, maybe you should take into account other factors as to why people are driven to these deadly drugs," Caitlyn snapped back.

Ethan held up his hand to stop the confrontation.

"You both have good points, but I agree with Steven that you, Caitlyn, need to stay out of harm's way. I also take heed to your suggestion as to how we get to the root of the problem. We know that during a period in our history, painkillers were viewed as the miracle drug. Doctors had something to help their patients manage pain, not knowing it would create even more pain down the road in the form of addiction," Ethan added, remembering Doc Morse's confession. "We have to find the suppliers, and shut down the supply line. At the same time, we have to provide a safe haven for users who overdose or are caught. Going after root causes is not our job."

"Don't forget, we are also dealing with the dark web," Steven added. "It's not just about your friendly dealer on the street anymore or an unscrupulous doctor handing out prescriptions. Those who need these drugs can get them from various sources. I think I've figured out who the person is running the operation in Central New York and it is not who you might think."

"Who is it?" Caitlyn asked, sliding forward in her chair, forgetting how tired she was.

"I can't say," Steven replied. "But now that this person knows I know, and realizes I'm no longer in that igloo, sparks are bound to fly."

Disappointed that Steven wouldn't name the area's drug dealer, Caitlyn couldn't hold her eyes open any longer. Summit would wake soon and wonder where she was. If he scratched at the door—why hadn't she thought of that before? She had to get back to her aunt's house. She grabbed her bag, and stated, "I have to go. I hope we can talk more later." It was wishful thinking, because the men made it clear she wouldn't be in the loop. She'd see about that!

~

After Caitlyn left, Ethan turned to Steven and said, "You can't go back to Tracy's house. They, whoever 'they' are, will find you there. I think it's best you stay with me. I'll ask my deputy to get you a rental car and have it delivered here. I have a detached garage. Park in there, just in case."

"Sound's good. I'll rest a bit, and then I have to get back to work."

"I'll call Tracy and let her know you're all right. I won't tell her where you are. We don't know at this point who we can trust," Ethan responded. "Now, let's get you set up on the sleeper sofa in the den, and get a few winks. I'll call Tom and get him started on the rental. By the time you wake up, the car will be parked in the garage."

"Thanks so much, Ethan, for all your help, and for rescuing me from that horrid place. It was only a matter of time before I would no longer be of use to them."

"Let's not think about that. I'll be back later and we can decide the next steps."

"One more thing, if you don't mind. Since you are in contact with my superiors, can you notify them with an 'A-OK?' And then get my stuff from the house?"

"Sure. Consider both things done," Ethan responded. "Now, get some rest."

~ FIFTY-SEVEN ~

Verna parked her car two blocks away from Doug Mitchell's house. She needed the walk to emotionally prepare for the meeting.

Doug said he had more information to share. She sat in her car, looking up the street, and was no longer sure she wanted to know what he had to say. The need to know had kept her going, and if truth be told there was also comfort in not knowing. She remembered her mother saying, "If ignorance isn't bliss, I don't know what it is." And her mother was usually right.

Verna got out of her car, locked it, and with a straight spine walked up the street to the office of the town historian.

~

Doug Mitchell whistled as he put the teakettle on to boil. He was excited about sharing information on his first assignment. Genealogy research is never finished, and this project certainly wasn't, with the number of boxes he still had to go through. But he'd found enough about Verna's ancestry that he couldn't wait to share it with her.

The teakettle whistled just as the doorbell rang. He turned off the burner, straightened the digestives he had arranged on a plate, and ran to welcome his client.

"Hello Verna. It's so nice to see you," Doug said, with a bounce in his step.

"Yes, you too," she murmured. She pulled herself together. Stiff upper lip and all that.

"Please, come in. We'll sit in our living room, because," as he swept his hand around his office still littered with boxes—most had been opened with papers spilling out—"this room is still a work in progress," he laughed.

Verna smiled, nodded, and followed him into the living room, which she agreed was a much more comfortable area.

"I've made us some tea. Let me get that, and then we'll get down to business," Doug said with a smile.

Verna wished the man weren't so cheerful. Her mood was in stark contrast. He must think she was a strange duck.

She sat, head down, hands clasped in her lap, as if she waited for what she considered something similar to a jury verdict.

She watched Doug arrange the tea service on the table in front of them. He poured a cup and handed it to her.

"I'll be right back. Have to get my folders."

Verna's nerves were firing giving her eye a slight twitch. She steadied her hand so as not to spill her tea.

Be calm, my dear, her conscience said. This was the moment for which she had long waited. Or was it? Again, doubts crept in. Did she really want to know what happened to her brother or was it more about the chase?

"It was fun tracing your family," Doug stated.

"I'm glad you enjoyed the research," she replied. She hesitated, "Did you find any information on my brother?"

"Not yet."

Doug noted Verna's concerned expression and continued, "I'm still working on that portion, but as you saw from the mess in my office, I have many papers to go through. However, I have traced your family history, which I think will help us put together the pieces of your brother's life."

Verna nodded, giving Doug permission to continue.

"I used several sources to trace your family," he said as he pulled a family group sheet from one of the folders. "When tracing a family, you need to start with the living person. That's why when we first met I asked you for the names and geographic locations of every family member you remembered. I used that information to trace the census back every year from 1940."

"Why not from a later year?" Verna asked.

"For privacy reasons, census data is available starting seventy-two years ago and earlier. Each census asks for different information, but the main reason for the census is to determine representation in the House of Representatives. I bet you didn't know that!"

Doug noted from Verna's expression she didn't care about why the census was taken, so he continued.

"I located your parents and then their parents, going back every ten years, finding the next generation. It was helpful that they stayed in New York State, because from 1825 through 1925 New York took their own census on the five's, except when they did it in 1892, for some reason."

"And why do we care about that?"

"Because the 1890 federal census was destroyed by fire," Doug replied, getting exasperated with Verna's lack of enthusiasm for all the work he had done.

"How does this help with finding Palle?" Verna asked, no longer hiding her annoyance.

Doug moved forward on his seat and said, "Verna, I think it's important to know about your ancestors, because it's that stock from which *you come*. Further, this process lets me look at the branches on your tree, which include, whether you like it or not, Palle's wife, Edda."

"I wish we didn't have to go there," Verna replied.

"I know," Doug said. "But it's necessary. It is quite a story. I used a lot of sources. It was good training," he said with a chuckle. He glanced up from his paperwork and noted Verna wasn't smiling.

"Oh, sorry. I know this is serious business for you. Guess I got carried away."

"That's okay. I'm a bit anxious. It's been a long time, you know."

The silence said it all. Doug pulled out the first folder and spread out the family tree he prepared for Verna. He figured he would start introducing her to her ancestors. He would then go into some background, before giving her the news that she waited so long to learn.

Doug cleared his throat.

"Verna, Your family has a wonderful history. They go back to the Walloons who settled in the Hudson Valley in the 1600s."

Verna didn't want to deflate Doug and make light of the research he'd done, because he was delighted with his findings. She didn't care a whit about her ancestors. She cared about her brother, and that was what she asked Doug to find out. It was obvious he had gotten sidetracked with the project. On second thought, it might be worthwhile to get ancestral information on Edda to see if in fact the family lore was correct about the Villettas.

Doug waited for Verna's response and realized the family ancestor sheets he prepared did not contain the information she desired. He kicked himself for getting distracted and going down a research path that his client didn't want or need.

Doug put the papers down on the table and sighed.

"I'm sorry, Verna. I got so caught up in the easy part, tracing back through the census, and reading books online through *Google Books* or *Archive.org* that I didn't come up with the information you wanted. It's not so easy to research in the near times, but there are ways, and I promise you I will find out what they are and when you come back I will have information on Palle," Doug assured her. At this point he didn't want to tell her he actually had found Palle buried in the family cemetery. He wanted to collect more information on Palle's life before he shared that with her.

"That's okay. This is interesting. Do you mind if I take these papers home? I'd like time to study them," Verna replied, giving Doug a weak smile.

"Yes, please, and I hope you enjoy reading what I found."

Verna gathered her things, turned to Doug, and said, "Thanks. I look forward to hearing from you."

~ FIFTY-EIGHT ~

Caitlyn felt a headache coming on. She'd been able to sneak into the house without her aunt knowing, and thankfully Summit was still sound asleep. If nothing else, he was a good sleeper.

She slept a couple of hours before she woke from the adrenalin that flowed through her system. She realized how isolated she was from the realities of the world around her. When she read about the problems with drug abuse, it was as though this wasn't *her* world and it was easy to keep an arm's length from the victims and the suffering. Not any more. She now faced reality from what Steven shared in the brief time they were together last night. The suffering of the victims, their families, friends and colleagues could no longer be calculated. It was off the chart.

She hoped the fresh air during her walk with Summit would relieve the pain in her head. Before she left the house, she grabbed a cup of coffee. If those two things didn't work, she'd have to make a trip into town for some aspirin. Her aunt left a note on the table saying she was at an early morning exercise class and that if Caitlyn went into Renwick, could she pick up a few things at the grocery store.

Looks like I'll have to go into town anyway, Caitlyn thought with a sigh. What she wanted to do after walking Summit was to crawl back under the covers, but that was no longer an option.

~

Caitlyn found a parking spot only a block away from the drug store. She walked up and down a few aisles before finding the over--the-counter pain relievers. As she turned to orient herself, she noticed Mr. Johansson in the back corner of the pharmacy in a serious conversation with someone. If only she could see who it was. His mannerisms were not that of a pharmacist advising a patient. Instead, he seemed anxious, agitated. She wondered whom he was talking to and what the conversation was about? There was something about that man. She walked down another aisle to see if she could find a better position to overhear the conversation. She found just the right spot and pretended to focus on the items in front of her.

~

"Can I help you find something?" A voice behind her said.

Caitlyn jumped and turned, coming face-to-face with a pimply-faced teenage boy who wore a green apron with the logo 'Johansson's Pharmacy' across the front. His nametag told her his name was "Billy." His long blondish hair flopped over his forehead, but what she noticed the most was a cowlick that stood straight up at the top of his head. Startled by his approach, Caitlyn controlled herself from laughing at his appearance. It was then, for the first time, she noticed the merchandise she was standing next to in order to listen in on Mr. Johansson's conversation. The shelving unit right next to the pharmacy was filled with all varieties of condoms.

Caitlyn's face turned red, and she stuttered, "Oh, no thank you. I was looking for aspirin."

The young man tried to hide his smile.

"Right this way, miss. That's down aisle eight," as he led the way. He was used to customers like her.

As Caitlyn turned to follow the young clerk, she caught a glimpse of the person Mr. Johansson was talking with, and the word "warehouse." This was the same person Ethan wanted to avoid the night they had dinner at the lake.

Brian Philips.

~ FIFTY-NINE ~

Ethan strolled into the office as if arriving late were a normal event. He nodded a good morning to Maddie, and noticed her head nod towards the reception area. Ethan turned and saw a young man sitting there.

Damn! He didn't have the time or patience for citizen complaints this morning.

The man stood up and offered his hand. Ethan approached and shook the man's hand, introducing himself.

"Good morning, sir. I'm Sheriff Ewing. What can I do for you?"

"Good morning, Sheriff. It might be what I can do for you. I'm Matt Miller, the editor of *Watchdog,* an online newspaper that tracks events happening in the state."

I should have known the media would catch up with us.

Ethan had been lulled into a false sense of security with media requests directed to the public relations department at the main precinct. So far, reporters had not honed in on Riverview, and for that he was grateful.

Ethan stood with arms crossed. He would not get into a game with this guy about information sharing.

"I suspect you know a woman by the name of Caitlyn Jamison?" Matt inquired, watching Ethan's expression.

Now I know why this guy is here.

Ethan was furious with Caitlyn for sharing information with a reporter. He thought she'd know better. Keeping his anger under control, he replied, "Yes, I know Ms. Jamison. What does she have to do with you being here?"

"Well, actually, nothing. She was in touch with me about what progress the state was making on some legislation. I wasn't able to tell her much. Then I noticed an AP bulletin come across about a death in Riverview of State Senator Richard Kent's son. That's news, and from what I could find, no one had any detailed information about this young man's death. So, I thought I'd drive down and talk to you myself. Things are much better done in person, don't you think?"

Ethan was cornered. The guy had a point, and Ethan's policy was to always talk to the press. Give them something. Because if you didn't, they'd either make it up or get it wrong. He believed a good relationship with the media was healthy for everyone, even if the top brass didn't think so. That was especially true in this situation where the victim was the son of a state senator. There could be repercussions. For some reason Ethan trusted Matt Miller, and saw him as a potential ally.

And he should not have misjudged Caitlyn.

"Okay, come on back. I can give you some information, but as you know, I can't share everything as we are continuing with the investigation."

The two men walked to Ethan's office, and as they passed Tom's desk, Ethan noted Tom had picked up on the conversation. Good.

~

Ethan saw Matt Miller to the office door and they shook hands. A partnership had formed, and Ethan was sure that partnership would benefit them both. In the current climate, the press focused on selling stories, not investigative journalism. Matt Miller was different.

Ethan watched Matt leave, and noticed a hesitation before he composed himself, and then walked swiftly out the door. Ethan studied the two men in the waiting room to see what had disturbed the reporter.

A well-dressed man sat in the waiting area. Another man, with suit and tie, stood near the door, surveying the office. The seated

249

gentleman glanced at Matt as he passed by, and as soon as Matt was out the door, the gentleman stood and came toward Ethan with hand out.

"I'm Richard Kent, Sr. and you must be Sheriff Ewing?"

"That's correct. You are the victim's father, I assume. I am very sorry for your loss."

"Thank you. I'm here to talk to you about your investigation."

"I'm afraid you'll need to talk with Captain Robertson in Renwick. He is covering all the press inquiries and has a liaison assigned to talk with the family," Ethan replied.

Richard Kent, Sr. looked around the office, noting Maddie and Tom. He turned to Ethan and said, "Do you mind if we talk in your office?"

Ethan was stuck. There was no way he could turn down the senator's request, at least without repercussions.

"Sure, come in," Ethan said to the senator while noting the other man at the door.

"John will stay by the door. He's with me to make sure nothing happens, if you know what I mean," the senator explained.

Ah, his own security guard. I wonder who's paying for that?

When the senator was seated, Ethan spoke first, taking control of the situation.

"I assume you know I have ruled your son's death a homicide. I've talked with your ex-wife, and she provided me with Richard's health history and how he got hooked on drugs. I need to find out what Richard was doing on Old Mill Road, and how he got a massive overdose of drugs in his system. I also need to find out what his connection was with a man whose credit card Richard had in his pocket. Do you have any of those answers?"

"The only answer you need, Sheriff, is to not pursue this investigation. I will have my men investigate and bring the culprits to justice."

"With all due respect, Senator, you know that is not how things work."

Senator Kent ignored Ethan's response.

"It's unfortunate that Richard was unable to get off painkillers after his accident, and I blame my ex-wife for that. She should have kept a closer eye on him."

"Don't you think that is a bit unfair, Senator? Your son was a grown man. He was pursuing his degree, and your wife was teaching full time. She shouldn't be his keeper."

Senator Kent rose, indicating the conversation was over.

"You've heard my request. You are entering dangerous territory, and we are better equipped to handle the situation. I expect you to stop your investigation. I also expect that neither I nor my family will be pestered by the press."

Ah, so he did recognize Matt Miller.

Ethan rose as well. He was glad to get rid of this arrogant man.

"I will do my best to honor your request in keeping your family out of the media, but I intend to continue my investigation. Good day, sir," Ethan said as he walked the senator to the door.

~

After the senator and his security guard left, Ethan approached Tom.

"Did you get the car arranged for our guest? Any further information from Doc or Carrie on Richard Kent?" Ethan asked.

"Yes to both. Doc just called, and said they found signs of a struggle, so he's reevaluating his initial cause of death. It's interesting the senator showed up, because I was going to tell you that Doc agrees with you. The cause of death will be ruled a homicide. Doc and Carrie are gearing up for a political fight, not something they are looking forward to."

"Keep me posted on any developments. I've got to get to a task force meeting and I know this will be the number one topic. We will be under a lot of pressure to solve this. Any ideas?"

"As a matter of fact," Tom said, getting up from his chair. He walked around to the front of his desk where Ethan was standing to put them on equal footing.

"I've been thinking through the circumstances since Doc's call. None of this makes sense, unless you consider the scenario that this

251

kid bought from a trusted source, and then that source decided, for whatever reason, the risk was too great. The kid was a senator's son, after all. The source may have sold the kid a large amount to carry him over until he could find another seller. If Richard Kent was distraught about losing his source, he may have overdosed on purpose. Or, if the stuff was stronger than he was used to, it could have been an accidental overdose," Tom said.

"I agree. If the stuff was laced with fentanyl and other powerful synthetic drugs, the kid's source may have wanted to get rid of him."

Tom sighed. "Yes, I guess there're just too many possibilities, and until we locate that source, we won't have our answer."

"Let me know when the forensics are back from the knife we found at the scene. There has to be something there. And put the crime scene photos on my desk. I want to look at them again."

"Will do," Tom replied. "The good news is I'm almost done with the cold case project. I heard from one of the other departments that once the cases are digitized, each station will be assigned a few to work on. Like we have a lot of free time."

"The bureaucracy never ends. If we weren't so loaded down, it would be interesting to take on some of these cases. Maybe someday," Ethan replied. "Gotta run; task force meeting in a few minutes. Thanks, Tom."

~SIXTY ~

Fifteen minutes after Ethan left for his meeting in Renwick, Caitlyn rushed into the sheriff's office. Looking around, she said in a rush, "Where's Ethan? I've got to talk with him."

"He's gone to Renwick; you just missed him," Tom replied. "Is there something I can help you with?"

"I think I've got a connection," Caitlyn said, still breathless from her race up the steps.

"A connection to what?" Tom asked. He could never be sure what issue Caitlyn was talking about, and he didn't want to make an assumption and accidentally give out sensitive information.

"With the illegal drugs, of course," Caitlyn responded. "I overheard a conversation in the pharmacy and I think it's relevant."

"Okay." Tom picked up his phone and sent Ethan a text. "I've asked him to call you as soon as he can."

"Great. In the meantime, I've got something to check out," Caitlyn responded as she raced back out the door.

Oh lord, not again. Tom thought. He debated what to do. Should he follow her to make sure she wasn't putting herself in danger? No. Better stay put and follow-up on Ethan's instructions.

~

Caitlyn was sure she'd figured it out. Her headache forgotten, she raced back to Renwick to find the warehouse run by Brian Philips. Ethan mentioned he was one of the task force members, had a warehouse, and was donating funds for the first clinic. He was also the person she overheard talking with Mr. Johansson about warehousing, and she assumed that meant drugs. It had all come together for her. The articles Steven Sullivan was collecting on

253

unhealthy snack foods, and the maps Dr. Jordan mentioned. She bet that Steven Sullivan was zeroing in on Brian Philips, but didn't have enough information yet to act. Or did he? Was he getting too close and that was the reason he was kidnapped? So many questions—Caitlyn had to find those answers.

In trying to find the warehouse, she took a wrong turn and was lost. She pulled to the side of the road and pulled up Maps on her phone. She was able to see where she went wrong. She doubled back and found the turn that led to the warehouse.

She pulled into the parking lot and noted the size, number and color of delivery trucks parked there. She wondered if there was any significance to the differences. They all said *Philips OnTime Delivery*. She was sure Brian Philips would be at the task force meeting, so she'd be able to look around before anyone noticed her.

She sat in the car a few minutes to watch for any activity. For a supposedly busy warehouse, there didn't seem to be anyone around, at least from what she could see. She needed a cover story, and that was easy to develop. She grabbed a notebook and pen from her backpack, straightened her posture, turned her phone to vibrate, and walked into the warehouse as though she belonged there. If she ran into anyone, she'd say she was writing an article for a women's magazine.

The warehouse was a huge sprawling building containing row after row of floor to ceiling shelves. Each of those shelving sections carried a label. How in the world was she going to find any evidence of drug activity in this massive space?

~

When Ethan settled himself into a seat next to Pamela West, she was talking with one of the Renwick city officers. Ethan listened with one ear while scanning the table to see who else was there and study their body language. You could tell a lot from body language and Ethan was getting good at it. He noted the mayor was acting nervous today as he shuffled papers back and forth, eyes darting around the room. One of the other city police officers was checking his phone for messages and looking particularly bored. When the pharmacist, Johansson walked in, Ethan noted the man looked stressed and a bit weary. Pamela West interrupted Ethan's observations when she leaned over and whispered, "How're things in Riverview?"

"Could be better. An overdose victim in the morgue and not much evidence from the scene, a missing academic, robberies reported several times a week, noise complaints, you know, the usual," he responded.

The situation wasn't funny, but Penny had to laugh at his response.

"I was sorry to learn about the overdose victim. His mom's a professor and she's devastated," Pamela replied. "I hear the victim's dad is hounding the captain, and even got the governor to call. Pressure is mounting."

"I had a visit from the dad as well. He 'requested' I drop the investigation into his son's murder. Said he would take care of it."

"Well, that's crazy," Pamela responded.

"I agree. Some politicos think they can rule the world. It's a tragic situation, and I guess that's why we're sitting here. We've got to get solid plans in place. I'm tired of sitting here tossing ideas around, getting nothing done."

"Maybe today," Pamela replied with a sad smile.

The arrival of the captain interrupted their conversation.

"Brian will be late to our meeting, so I'll call the meeting to order and provide you with an update on what's been done since we last met."

Ethan slipped his phone out of his pocket and read the text Tom sent. What could Caitlyn be up to that needed an immediate call? He sent her a text asking how urgent was her problem. When fifteen minutes passed and there was no response, Ethan became concerned. He sent Tom a text asking if he had any idea where Caitlyn had gone. Tom replied he didn't except she said she had something to check out. Chills ran down Ethan's spine. He assumed she would have been exhausted after the long night, and be at her aunt's, safe in bed. Instead, she was out somewhere doing something related to the case. He had a bad feeling what that something was. It also concerned him that Brian Philips was not at the meeting. Were the two related? He squirmed in his seat. The topic on the table was where the clinic would be located and what the name should be.

Ethan admitted he didn't do well on committees and had honestly tried his best to be a team player. With Caitlyn in possible danger, and this task force was discussing the pros and cons of a facility name, he had had it. He stood up, leaned on the table and said, "Enough! We're here to find solutions to a problem that is overwhelming our society. It doesn't matter what we name the damn place or where it is located. Just get it done!"

With that said, Ethan walked out.

~

Caitlyn assessed the product aisles and thought if she were shipping drugs out of a facility like this, where would they be located? She was surprised that she hadn't run into any employees, and wondered where they were. She stayed close to the shelving units, working her way towards the outside walls and to the back end of the facility to the loading areas. She stopped when she heard voices. Acclimating herself, she figured there must be an office nearby and a meeting going on. When she got closer, she pushed herself up against the wall, and peeked through the crack in the door. Sure enough, a number of men were seated listening to someone giving instructions. As she scanned the group, her blood ran cold. She recognized a few of the men from those gathered in the park's outbuilding several days ago when she and Abbie were walking the gorge trail. *Oh, my God. I'm right.* She recognized the voice of the man talking. It was the same man she overheard talking with Mr. Johansson in the pharmacy—Brian Philips.

Isn't he supposed to be at the task force meeting?

She had to get out of there. She backed up, careful of her footing, until she hit something solid. A man with strong arms, and stronger body odor trapped her in a steel embrace.

"What do we have here?" Whispered a gravelly voice.

Caitlyn almost forgot her cover story.

"I'm . . . well, I'm writing an article. Something for a women's magazine on the best snacks for kids," Caitlyn stuttered. "Please, let me go." She was suffocating from his grip and his smell.

The man's rough embrace loosened and he pushed her toward the open door.

~

Ethan thought he'd figured out the unholy triangle. Watching those seated around the table today confirmed what he suspected. He also suspected Caitlyn had figured out at least part of it. He didn't know how, but he feared for her safety. The fact Brian Philips had not shown up for the meeting was alarming. Something was going down, and it had to be at the warehouse.

~ SIXTY-ONE ~

Verna braced herself for whatever Doug Mitchell had to report. He called and wanted her to return that very afternoon. He sounded excited about what he found, and warned her it might be an emotional time. Did she have someone who could come with her? Verna didn't want anyone else to know about her family's history.

~

Doug opened the door before Verna could knock a second time.

"Verna, thanks for coming back again," he said with a smile as he waved her into his office.

"So what do you have for me?" Verna asked, unable to hid her anxiety.

"Of course, let's get on with it," Doug replied. He hoped all his clients wouldn't be this way, or he'd have second thoughts about the town historian job.

After Verna settled herself in the chair next to the desk, Doug cleared his throat and began the story as he had discovered it.

"Verna, after you left, I traced your sister-in-law's family back through the census and then in online books in order to verify the stories you heard. I learned that in the 1700s some of Edda's family, along with others, died from what appeared to be mold toxins. These were later identified as fusarium, which are natural toxic chemicals mostly in rye. There is no proof that any of Edda's ancestors were intentionally poisoned this way, but the reality is, we may never know. During cool and wet growing seasons, the rye wouldn't dry out and toxic molds developed. When people ate the grain, the mold caused effects like nervous dysfunction, tremors, and then death. Edda's family was poor, so they had few options as to what grains they could use for food. By the time the 1800s came around corn and potatoes became more available."

Verna nodded, taking in the information.

"So I believe the question you have is, did Edda have a predisposition to murder? Is that even possible? I think the jury is still out on that one. Personally, I didn't believe in those things, but . . . I'll get into that later."

Doug had Verna's full attention now, and he dreaded sharing the information yet to come. He'd experienced sleepless nights wondering what can of worms he was about to open. He struggled with his ethical responsibility and prayed the situation would resolve itself. For now he'd continue on course.

"Using more recent sources I found your brother and his wife Edda had a daughter named Villetta. You will recognize it as Edda's maiden name. Using the library's microfilm of local papers, I found that in 1969 Edda joined a commune located a few miles from here. And yes, before you ask, there were three communes in the area. The university was a great spawning ground for radicals during that period of our history."

Doug hesitated, waiting to see if Verna was following him and if he should continue. He noticed a small nod of her head that he took as permission.

"That article about joining the commune did not mention a husband or baby. I think Edda joined the commune by herself. In a later newspaper article I found a marriage announcement for Edda van der Molen and a Jon Philips. I didn't find a record of divorce."

Again Doug waited to see if the name meant anything to Verna. There was no response, so he went on. The implication was obvious. Palle must have died. Or was Edda a bigamist?

"I did a Google search for Jon Philips. Do you know what a Google search is?"

"Of course I do," Verna snapped. "Do you think I'm completely daft?"

"No, Verna, I don't. What I know is that this information is difficult and I am trying to be sensitive to that."

"Go on," was all Verna could reply.

"Jon Philips was the son of a wealthy Midwest newspaper man who was on the board of one of the biggest pharmaceutical companies at the time. As you know, board members of most large companies get paid a healthy stipend with lots of perks.

Apparently, Jon didn't agree with his dad's way of life. He came to this area and started a commune. I think his father was happy to have the kid out of his hair, and it appeared that daddy underwrote the whole thing."

"So where was Palle?" Edda asked. "You know I don't care a hoot about Edda. Never liked her anyway."

"I realize that, and I'm getting to Palle. But Edda's story is important and in a moment you will know why," Doug replied, controlling his patience.

"A son, Brian, was born to Edda and Jon. I traced Brian, again through newspaper articles. I believe Edda's son Brian Philips is living in Renwick and runs a large warehouse operation there."

Verna's head jerked up at this news.

"Do you know what happened to the . . . other child?" Verna asked hesitantly. The information was unsettling, and he still hadn't told her about Palle, which made her uneasy thinking Doug was leaving the worst news for last.

Doug hesitated. God, he hated this part. He took a deep breath before continuing.

"I believe Edda gave the baby to a friend. A society note in one of the papers of that time period mentioned Mr. and Mrs. Connor adopted a baby girl they named Tracy Villetta Connor. If it's the same person, and the naming pattern suggests it is, there's a Tracy Connor living in Riverview and running a real estate agency in Renwick. So, Verna, if my research is correct, you have a niece and her step-brother living nearby."

~ SIXTY-TWO ~

Ethan arrived at the warehouse and drove around the parking lot. Trucks were backed into the loading dock awaiting their cargo.

He then spotted Caitlyn's Prius.

Dammit! He knew she would be here.

What was she thinking?

He surveyed the building looking for all entrances, guessing which door she might have entered. A personnel door in the middle of the long warehouse was flanked by large overhead loading dock doors made the most sense. She wouldn't have climbed up onto the loading dock, but with Caitlyn you never could tell.

Ethan entered the warehouse and scanned the aisles. Because he entered the building midway, he had to guess which way to go. It was suspicious that a facility this large, and this busy, would be so quiet. Something was going on. There were no workers around that he could see, and no forklifts moving merchandise. He listened and heard voices at the far end of the warehouse. He made his way through the maze of shelving towards the voices.

Nearing the end of the shelves, Ethan peeked around and saw a door ajar. There were several men inside talking, but the predominate voice he recognized was that of Brian Philips. What was so important that Brian blew off chairing the drug task force meeting? He wouldn't only be delayed; it appeared Brian was not planning to attend at all. It was then he heard Caitlyn's voice.

"Let go of me," he heard her say. "I'm only a reporter for a magazine."

Isn't that just like her to have a cover?

~

Brian Philips was furious. This meeting with his "team" had not gone as planned. One of them let slip that they had met with a Harvey Davis and the assignment he gave them. Brian wanted these guys, his trusted drivers, to be under his control only. He now knew that the pharma company he worked for had violated their agreement with him and had secretly engaged *his men* to eliminate the cartel operating in the area. Using his men to get rid of the competition was not part of the deal.

Then he was told the federal agent had escaped.

~

His day couldn't get any worse, and now this girl reporter listening outside the door. He doubted her story, and intended to detain and break her into telling him who she really was and what she was doing wandering around his warehouse without an appointment.

"Guys," Brian yelled to get their attention.

"Bugger, let the lady go."

The men didn't settle down. They were eager to get out. Their boss was angry, and they were nervous about what this woman might have heard. Would they be asked to quiet her for good?

"You have your delivery assignments. The supervisor will check off the inventory as your trucks are loaded," Brian said, dismissing the men.

The men scurried from the room, their metal chairs clanking against the concrete floor.

"Want me to stay, boss?"

"No, I can handle this. You make sure everything's okay in the warehouse."

Brian turned to Caitlyn.

"Haven't I seen you someplace?"

Caitlyn had to think fast. Did he see her and Ethan at the restaurant? Did he notice her in the pharmacy? She didn't think so, but her heart pounded. Who else was in this tangled web of the drug trade? She'd been on campus, and had probably been seen with Ethan. Did Brian have informants around town?

"I don't think so. I'm in town working on a story," Caitlyn said, struggling to keep the stress out of her voice. How was she going to get out of this situation?

"What kind of story?"

"About what companies are doing to make healthier cereals and snacks," Caitlyn responded.

Brian wasn't buying her coy response, but he wasn't absolutely sure whether she was telling the truth or not. What if she really was a journalist, and was being treated this way. This simpleton reporter could blow the whole operation wide open if she printed a story about her experiences in the warehouse. Either way, it was a no-win situation.

He grabbed her arm, shook her, and said, "Tell me who you really are and what you are doing here."

~

Ethan stopped holding his breath when he was sure the last man left the room. He was lucky that not one of them turned their head to look down the aisle where he was hiding. From the little he overheard, this group of drivers was the delivery system for illegal drugs distributed throughout the rural upstate towns.

It was beginning to fit together. He'd better alert Steven Sullivan. Ethan pulled out his phone and sent a text, with no idea if it would be received, and if it were, how long before Sullivan would arrive at the warehouse. Even if he and Caitlyn escaped, how would they be able to exit the building without being seen by that group of thugs? It was his responsibility to get them out of there alive.

When Ethan was sure all the men had reached the far end of the building, he stepped out into the aisle and walked up the steps to the elevated room where Caitlyn and Brian were located.

"Brian, we missed you at the task force meeting," Ethan said, leaning against the doorframe, trying his best to stay calm. He decided that was the best tact to turn Brian's attention to him and way from Caitlyn.

Brian Philips looked up, startled by the sheriff's arrival. He let go of Caitlyn's arm.

"I had important business matters to attend," Brian responded. He looked beyond Ethan hoping one of his men would come back to check on him. He shouldn't have let them all go.

"I can see that. Caitlyn, come over here."

By Ethan's side, she continued to rub her arm.

"Now, you and I can talk," Ethan said, fingering his holster to get his point across.

"I've nothing to say to you, and you don't have any authority in this town. You're nothing but a hick cop that no one takes seriously," Brian said sneering, trying to get control of the situation.

Ethan lunged at Brian, grabbed him by the collar, and pushed him up against the wall.

"I'd say I have a lot of authority here, and . . ."

"Ethan, stop!" Caitlyn yelled. She knew how furious he must be, and she was afraid of what he might do.

"Wait," another voice yelled. Standing in the doorway was Steven Sullivan.

"I got your text," Steven said to Ethan. "Thanks for letting me know you were here. If you hadn't, it could have gotten hairy because a raid was scheduled for this warehouse just as the trucks were leaving. In fact, we stopped them as they exited the parking lot onto the street, off warehouse property. The drivers have been arrested, the trucks seized. We found bags of heroin in among the boxes; too many bags to ascertain their value at the moment. We have men surrounding the building, and I will arrest Mr. Philips for running an illegal drug distribution center."

Ethan breathed a sigh of relief, but still held Brian firmly up against the wall.

"You can let him go now," Steven said in a firm tone. This was his case, and he was in charge. He turned to one of his agents, who immediately handcuffed Brian and walked him from the room.

Steven waved another agent into the room, and said, "Escort Sheriff Ewing and Ms. Jamison from the building. We don't want them to be confused with our band of thieves."

~ SIXTY-THREE ~

Safely by her car, Caitlyn turned to Ethan with her finger up to silence what she expected would be a long harangue about what she had gotten herself into, again.

"Don't say it. I know I put myself in unnecessary danger. But how the hell was I to know Steven Sullivan and his army of agents were also onto Brian Philips? But listen . . ."

Ethan's fisted hands were shaking as thoughts of what could have happened went through this mind. There was nothing to gain by yelling at her, so he got control of himself, took a deep breath, and veered the topic in another direction.

"A 'friend' of yours, Matt Miller, stopped by for a chat."

Caitlyn's mouth dropped. "Oh?"

"Can I assume you haven't told him anything about our investigations?"

"Of course not. I hope you know me better than that," Caitlyn replied, shaking her head, indignant he'd think such a thing. "But I need to tell you something . . ."

"Matt and I had a little chat. He suggested I check out Brian Philips and this warehouse. That, and the fact Philips didn't show up for the meeting this afternoon was when I figured this was where you were headed. After your email to Matt, he did more research and networking with certain informants and found out that the 'kingpin,' if you will, was located in or around Renwick. And here we are."

"I know, and that's what I want to tell you," Caitlyn cried.

~

"Excuse me, sir, but Steven Sullivan needs you inside. Now."

Ethan turned to see the agent who escorted them outside standing close by.

"Okay, I'll be right there."

He looked at Caitlyn, leaned over and opened her car door. "Go home. We'll talk later."

"But Ethan, I need to tell you . . ." Caitlyn said to Ethan's back as he had already left to accompany the agent back into the warehouse.

~ SIXTY-FOUR ~

Doug had talked for almost an hour explaining her family line, but still no information was forthcoming on what happened to her brother. Verna was stunned by the information that she had a niece and nephew, though she didn't consider this Brian person any relation. He wasn't her brother's child. But the girl, well, she would have to think about whether she wanted to meet her or not.

"I know you are anxious to know what happened to Palle," Doug stated, sitting back in his chair.

"I checked every website in order to trace him and came up blank. I went back to the microfilmed newspapers for the years surrounding the time Edda joined the commune and married Jon Philips. There was a death notice in the paper, so I went to the county clerk's office to see if they had his death certificate. There was a record, but they were reluctant to show me, so I pulled in some favors and at least got the information."

Verna waited seeing that Doug was having trouble continuing.

"I verified that Palle died in January 1969. The death certificate states he died of 'heart failure.'"

"So, a heart attack then," Verna stated with stiff upper lip.

"Not exactly," Doug replied. "Everyone dies of 'heart failure.' I think the attending doctor or medical examiner was lazy. They didn't look into the real cause, which was recorded as a secondary note on the death certificate. That stated 'nervous dysfunction.'"

"What does that mean?" Verna asked.

"It means he developed a condition that *might* have been caused by ingesting mold toxins. Palle worked in a mill. He could have breathed in the toxins, or he may have taken home grain, either as part of his compensation or sneaking it out in order to make ends meet."

Verna's eyes widened. "Oh my God. I went into the house the other day. After all these years, I found a bag of grain on the counter. I was amazed that the wildlife hadn't gotten into it."

"Animals have instincts when food is bad. They must have known it was full of mold toxins," Doug replied.

"Do you think Edda poisoned Palle?" Verna asked.

"That is not for me to say. He definitely had symptoms of poisoning, but whether it was intentional or not only Edda can say."

Doug turned back to his computer and turned the screen so Verna could see.

"The website I have here is Findagrave.com. Volunteers supply the information and sometimes add photos of the gravestones. When I tried to find Palle's grave, I couldn't at first. There is always the possibility that a person is buried in what's called a home plot, and that is where I found him. Yesterday I went to the homestead on Old Mill Road and walked around through the brush looking for periwinkle that grows in abandoned cemeteries. I found a depression and a small marker that just said, 'Palle.' I don't know who buried him or how many others might be buried near him. That is a task for another day, and another group more familiar with old cemeteries than I. But I wanted you to know when and where."

Verna let the tears flow. All these years she wanted to think about her brother as if he were alive. She didn't want to face the fact he was not. Occasionally, she'd wonder what he was doing. Was he retired? Was he enjoying grandchildren?

How many times had she walked by the house, by where he lay and didn't have a clue? Her heart clenched, and she turned pale.

"Verna, are you okay?" Doug asked. "Can I get you some tea?"

"I'm fine. Thank you for all your work and for finding my brother. It wasn't the answer I was hoping for, but I guess I shouldn't be surprised," she responded.

Verna got up, thanked him, and hastened from the house.

~ SIXTY-FIVE ~

Caitlyn was furious Ethan wouldn't listen to her. She understood he was upset about her going to the warehouse, but her instincts were correct. Brian Philips *was* a major player in the illegal drug trade. But he wasn't the 'kingpin' as they termed the head of the hydra. She knew who it was . . . or *thought* she did. One slip of the tongue by Brian made it click into place. The university was the perfect setting—hiding in plain sight. Brilliant.

This time, Caitlyn had no trouble finding a parking space in front of the science building. Having just escaped a dangerous situation, she considered what she was about to do. The adrenalin pumping through her veins pushed her to respond, even if it was reckless. Ethan and Steven were busy at the warehouse. The news about the raid would spread through the drug network and the major players would be gone. There was only one option. She had to go in alone and hope for the best. She called Maddie to alert Tom, and to contact campus security.

~

"What're you doing here?" Deborah Kent asked, startled at seeing Caitlyn at her door, as she slipped her laptop into its case.

"You know very well why I'm here. Is there something you need to tell me?"

"No," was the curt reply.

"Then let me fill in the blanks. When we first met, you were clear you didn't know Steven Sullivan or socialize with the new faculty. Part-time lecturers seemed particularly distasteful. But in fact, you let slip that Steven Sullivan was researching the possible effects of genetically modified foods. How would you know that if you knew nothing about him as you claimed?"

269

"You're crazy. I said nothing like that, and if I did, it was just idle gossip."

"I don't think so. I think you are the one responsible for kidnapping Steven Sullivan *and* for the death of your nephew. He knew you were the conduit. Did he tell you he planned to share that information with Steven Sullivan? And it was you who sent someone, possibly Brian Philips, or one of his goons to take care of the situation. And now you are packing up. Your desk is unusually clean. The last time I was here it was covered with papers. Going somewhere?"

~

Deborah's right hand rested in her pocket while Caitlyn laid out the scenario. It was amazing this amateur had figured it out when the government had sent in their best teams and failed. Her hand slid out of her pocket and a small-caliber pistol appeared.

Caitlyn expected as much, and prayed that Tom or campus security would arrive soon. She needed to stall so she decided to engage Deborah in conversation.

"Look at you. A perfect example of why we need common sense firearm legislation in this country. Gun ownership comes with responsibility, and *you* don't fit that bill," Caitlyn said in disgust. She had to keep Deborah distracted long enough for authorities to arrive.

"You won't live long enough to see any legislation," Deborah said with one eye on Caitlyn as she continued to stuff papers into the computer's case. "Move over there, next to the bookcase."

Caitlyn did as she was instructed.

"Tell me why. Why would someone of your education and talent want to destroy people with drugs?" Caitlyn asked.

"You really are stupid, aren't you?" Deborah replied. "It's simple. Money. And power. One of the pharmaceutical companies approached me years ago to manage their warehousing business. I once worked in that industry and had a lot of contacts. The money was good, much better than I could ever earn teaching a bunch of lazy college kids. The company realized it could capture both sides of the market with pain relievers and then sales of recovery products. The same with diabetes, hypertension, any number of diseases."

"But your own nephew? How could you?"

"That was difficult, I admit," Deborah responded without emotion. "He called early that morning and said he couldn't do the drugs anymore. He said he was going to meet with an agent, so I had Richard followed. I guess Richard was giving me fair warning. But leaving town wasn't in my plan. It's too bad, but . . ."

Caitlyn had heard enough. This woman disgusted her. No remorse for having her nephew murdered. She was driven by power and greed.

Deborah picked up her computer case, pointed her gun at Caitlyn, and indicated she should move towards the door.

Caitlyn didn't move. She had to keep Deborah talking.

"You need to give yourself up. Campus security officers will arrive before we even get down the stairs."

"Don't count on it. They patrolled through here a half hour ago. They won't be back in this area for another ninety minutes," Deborah replied, grabbing Caitlyn's arm. "Now, shut up and move."

Caitlyn's muscles started to twitch from the stress. She *really* had done it this time. If Deborah was right, and campus security officers wouldn't come around for a long time, there would be no one to notice them leaving the building. Caitlyn realized she might end up on an abandoned road just like Richard Kent.

Deborah let go of Caitlyn's arm as she pushed her out the door. Deborah held the computer case in her left hand, the gun in her right, pressed into Caitlyn's back.

"Walk normally or you won't even make it to the car."

"Professor Kent!" A young woman approached them from behind. "I was hoping to catch you before you left for the day. I know it's late, but I was hoping you might let me into your seminar. I love your work, and you have such a great reputation on campus,

271

and it is so nice to finally meet you," the young woman blathered on.

Caitlyn tried to figure out what she could do to alert this woman who was gushing all over the professor.

If she only knew what was really going on.

"See the secretary. I don't have time right now. Late for an appointment," Deborah replied, sharply, giving the young woman a stiff smile. Deborah continued to push Caitlyn along, with the gun as an incentive.

The young woman wasn't put off. She followed them, talking about how much she admired the professor, on and on. Caitlyn was thankful that the student had slowed their progress out of the building, but when she saw the door to the parking lot she realized her time was about up. She had to come up with a plan to detain them from leaving the building. Just as she was about to make a move, Tom entered.

"Professor Kent, stop where you are," Tom instructed.

The young woman trailing them grabbed Deborah from behind and knocked the gun from her hand. It went sliding down the hall, to the shock of the students hurrying to class.

Tom yelled, "Don't touch that!"

He then turned to the woman. "Thanks, Pamela. You've been a big help," Tom said as he handcuffed Deborah.

"Anytime partner," Pamela replied. "If you've got the situation under control, I'll head off to class."

Caitlyn turned from one to the other.

"Are you the Pamela from campus security that serves on the task force with Ethan?" Caitlyn asked, amazed at how all this came together.

"Yes, the same. The dispatch in Riverview briefed our office on the situation. I was in the vicinity, so I responded. I'm in plain clothes today because I'm scheduled to speak to the beginning law class and I'm more comfortable this way."

"I, for one, am thankful for that," Caitlyn replied.

~ SIXTY-SIX ~

Ethan leaned back in his office chair, hands clasped over this stomach.

"You look pretty content," Maddie commented as she entered the room, handing him a cup of coffee.

"I am," Ethan replied. "We've accomplished what few others have. We've run the bad guys out of town, as they'd say in the Wild West."

Caitlyn, Tom, and Steven entered the office and vied for seating in the limited space. Maddie, always on duty, stood at the doorway keeping an eye on the front door and the switchboard. As the group assembled, Ethan sat up and turned the meeting over to Steven.

"It's not agency policy to do a debriefing with locals after one of our assignments," said Steven. "But you four went above and beyond to close down this multi-faceted drug ring. I think it is only appropriate to fill you in on the rest of the story."

Steven paused, searching each of their tired faces.

"First, I want to thank Caitlyn and Ethan for rescuing me. I was embarrassed to have been put into that situation. I should have known better. I'd been cultivating contacts on campus and one of them was Richard Kent. He hated being hooked on drugs. Each hit made him crave the drugs even more. He was intelligent enough to know what was happening and agreed to help me. We met for drinks one evening, and he told me he could identify his supplier. He was hesitant and needed more time to think about it. I knew he was conflicted, and there was more to his decision than drugs, though it never occurred to me it would be family. We finally set up a meeting, though I wasn't sure whether he'd show. I now know why he was conflicted and needed more time. He was going to give up his aunt. She found out about the meeting and called Brian. It was he who ambushed me and gave Richard the fatal dose."

"How'd he get your credit card?" Ethan asked.

"That was just a mix-up. We both wanted to pay for the drinks that night, so both cards went on the table. After some scuffling we decided the hell with it, we'd pay cash. We grabbed our cards, but in the scuffle, we picked up each other's cards. I just noticed that I have his card in my wallet."

"So where does Mr. Johansson come in?" Caitlyn asked.

"As a druggist, Johansson partnered with the pharmaceutical companies for years. It's the pharmaceutical companies that wanted the monopoly on the drug traffic through Upstate New York. They wanted the cartels out. The pharma companies ship large quantities of opioids and other drugs to certain warehouse locations, like Brian's, for doctors to prescribe. When patients became addicted, then the pharmaceutical companies supply the naloxone and other reversal drugs. Mr. Johansson receives what we refer to as payment in kind for all the drugs he sells. He works with some of the area's doctors in pushing certain brands. Then there are the doctors who are in the business of over-prescribing, and we are in the process of rounding them up. Sometimes it takes years before enough evidence is gathered, but we're trying."

Ethan understood and said, "The pharmaceutical companies want complete control of the area's drug supply. They can also control the price of the reversal drugs, knowing a good portion of the overdose population with fall back into dependency."

"That's correct," Steven agreed. "They were up against stiff competition with the cartels. They wanted the cartels out so as to limit the amount of attention to the warehousing."

"Money and control," Ethan offered.

"Correct again," Steven replied.

"How did you learn about the warehouse operation when the agents before you couldn't?" Tom asked.

"I figured it out when I was locked up. The sides were stacked with boxes and men moving boxes in and out every couple of days.

To me that said 'warehouse,' and then it clicked. How could they deliver all those drugs around the state? Trucking company, of course. That put me on the trail of Brian Philips."

At this point everyone looked at Caitlyn.

"Okay. I know I shouldn't have gone to the warehouse. But it was there that I overheard Brian say a simple phrase, something like, '*she* isn't going to be happy.' I thought that was a strange comment until I remembered the notes I had taken of my conversation with Professor Kent and how off-putting she was about the lower class lecturers. She claimed to know nothing about Steven, but then mentioned his research into various food types. I also recognized some of the guys at the warehouse were the same I saw at the park. I remembered when the last man came out, talking on his cell, and he said, 'ma'am' it fell into place. I just hoped I was right. Actually, I hoped I wasn't. When I entered Deborah Kent's office I wanted her to be sitting there working on a course syllabus or counseling a student. Not hurriedly packing a bag for a quick getaway."

"I can't condone what you did, but a female heading up the drug trade wasn't on our radar though it should have been. From now on *you* need to leave law enforcement to the professionals."

Caitlyn nodded looking at Steven to continue.

"We are now in the process of locating and shutting down the pharmaceutical warehouses in Central New York as well as in the other states. The cartel has gone underground, but we'll flush them out. Things should be looking better in this area very soon," Steven added.

Ethan sat forward in his chair. "In your opinion, Steven, do you think Mayor Goodrich had any part in this?"

"Not from what I can tell. I think the mayor is doing his best to serve the people of the community. His ideas are good, and I think you should support the clinics he is suggesting. It's not the best answer to the drug problem, but a positive first step."

"What are your plans now?" Ethan asked.

"I have to get back to Boston for the debriefing and share what we learned of the operatives in Upstate New York. We'll have to adjust our modus operandi and we have you to thank for that. Then I plan to take time off, come back here and do a little fishing," Steven replied with a smile.

~ SIXTY-SEVEN ~

Verna pulled back the living room curtain just enough to peek outside. In the driveway was a shiny gray car. A woman got out, hesitated, and then headed to Verna's front door. The woman's gait was familiar. So familiar it brought forth distant memories. She shook herself. This was too much. Could she go through with it? When her doorbell rang, she knew it was no longer a choice.

Verna let the curtain fall and headed to the front door, bracing herself for whatever this woman had to say.

When the door opened Verna saw a reflection of her younger self.

"Hello Aunt Verna. I'm Tracy, Palle's daughter."

~

The two women sat in Verna's living room with a tea service on the antique oak table in front of them. Neither knew where to start. Finally, Tracy broke the silence.

~

"I was told I was adopted as soon as my parents felt I'd understand what that meant. They told me I was their choice and they loved me unconditionally. When I was fourteen, I started asking my mom about my birth mother. My mom was secure in her position as my 'real' mother, so she didn't hesitate to tell me how the adoption came about."

Tracy took a deep breath and then a sip of her tea.

"Go on," Verna encouraged, bracing herself for the information she was about to hear.

"My birth mother, Edda, met a man from the commune. He came around every week selling fresh vegetables. My birth mother

277

was pregnant with me and in much discomfort. This young man gave her a packet of homegrown marijuana and told her it would make her feel better. It did, I guess. Unfortunately, it gave me some growth issues and I had trouble, early on, retaining what I learned. I was lucky I escaped leukemia and other more serious side effects that marijuana use brings about.

When Edda left my dad, she went to live at the commune and gave me and the cat to the Connors. At first the Connors thought it was a short-term arrangement, but after a couple of years, they applied for adoption, even changing my name, and Edda didn't contest it. In the meantime my dad was ill, suffering from convulsions and things like that.

Apparently my grandparents decided the Connors would be better equipped to care for an infant than they were. And I believe they made the right decision."

With Tracy's story told, the women sat in silence.

"Do you know what happened to your mother?" Verna finally asked, carefully wiping away a tear.

"She's in a Renwick nursing home. I've been told she has dementia and whether she does or not I have no desire to see her," Tracy replied. "I have my parents, the Connors, and I love them dearly. There is no room in my heart for a woman who thought more of her infatuation than her newborn child."

Verna noticed a slight tic in Tracy's facial muscles. Even though she claimed she didn't care about her parents, something inside her was crying out for them. Verna then approached her own sensitive area. She hesitated, not knowing if she could follow through with the question.

"And your father? Did you ever know him? Do you ever visit his grave?" Verna asked.

"No. I was too young when he died and the Connors never talked about him. If I knew where his grave was, I would visit," Tracy responded, finishing her cup of tea and getting up.

Before Verna could respond or ask more questions, Tracy said, "It's nice to meet you, Aunt Verna. I hope to see you again, but I think we've had enough emotion for today."

~ SIXTY-EIGHT ~

Caitlyn looked forward to the Vietnam Veterans Memorial
Dedication ceremony in Riverview Park. She found a convenient
parking spot on Main Street not far from where the event was to be
held. Her parallel parking skills were rusty, but on the third try she
figured the car was close enough to the curb so it wouldn't be hit by
passing vehicles.

Caitlyn put Summit on leash and walked down the main street,
peering into the various storefronts. She stepped carefully around
the water bowls on the sidewalk, placed there to serve thirsty dogs.
Summit stopped at one of the bowls to take advantage of this
kindness and enjoyed a long drink.

They stopped in front of Notions and Things and admired the
window display. Anna Jones's dream of opening her own store had
become a reality and Caitlyn was happy for her.

The door jingled as they entered.

"Anna?" She called.

An attractive woman in her early sixties, with her silver hair
pulled back in a neat bun, appeared from the back of the store.

"Caitlyn! What a surprise to see you," Anna said as she rushed
forward to give Caitlyn a hug. "I heard you were in town, but
haven't had a chance to catch up with you."

Anna hesitated, her eyes starting to tear, as she stood back and
looked at Caitlyn.

"Are you here for the . . . dedication?"

"Yes, Anna. When I heard there was going to be a Veterans
Memorial Dedication in Riverview Park, I wanted to stay for it. It's
the least I can do for your brother Clyde. He fought valiantly for his
country and then suffered for years because of it."

Anna folded Caitlyn into her embrace and both women cried for the man who suffered long-lasting scars from his service to the country.

"We used a portion of Clyde's inheritance to purchase the memorial, landscaping, and benches. The memorial features the names of all the area's veterans, but Clyde's name will have a special plaque. The surrounding benches will allow people to view the monument and remember the sacrifices these young men and women made for all of us, for our way of life," Anna said. "I hope today's ceremony will bring our family peace."

~

"I like your store. I see your loan came through from the bank," Caitlyn said with a smile. She remembered Anna telling her about the hoops Uncle Jerry had put her through when he was president of the bank.

"Things worked out. As you know, before I got the paperwork together your uncle was appointed to fill Senator Smith's seat in Albany, so I dealt with a new bank manager. The new manager is a woman and she was all for a notions store in Riverview, and we were right. Business is good and with the influx of students I've expanded my inventory to include art supplies to meet their needs."

She looked at her watch.

"It's time. Will you walk with me to the park? All the emotion is making me feel a little wobbly," Anna said.

"Absolutely, and I'll be by your side the entire time. Clyde will be with us in spirit, you know," Caitlyn said as she took Anna's arm.

~ SIXTY-NINE ~

"The ceremony was lovely," Caitlyn whispered, turning to Anna.

Anna nodded, wiping a tear.

Caitlyn looked around at those who remained. Tom stood at the periphery with Carrie Young by his side.

Interesting. I wonder if this is the start of something . . .

"I hate to interrupt," Caitlyn said as she approached Tom and Carrie. "I thought Ethan would be at this important community event."

"He planned to be, but something must have come up," Tom replied, nodding to townspeople as they milled around the monument.

Caitlyn put her hand on Tom's sleeve and moved him to the side, asking Carrie to excuse them.

"Tom, look at me! What duty could be more important than attending a service for our veterans?"

Tom looked down at Caitlyn and sighed. She hadn't changed, and she'd keep at him until he told her.

"I'm not supposed to say anything, but he left a couple hours ago to meet with an attorney in Renwick. Personal business, he said. Then he was to meet with Verna Adams and Tracy Connor. Ethan thinks there's enough evidence that Edda van der Molen caused her husband's death. But that can't be determined unless they disinter the body and run tests on the bones, assuming anything would show up after all these years."

Caitlyn shuddered at the thought. "So what will happen?"

"Edda is in a nursing home in the middle stages of Alzheimer's. Ethan doesn't want to cause the family any more distress, so he called an emergency meeting with Mrs. Adams and Ms. Connor to ask them how they'd like to proceed. Ethan knows he should go by rule of law, but he's sensitive to the family. And what good would it do to arrest Edda at this point?"

"I agree. He's in a tough spot. The rule of law versus compassion."

But an important question remained.

"What do you think he is seeing an attorney about?"

Tom shook his head, not providing any further information. If Tom knew, he wasn't telling.

"And what are your plans?" Caitlyn asked. She sensed more changes coming to Riverview.

"Actually, we've had some good news. We got approval for more budget money, so Ethan is adding a detective position and asked me to fill it. We'll hire another officer, and a part-time staff member to help with general office work and to finish the cold case digitization project."

"That's wonderful news," Caitlyn exclaimed, giving Tom a hug. "And it looks like maybe you and Carrie are hitting it off?"

Tom gave her a shy smile. "At least she understands my workload, and we've found we have a number of things in common."

"Stay in touch and let me know how things are going with you, both personally and professionally."

"I promise," Tom replied.

Caitlyn took a last look around the park and sighed. "If Ethan doesn't make it back before I have to leave, tell him I said good-bye."

"Will do," Tom said as he headed back to where Carrie stood patiently waiting.

~

Caitlyn was devastated. She understood why Ethan hadn't attended the ceremony, but it didn't diminish the hurt she felt that he hadn't made an effort to see her before she left. Would they ever come to some resolution about their relationship? Was it something that could be nurtured long distance? If so, there'd come a time

283

when one of them would have to relocate. Careers could be the breaking point in a relationship. There was so much she wanted to say to him, but she couldn't stay in Riverview any longer. She had an important client meeting early tomorrow morning. She had to get back to D.C.

She put on a brave face and went back to her friends.

~

She bade Abbie and Tim farewell and gave her Aunt Myra a long hug.

"Take care, Aunt Myra. Thanks for letting me stay with you, and I hope I can come visit soon. And next time *without* a murder in Riverview!"

They both laughed.

When most of the residents had left the event, Caitlyn noticed the marine biologist, Chad Owens, standing at the monument, head bent. She decided not to interrupt his private moment, but just as she turned away, he called her name.

"Caitlyn, wait," Chad called.

"I've been called back to Long Island. There's a situation in the sound that needs my attention. I'll miss the folks here and hope to be back soon. Maybe we'll meet again?" He said in a hopeful tone.

"Dr. Owens, I'm sorry we didn't have the opportunity to get to know each other better. I never had the chance to explain that I live in Arlington, Virginia, and was only here to work on a brochure for the local winery."

Chad's face fell, but he recovered quickly. "Well, if I'm ever in the DC area, I'll look you up. I know my wife, Emma, would love to meet you."

Caitlyn watched Dr. Chad Owens walk away. He was an enigma. There were moments when she thought he might be part of the investigation either with regard to Richard Kent's death or Steven Sullivan's disappearance. He still could be, though she suspected he was only what he said he was, a marine biologist with a quirky personality.

Caitlyn walked over to Anna who continued to stand by the monument featuring the plaque in honor of her brother.

"It's time for me to head home, Anna. Shall we walk back to your store?"

Caitlyn took Anna's arm and they walked back to the store where they shared a heartfelt good-bye, not knowing when they would see each other again.

On the way back to her car, Caitlyn stopped outside the florist shop to admire the display. On a whim she entered and headed to the refrigerated section.

"I'd like a dozen of those pink sweetheart roses," she told the clerk.

With the bouquet of roses in one hand and Summit's leash in the other, Caitlyn knew what she had to do next.

She placed Summit on the front passenger seat, and placed the roses in the back. Caitlyn turned to take one last look at Riverview before she drove off.

~ SEVENTY ~

Caitlyn had to make one last stop before she headed out of town—her cousin's grave. She needed to share with him her confusion about what was happening in the country. She needed to make sense of things.

She drove into the cemetery, past the small stone chapel, and slowly made her way down the winding dirt road in order to find the narrow lane that would take her to Todd's burial site. The sun was at just the right angle on this early fall day so the remaining golden leaves provided a colorful contrast to the gray stones that dotted the cemetery landscape.

~

The cemetery was well cared for, and the winding narrow roads well marked. Leaving Summit in the car with the window open for air, she picked up the bouquet of pink roses and walked the few steps to the monument erected in honor of her cousin. She didn't know where to start or what to say. Her emotions were in such turmoil.

"Todd, I've just been through the most upsetting week. Nothing makes sense. Why do so many want to escape from their reality? There is so much sadness, so much pain," she said to the granite tombstone that marked the final resting place of her young cousin.

"Why does greed and power continue to be driving forces? Have we learned nothing from history?"

Todd remained silent. He had no answers for her.

"And why," she hesitated, "can't Ethan and I talk about our relationship? What's holding us back?" With one hand on the top

286

of Todd's monument, Caitlyn felt a shiver go down her spine as though an answer was coming up through the stone.

Was there someone else?

"Oh, my God. I had never thought of that."

Todd's tombstone wasn't providing the answers she needed, but that didn't matter. Being near him and talking about her feelings was enough.

"You know, I, too, question life and where I might be happiest. Something draws me back to Riverview, even though my life is in Virginia. I want to be with Ethan, but I don't know if a relationship is possible with him. Relationships are built on trust and how can I trust him if I suspect he's holding back something important?"

Caitlyn was talked out. She looked around the cemetery and sighed as she noticed the number of recent burials, knowing the cause of the recent deaths.

She patted the top of the tombstone, bent over and placed the pink roses at the base.

"Goodbye, Todd. Thanks for listening."

~ SEVENTY-ONE ~

She checked her phone one more time, still hoping to hear from Ethan, but she couldn't wait any longer. He was probably busy sorting through the details associated with the deaths of Richard Kent and Palle van der Molen. Those tasks would keep him occupied for weeks.

As these thoughts flitted through her mind, her phone rang. Without checking caller ID, hoping it was Ethan she answered in her softest tone, "This is Caitlyn."

"Caitlyn, it's Mom," Ann Jamison yelled into the phone.

"Why are you yelling?" Caitlyn asked, not immediately recognizing her mother's voice. This can't be good. Her mother never called during the week.

"Mom's what's wrong?"

"Well, I don't want to bother you . . ."

"You aren't bothering me. What's wrong?" Caitlyn did her best to stay calm.

"Your father had a little heart attack and he's in the hospital. I wanted you to know in case you called the house. I'm here with him most of the day."

"A *little* heart attack? Should I come down?" Caitlyn asked as her mind raced. Her first instinct was to hop a plane. But she was in New York, not DC. She had Summit and her clients to worry about. Her mind raced thinking of the quickest way to get to Florida, serve her clients and figure out what to do with Summit.

"No, don't come. He'll be home in a day or two. But, well, what we wanted to talk to you about was our future plans."

Caitlyn took a deep breath. This can't be good. When her mother started a conversation like this, it usually meant something life changing.

"Okay, mom, so what are your future plans?"

"Your father and I have had a couple of medical issues lately, and though we live in a supportive community, there are several months during the summer when people aren't around."

"Mom, what medical issues? You haven't mentioned them when we talked."

"We just don't want to bother you with the little things. You know, as a person ages, the body starts to wear out. Just like any old machine," her mother said with a forced laugh.

Caitlyn waited for the other shoe to drop. She knew her mother was just warming up.

"We know how busy you are, and how difficult it is for you to get here."

Her mother paused.

"Mom . . ." Caitlyn started to say, but was interrupted by her mother.

"We've decided to move to Virginia. That way if we need help, you'll be close by . . . you won't have to disrupt your life every time we have an episode. We also miss you, especially on holidays."

Caitlyn was silent, thinking about her parents' decision. It made sense. She couldn't help worrying about them and hated the fact she'd have to hop a plane each time they needed her. She couldn't be there in a hurry if something drastic happened.

"I think that's a great solution, Mom," Caitlyn said. "Do you want me to check into communities here?"

"Actually, we've always longed to live on the Chesapeake Bay. Once your father feels better, we'll drive up and shop around. Don't worry, we're still mobile and your father's condition is just a momentary setback. Take care, dear."

The call ended. Her mother was like that. As soon as she finished talking, she hung up. It didn't matter if the other person had more to say.

Caitlyn laughed. Her mother was a character and Caitlyn loved her for it.

Although conflicted about her parents move to Virginia, she had to admit it would make life easier.

More adventures with Mom and Dad.

Caitlyn started her car and with Summit snuggled in his travel bed, she headed south.

Author's note

An idea for a book can come from anywhere and sometimes from the most unexpected places. And that is exactly what happened with this story. When the seed is planted, it takes root, and there is nothing the author can do.

The main plot line was difficult for me. Dealing with the current opioid epidemic was not in my comfort zone. But as with my first book, the characters took over and developed the plot line for me.

In doing research for this book I began to wonder if there were additional root causes of the current drug epidemic. I worked some of that research into the story line with the hope it provides food for thought.

I like to think of myself as a family historian, and that is why I wanted to include a genealogy subplot in order to share how genealogy research is done. Not only does Verna Adams play a vital role in discovering the body, she is the catalyst for the ancestral research as she learns the truth about her brother.

As for the white deer, 7,000 acres of the Seneca Army Depot property has been purchased and bus tours sponsored by the nonprofit *Seneca White Deer* will begin in fall 2017.

The cover photo is of Grove Cemetery in Trumansburg, New York. When I searched for just the right picture for this book, I wasn't looking for this type of photo, but when I saw it I knew it was the one. Ironically, the day after I found the photo and got permission from the photographer to use it, I received the Ulysses Historical Society newsletter. The feature story was of Grove Cemetery. Grove cemetery was incorporated on April 27, 1847, is still active today, and is where a number of my ancestors are buried. Hmm, makes me wonder.

Acknowledgements

Unbeknownst to her, Karen Armstrong Royce planted the seed for this book one summer day several years ago. She never knew that her casual comment surprised me, took root, and wouldn't let go.

I'm blessed to have a friend with whom I can share my frustrations and successes, so I am grateful to Andrea Zimmermann for her steadfast support and constant encouragement as I worked my way through another story. Whenever I had a down day, Andrea would advise, "Write for yourself." I did, and I came to love this story.

Experienced beta readers are another blessing bestowed upon me. My heartfelt thanks go to Lucille Anderson, Michelle Jackson, Elizabeth Spragins, Cheryl Wicks, Marian Wood, and Andrea Zimmermann.

I thank Joseph Scaglione III - Joe Scaglione Photography in Ithaca, New York for capturing the cemetery photo, and Suzette Young for turning that photo into a stunning cover.

Caitlyn Jamison mystery readers, *thank you* for continually asking when the next book was coming out. Your gentle nudges kept me going.

The support of my family, Melissa and Rebecca, and Brennen and Jessica means the world to me. Thank you for being there. My husband Ray provided support all along the way and . . . pouring me a glass of Finger Lakes wine after a particularly grueling editing day. I thank him for his IT support, and for schlepping books, computer, projector and all the paraphernalia needed for my author presentations.

I write for fun and for the challenge. I thank the above-mentioned support team that helped to make the book the best it can be. Any mistakes are mine alone.

Peace.

Bibliography

"A World of Pain," *The Economist*, 8 April 2017, p. 56.

Andrews, Travis M., "In just 32 hours, city gets 52 overdose calls." *Sarasota Herald-Tribune*, 15 February 2017.

Brokaw, Josh, "Addiction Services Not Enough…Yet." *Ithaca Times*, 3 February 2016.

Brokaw, Josh, "Selling Heroin: In Ithaca the Quality and Price Varies, but the supply is constant." *Ithaca Times*, 22 June 2016.

Choi, Candice, "Study details sugar industry attempt to shape science," *The Free Lance Star*, 13 September 2016, p. A5.

Chadwick, John, "Getting at the Root Causes of Drug Addiction," *Rutgers Today*, 21 September 2009. [http://news.rutgers.edu/issue.2009-07-17.9564201431/article.2009-09-21.5328747955#.WRhOpcm1vAI]. [Accessed 14 May 2017]

Dyson, Cathy, "Community Addresses Drug Epidemic." *The Free Lance Star*, 12 May 2017, p. 1.

Gable, Walter, *Written History of Seneca County, New York*, http://www.co.seneca.ny.us/departments/admin-operations/county-historian/written-history-of-seneca-county-ny/ [Accessed June 2016]

Goodman, J. David, "New York is a Hub in a Surging Heroin Trade." *New York Times*, 19 May 2014 N.Y./Region.

"How to Smack It Down," *The Economist*, 7 November 2015, p. 13.

Kang and Thiruvananthapuram, "The Problem of Pain," *The Economist*, 28 May 2016, p. 53.

Matossian, Mary Kilbourne. *Poisons of the Past, Molds, Epidemics and History*, New Haven, CT, Yale University Press, 1991.

Marzulli, John, "Narco Agents Weed Out Bad Apples Upstate," *New York Daily News*, 17 August 1998. [Accessed June 2016]

McDermid, Val, *Forensics; What Bugs, Burns, Prints, DNA and More Tell Us About Crime*, New York, NY, Grove Press, 2015.

Melinek, Judy and T.J. Mitchell, *Working Stiff*, New York, Scribner, 2014.

Platt, Richard. *Crime Scene*, New York, Dorling Kindersley, 2006.

Purcell, Kathy, "Drug deaths, arrests spill onto Anna Maria Island." *The Islander*, 22 February 2017, p. 23.

Roby, John R., "New Numbers Show Growing Toll of Opioids," PressConnects.com, 12 May 2017.

Quinones, Sam, *Dreamland; the true tale of America's opiate epidemic*, New York, NY, Bloomsbury Press, 2015.

Wilson, Keith D. M.D. *Cause of Death: a writer's guide to death, murder & forensic medicine*, Cincinnati, Ohio, 1992.

New York Office of Children and Family Services [Accessed 23 December 2015] http://ocfs.ny.gov/main/Opiate_Abuse/default.asp

Syracuse.com - http://www.syracuse.com/news/index.ssf/2014/05/heroin-gone-wild_in_central_new_york_causes_jumps_in_overdoses_deaths.html [accessed 23 December 2015]

The Associated Press, "Report, West Virginia Flooded with Drugs," *the Free Lance Star*, 20 December 2016, p. C4.

Wilber, Del Quentin, "VA's Radical Approach to Heroin ODs." *The Free Lance Star*, 4 November 2016.

CPSIA information can be obtained
at www.ICGtesting.com
Printed in the USA
LVOW03s1515141217
559733LV00012B/1199/P